BY KIERSTEN WHITE

HIDE

HIDE

A NOVEL

KIERSTEN WHITE

NEW YORK

Copyright © 2022 by Kiersten Brazier

Published in the United States by Del Rey, an imprint of Random House, a division of Penguin Random House LLC, New York.

Del Rey and the Circle colophon are registered trademarks of Penguin Random House LLC.

Hardback ISBN 978-0-593-35923-5
Ebook ISBN 978-0-593-35924-2

Printed in the United States of America on acid-free paper

randomhousebooks.com

2 4 6 8 9 7 5 3 1

FIRST EDITION

Endpaper map design by David G. Stevenson
Endpaper map illustration by Elwira Pawlikowska
Endpaper map copyright © 2022 by Penguin Random House
Book design by Simon M. Sullivan

To the youngest generations we've tasked with saving us all:
You shouldn't have to. I'm so sorry.

HIDE

THE AMAZEMENT PARK OPENED IN 1953.

GET LOST IN THE FUN! posters advertised, and it was true: Crowds surged through the gates in the morning and didn't stumble out again until the sun had set, and spotlights at the exit guided them free. The maps were useless, the You Are Here guides impossible to find. It was a park designed to swallow. Trees loomed over lush grounds. Signature topiary lined every walled and wandering path, adding to the sense of wonder. Roller coasters, swings, carousels, games, houses of love and fun and terror—though the house at the very center was always closed for refurbishment.

The park was open from mid-May until early September. WHITES ONLY was on signs in the early years, heavily implied when such a thing became harder to officially declare. And, for one week every seven years, it was free. The gates would swing wide, and the summer migrant workers and distant relatives of the wealthy townsfolk, normally too poor to enjoy something designed purely for escape, would wander in, wide-eyed. There were no ticket sales, no attendance numbers, just a joyfully packed park.

In 1974, during the free week, a prominent businessman from upstate decided to visit. He hadn't been invited, but he was considering investing since a cousin-of-a-cousin owned the park. He wanted to see the attractions for himself first, though. He brought along his wife and two children and made it a holiday.

Their little girl, five, was never seen again.

One of the migrant workers was arrested for her murder, but the negative publicity left a stain that didn't wash out. So the Amazement Park closed its gates.

Eventually, the rumors died. The plants grew. Nature slowly co-opted the buildings, the rides, the roller coasters. What didn't crumble rusted, and what didn't rust leaned, and what didn't lean sagged under the weight of ivy and neglect.

Somewhere, very close to the center—the house that was always closed, where few ever even got, owing to the odd layout of the park—a shoe had caught on the low branches of a topiary. Unchecked, the verdant beast slowly grew higher and higher until the shoe was eye level.

It was patent leather, dulled and cracked with weather and time. The perfect size for a five-year-old foot.

I*T TAKES MONEY TO MAKE MONEY*, her dad used to say.

He also once said *Come out, come out, wherever you are,* dragging the knife along the wall as music to accompany the dying gasps of her sister. Mack might have imagined the gasps, though. Who could say.

She couldn't, and even if she could, she wouldn't.

She's not saying anything right now, either, sitting across from the manager. The meeting was mandatory, a "shelter requirement," though she's been here several months now and this is the first one.

"Come on, Mackenzie. Help me help you." The woman's smile is painted on like her cheekbones and eyebrows, and just as artfully. Her expression doesn't shift at all in the face of Mack's silence. It's impressive. Does she do stamina reps in the quiet dark of her bedroom, lifting the corners of her lips over and over, careful not to disrupt her eyes?

The manager clasps her hands together, fingernails painted dark red. "I'll be honest with you. Things are going to change around here. I believe that we can help only those willing to help themselves. These shelters have stagnated—no hope, no progress. How can we live in a society without progress?"

The voice is animated, but the eyes remain untouched by the sentiments or the smile. Expressionless. Like they're hidden behind something. Mack feels an odd affinity for this woman, alongside an instinctive wariness. But she disagrees. The point of a shelter isn't progress. It's *shelter*.

"I've looked at your file." The woman gestures to a blank manila folder on the desk. Mack suspects it's empty. She hopes it is. "It's bad luck you're here. I understand. No social safety net to fall back on. A few months without a job, without rent, and it's hard to dig yourself out. You need to move on with your life. Contribute to humanity. All you need is a little good luck first."

"Donation bins could use tampons more than luck." Mack's voice is soft and dry with disuse.

The woman cracks, something triumphant behind her eyes. Mack shouldn't have spoken. The woman holds up an envelope. "It just so happens, some luck has come in the mail. Whether it's good is really up to you. Right now, it's an opportunity. And I think you're perfect for it."

Mack has never been perfect for anything in her life. *Perfect* feels like a foreign word, stiff and uncomfortable. But maybe it's a job. A little money to get presentable and she'll have an actual chance. As long as they don't pry. As long as they don't look too closely. She could make it work.

She takes the sheet of paper the woman slides across the desk. It's thick. It feels expensive. Mack is suddenly aware of her hands—her bitten fingernails, her shiny burned palms, her ragged cuticles. If she sets down the paper, will she leave a smudge? It's hard to be embarrassed at this point in her life, but the idea wriggles beneath her skin.

She's so worried about leaving a fingerprint—one that will somehow count against her in this imaginary job interview—that it takes her several seconds to process what she's reading.

"Is this a joke?" she whispers.

The woman's smile doesn't budge. "I know it sounds like one. But I assure you it's legitimate."

"Who told you?"

Finally, the woman's cheeks relax, and her eyebrows draw close. "What do you mean? Who told me what? That it's legitimate?"

About me, Mack thinks. *Who told you about me?* But the woman's confusion can't be feigned. Can it? If she can paint on a face, can she paint on emotions, too? Mack drops the letter. There are no fingerprints. But the words have left smudges across her mind.

"Why are you giving this to me?" Mack knows how lost she sounds, how scared, but she can't help it. "Why *me?*"

The woman laughs, a single dismissive burst. "I know it seems silly. The Olly Olly Oxen Free Hide-and-Seek Tournament. It's a children's game, for god's sake. But it's a chance to win fifty thousand dollars, Mackenzie. You could use that to actually move up in the world. You're young. You're intelligent. You're not a thief, you're not an addict. You shouldn't be here."

No one should be here. They all still are.

The woman leans forward intently. "It's run by an athletic company, Ox Extreme Sports. I can put in a good word and get you registered. There's no guarantee you'd win, but—I think you have a shot. It's more about endurance than anything else. Besides, you strike me as someone who's good at hiding."

Mack's chair scrapes back, jarring them both. But Mack can't be in this room, can't think, not while she's being looked at. Not while she's being *seen.* The woman doesn't know about Mack's history, and still, somehow she *knows.*

"Can I think about it," Mack states. It's not a question.

"Of course. But let me know by tomorrow. If you don't want the spot, I'm sure someone else will. It's a lot of money, Mackenzie. For a silly game!" The woman laughs again. "I'd enter it myself, but I can't go more than twenty minutes without needing to pee." She waits for Mack to laugh, too.

She's still waiting as Mack slides out through the door, not even a whisper in her wake.

Everything about the shelter is designed to remind them that nothing is theirs. There are no lockers. No alcoves. No closets. No bedrooms. In a featureless box of a space, the ceiling looming so far overhead a bird lives in the beams, there are cots. Each has the same stiff white sheets and scratchy blankets. The area beneath the cots is to be kept clear at all times. They are not allowed to use the same cot more than two nights in a row. Anything not cleared by nine A.M. will be confiscated and thrown out, so they can't even leave their meager possessions on the cot that is not theirs.

When the cots are all filled, Mack is as good as hidden. She's small. She's quiet. But now she feels as though a spotlight has been trained on her. Everyone else has already cleared out for the day. Some will go to whatever work they've found. Several will sit outside on the sidewalk until they're allowed back in at four P.M. The rest, who knows. Mack doesn't ask. Mack doesn't tell. Because she goes somewhere she doesn't want any of them to know about, either.

Hidden behind a half wall, choked with the scent of burning dust, an old water heater sizzles and rages. She has permanent shiny burns on her hands from where she scales the water heater, wedges herself between walls, and shimmies up.

The bird in the beams she has named Bert. It's been building a nest, finding scraps of trash, even hair. But what is it building it for? How will it find a mate, have eggs? Won't it live forever alone, safe and protected in the dusty dark up there? Mack lies on her stomach all day, three beams over from Bert, just existing. Patient and empty like the nest. And then when it's four P.M., she shimmies down and joins the weary throng claiming a cot that will never be their own.

She'll be able to think up in her spot by the bird, safe and hidden. But she has until tomorrow to decide. Maybe she won't think until then.

She stops midstride.

All the cots are stripped. Including the one she used last night. The one she left her pack on because she wasn't allowed to bring anything into her mandatory meeting. For *security* reasons.

Her pack is gone, which means she now owns only what she's wearing. Which means she can't even wash her clothes without standing over the sink, naked. And what public restroom will let her do that? She'll be noticed. She'll be seen.

She knows better than to ask the women who run the shelter to return her bag. They won't, and she'll be labeled trouble. Her time here is over. She can't sink beneath what little security she already had. She's seen what it looks like, what it costs.

Olly olly oxen free. A gradual corruption of the phrase "All ye outs come free." But nothing is ever free.

In the office, the blond woman's smile has not dropped a single millimeter, as though she was waiting. As though she knew.

"Okay," Mack whispers. "I'll do it." *Come out, come out, wherever you are,* he sings in her head.

She won't. She'll win.

And after all, her life doesn't depend on it this time.

FOURTEEN COMPETITORS. Seven days. The list is set. Arrangements have been made for delivery inside the park—food, gas for the generator, blankets and cots and whatever else is needed. Supplies have been gathered for outside the park. Cellphone jammers. Movies and books for the interminable wait. Power washers for the inevitable ending.

The list is distributed, along with photos. Everyone is expected to memorize it. Few do. The competitors are tacked onto the wall at Ray's diner one by one. No one is supposed to bet on the outcome—it's strictly against the rules—but it doesn't stop them from ranking, making predictions, picking a favorite. The competitors can be divided into two groups.

Those who are best described as aspiring:

A social media fitness model
A graffiti artist
A YouTube prank-show host
An app developer-slash-house sitter
A jewelry designer-slash-dog walker
A zealous CrossFit instructor
An actress with severe food allergies

Those who are best described as stalled:

A writer with severe people allergies
A boy equal parts banished and lost
The kindest gas station attendant in Pocatello, Idaho
A veteran
A solar panel salesman
An eternal intern
And Mack, who is nobody, if she has her way

Seventeen hours on a bus to another bus to a third bus to a glori-fied minivan, and finally Mack is delivered to the middle of the middle of nowhere. She often wonders which is more anonymous: a big city with so many people to notice that no one notices any-one, or the empty countryside where no one lives. Stepping off the van into a swirl of dust, greeted by no one, she suspects the former. She can see for what feels like miles in either direction down the road. Which means she can be seen, as well.

If she doesn't win, will they give her a bus ticket back? Or will she be stuck here? She doesn't even know where *here* is, unsure what state she's in. It's green, wildly so, with huge trees and dron-ing insects. It seems flat, but she can't see beyond the road or the trees.

She sits on the side of the road, clutching the Ox Extreme Sports duffel bag she was given. It contains seven shirts and four pairs of pants. They're all a weary shade of black. New but already faded, somehow. They feel familiar.

There's also a toiletries kit, which feels like a tender mercy. There were several granola bars and a bottle of water, but those disappeared a few hours into the seventeen she spent getting here. Hungry is hungry. No point in stretching out what she has when she can have the luxury of a full stomach once.

After an hour, her unease sharpens, pulling ever tighter. No one has come. The trees loom at her back. The road stretches, empty.

Has the game already begun? Has she already lost?

It could be worse. She's endless miles from where she knows, but she has clothes. Toothpaste, a toothbrush, deodorant, a comb. A sturdy bag. She's technically ahead of where she was before.

The protest of a much-abused automobile suspension greets her long before another van pulls up. She's resigned. It's here either to pick her up—*found!*—or to deliver her to the actual game.

It spews out three people and then unceremoniously continues along the infinite road. Two women and a man. A boy, really, Mack gets the sense. He can't be much younger than she is, and he's far taller, but something—the boyish part in his hair, the round face, the long-sleeved white button-up worn tucked into ill-fitting, cheap navy slacks—suggests he was dressed by someone else.

One of the women is put together with an artist's attention to detail. She is as much makeup and hair product as she is person, and Mack is dazzled by the visual perfection. It's almost hard to look at her. The other woman wears a black tank top over baggy cargo pants. She limps slightly as she shifts off the road and next to Mack.

The limping woman, her buzzed head emphasizing her large dark eyes, regards Mack without shame. The beautiful woman doesn't regard Mack at all. She scowls at her phone, holding it ever higher as though reception could be found that way. And the boy looks everywhere but at the women he is with. A fine sheen of sweat is on his forehead, wet spots at his armpits. He looks ready to flee.

Someone here is more terrified than Mack. It's comforting.

"Fucking kill me, there's really no reception," the beautiful woman finally says, still clutching her phone as some sort of talisman. "Lighting is too harsh, anyway." For the first time, she looks at Mack, who has shifted farther back from the road, almost to the tree line. "Did they tell you anything?"

Mack shakes her head. When the van picked her up at the bus station, the driver had only said, "Oxen Free?" He even asked her what it was, but she mumbled an answer and pretended to fall asleep.

"Ava," the woman with the buzzed head says.

"What?" the beautiful woman snaps.

"Ava."

The beautiful woman throws both hands in the air. "What?"

The buzzed woman lifts an eyebrow, patience wearing thin. "We didn't talk in the van, so I'm introducing myself. *I'm Ava. And you are . . .*"

Finally, the beautiful woman relaxes, snorting a laugh. "God, sorry, I'm such a bitch when I'm hungry. I'm Ava, too. That's why I was confused."

"May the best Ava win, Ava Two." Buzzed Ava's wry smile shows dimples deep enough to get lost in.

"I intend to." Beautiful Ava's tone is more playful than vicious. She retreats into the trees, snapping several selfies. Buzzed Ava turns to Mack expectantly.

"Mack." Mack offers her name as a complete sentence, hoping it will be accepted as such.

Buzzed Ava sits on the ground, stretching one leg easily in front of herself and manually positioning the other. "Good to meet you, Mack. I hope I beat you, and it's not personal."

Mack doesn't answer. It's a competition. Of course they want to win.

Buzzed Ava nods toward the boy, who has crossed the road and is standing on the other side, staring resolutely away from them. His shoulders are turned inward, his posture less anticipation than defeat. Already.

"That's LeGrand. He got picked up the same time as me, before Ava Two. When I took off my jacket, he twitched so hard looking away, I thought he'd break his neck. Poor kid is terrified of women. Might give him an edge. He'll be so desperate to avoid seeing us, he'll never come out."

"I think he's gay." Beautiful Ava sits on the ground next to buzzed Ava. Beautiful Ava is slender and bony. Buzzed Ava is thicker, strong looking. Mack admires and envies the line of her shoulders, the heft of her core. Her looks challenge in a different way than beautiful Ava's, but both draw attention.

Mack's own hair is cut short enough that she could be a guy, or she could be a girl. She wears oversize shirts and baggy pants, hands shoved in pockets to throw her shoulders forward and hide her breasts. Ava and Ava hide nothing.

Mack thinks she'll beat both of them.

"Not gay," buzzed Ava says, pulling up a long strand of grass and holding it to her mouth. She blows on it, but no sound comes out. "If he's that scared of female skin, he's gotta be interested." She leans back, squinting toward Mack. "What's your story?" There's something equal parts playful and appraising in the way a single bold eyebrow raises.

None of these people are Mack's friends. No one is her friend. No one will be. She can play nice and hope a mumbled answer satisfies buzzed Ava, but she doesn't think it will. So she goes for the other tactic.

"Fuck off," Mack answers.

Beautiful Ava scowls, offended by proxy. Buzzed Ava's look shifts, but not in a threatened or angry way. "Cool." She turns back to the road.

Mack retreats further into the shade, but in spite of her dismissal, both Avas eventually join her there. The sun is relentless and droning, like the insects around them. After an hour or two, another van bumps along to them. Beautiful Ava runs up to greet it, but it's the same story. Hired and dropping off. Over the course of the day, three more vans come until finally there are fourteen people waiting. They all seem around the same age, midtwenties, give or take a few years.

Mack feels more at ease now. With so many people there—several of whom are desperate to establish dominance and be noticed, talking and laughing loudly—she barely registers. Except to buzzed Ava, who brazenly stares at her and winks whenever caught.

When the last van pulls away, everyone looks down the road, waiting.

• • •

Five hours later and the mood has shifted considerably. Everyone is sweaty. There's nowhere to sit but the ground. No phones work. No one has any food or water—though one expertly muscled man increases monetary offers for food by the hour. One of the women, a brunette who looks like a toothpaste commercial with her dazzlingly white smile, cries. Several vow to leave scathing reviews of the experience online. A couple of the men suggest walking down the road to find the nearest town, but the fear of missing the competition keeps them in place. Everyone is short-tempered and angry. Except LeGrand, who stays at a distance, looking utterly lost, buzzed Ava, who is taking a nap with her arms for a pillow, and Mack, who knows she's two full days from being too hungry to function. A ghost of a smile haunts her face.

She can win this.

As the gentle bruise of evening spreads, a bus arrives. Apologies are delivered with water bottles and sandwiches. Their hostess, a woman well past middle age with a jewel-toned pantsuit and hair that exists in defiance of gravity, is so genuinely excited to greet them it's hard to hold the scheduling mix-up against her. A P.M. where an A.M. should have been, missed emails, no service, a litany of excuses made softer by calories and hydration . . . though several of the women will never forgive her for the indignity of having to pee in the woods.

Everything will be explained, the woman promises. But they have a long drive ahead of them, and if they could file into the bus quickly quickly quickly, so much to discuss, so much to prep, such a thrilling week ahead of them!

Water is gulped, food devoured, jokes exchanged. The bus toilet is gratefully and extensively taken advantage of. Seats are claimed, already sorting the contestants. LeGrand sits alone. Beautiful Ava no longer sees Mack, focused on those more on her level. Buzzed Ava follows Mack to the middle of the bus and sits next to her without asking. It's a problem. Mack wants to be invisible, wants to be underestimated, wants to be unseen. It's a hide-and-seek competition, after all.

Night arrives. The bus starts. Fourteen heat-exhausted and re-hydrated heads bob in near unison.

No instructions are delivered. Everyone is already asleep.

While they sleep, a tour.

Buzzed Ava's dog tags fall free of her tank top. One set her own. One set not. Her head falls onto Mack's shoulder. Mack's head rests against the soft fuzz of Ava's. It's the most human contact either of them has had in years. They sleep through it.

Beautiful Ava, aspiring Instagram model, has found beautiful Jaden, aspiring CrossFit gym owner. She has no sponsors and he has no gym, but they are lovely with hope and promise. Beautiful Ava's head rests against the window. She snores. She would be mortified to know she did it in public, but no one except the driver and their hostess is awake to hear. The driver keeps his eyes on the road with aggressive determination. He wields the steering wheel like a shield. The hostess wanders the aisle, touching each forehead with feather-soft fingers, like a blessing or a benediction.

The benediction misses LeGrand, tucked in the back, lost and alone even surrounded by people. This is not his world, and he doesn't know how to exist in it. Nothing, *nothing* makes sense. He dreams of digging for vegetables, his fingers hurting, digging deeper and deeper and finding nothing, knowing he should find something, should be looking for something, but all he can do is keep digging in the dark and the dirt. He's not looking for vegetables. He's digging a grave, and it hurts, and he hurts, and he's terrified he knows whose grave it is.

Ian has a notebook on his lap. His pen, the most expensive thing he owns, has fallen on the floor. He won't realize it until they're off the bus and he's already lost it. How can he write without it? He doesn't manage to write anything with it, either, but he'll be convinced it's the lack of pen holding him back. He came for inspiration. Also for money. A little bit of money, a little bit of security, and he could write the great American novel.

Brandon looks pleasant even in his sleep. There's something

wholesome and helpful in the way he slumbers completely up-right, as though ready to dive into service should someone need help. Regardless of what else happens, he's already had a great time and will be happy with the results. Honestly, he doesn't even know what he'd do with the money if he won. He can't quite imagine beating everyone else. It feels petty to want to win, almost mean. Because him winning would mean thirteen people lose. This is an adventure. A vacation. He hasn't taken a day off since he started working at the gas station at fourteen. But Grammy isn't waiting for him anymore. He's been a little lost since she died. An adventure is all he can ask for.

His seatmate slumps, head lolling for hours. There's still paint on his hands from where he tagged the last bus station. He's ready to leave his mark on the competition. Hopeful that he can create something here that will follow him back out into the world. He'll be the next Banksy. *No.* He'll be the first Atrius. (His real name is Kyle, and he hates it and everything Kyle was and could be. But he made the mistake of spelling Atreus wrong, so any chance he has of being googleable is taken by a health insurance company. A branding failure by someone determined to exist outside of brands.)

Christian fell asleep with a smile but secretly despairing. No one here seems like a good contact. His idea to do this for potential business opportunities seems as unlikely as actually winning the stupid thing. Maybe he'll meet someone from Ox Extreme Sports. Everyone needs a good salesman. If he has to knock on one more door and smile while asking about solar panels . . .

YouTuber Sydney and app developer Logan connected in the forest in the way Christian wished he had managed to with some-one. They're going to make a new app together based on Sydney's fledgling YouTube prank show. A national prank competition. It's gonna be huge. They're glowing even in sleep, secure in their imagined brilliant future. Dinners with Musk, charity summits with Gates, partnerships with Frye Technologies, and so many terrible pranks to get there.

Rebecca has priced out exactly how much it would cost to go from an A to a C. She thinks C is big enough. The agent she met with told her she had potential, but she'd need a little more up top for him to be interested. She's never been able to settle on whether he meant professionally interested, or casting couch interested. C is the letter that will get her her dreams, and $50,000 is the number that will get her to the letter she needs. She sleeps with her EpiPen-filled purse clutched against her chest like a security blanket.

Rosiee just wants to sell some fucking jewelry. Just once. Just to prove she's not the loser her mother always predicted she'd be. But silversmithing requires silver, and silver requires money. She's been hiding from her ex for four years. She can hide for a week, no sweat. Her ear is so heavy with jewelry, it clinks against the window where her head rests. The hostess's eye lingers over the snake twined around Rosiee's wrist. So pretty. She actually has talent.

In the front of the bus is Isabella, the eternal intern. She's interned at more places than she can remember. She wants face time with Ox executives, too. She needs a salary. God, she needs dental benefits. Fifty thousand dollars won't even cover her student loans for the education she borrowed herself into the ground for. The incredibly expensive degree that has yet to land her a single income-producing job. She grinds her teeth in her sleep.

The bus bumps along the deep tunnel of night, sealing in fourteen desperate dreamers against the world.

FOURTEEN PAIRS OF BLEARY EYES OPEN. They assume the bus stopping is what woke them.

They're wrong. The bus stopped hours ago. While they slept, half a dozen people climbed on, checked names and photos, marked them off on a list. The jewel-toned woman drifted up and down the aisle again, pressing her fingers to each forehead in benediction before rejoining the others outside of the bus. She insists on the pageantry of it, the formality, as they all bow their heads in a minute of silence. A few shuffle their feet, eager to leave. A few roll their eyes. And a few close their eyes in fervent gratitude. Then they're done, and off to finalize all the logistics, or take their posts, or shut themselves inside their houses until the next meeting before it's over at last.

With no evidence remaining of their visitors, the passengers stretch. Eleven phones are pulled immediately from pockets and purses. "No service?" Isabella asks, feeling panicky. What if she has a job offer? What if one of her infinite résumés has been flagged for potential? What if someone wants to connect on LinkedIn? No one has ever hoped to receive an email from that morass of despair more than Isabella.

"What provider do you have?" Jaden drapes his arms over the bus seat to best show off his biceps. He used to do these things deliberately, but now it's reflex. He's trained himself and his body to perfection.

"Verizon."

"T-Mobile. Nothing."

"AT&T," beautiful Ava says, scowling. "Nothing either. Even the Ox Extreme Sports app we had to download isn't working. I was going to go live on Insta."

"What about the NDA?" Isabella says.

"Well, obviously I wasn't going to say anything specific." Beautiful Ava scowls.

"Yeah, that was the most intense NDA I've ever seen!" Jaden says. Most everyone else laughs and nods, though in reality not a single one of them has ever been involved in something important enough to have a nondisclosure agreement. But none of them are going to admit it.

"I have four bars," Sydney says. She's met with hungry—almost desperate—stares. "Prank you very much!" She cringes as soon as it leaves her mouth. She really needs a better tagline for her YouTube show. And now everyone hates her as they slump back into their seats. Even Logan leans away from her. So much for their genius app partnership. In the full light of morning, it all feels less likely.

"No one has any service? Really?" Rebecca walks down the aisle, a bit wobbly, EpiPen purse carefully clutched. Everyone holds up worthless phones. Rebecca stops at Mack and Ava. Neither of them have a phone out. Ava's eyes are wide, her olive face pale.

"Phones?"

Mack shakes her head. Rebecca interprets it as Mack not having any service, not as Mack not having a phone.

"Your phone?" Rebecca asks Ava. "Do you have any service?"

"Leave me the fuck alone," Ava mutters, not looking up. Ava had been so calm, so cheerful. This shift unnerves Mack. Rebecca continues her journey to wake up fake-sleeping LeGrand. He doesn't have a cellphone, either. Those around him are struck with a bone-deep nervousness at the very idea. Their hands spasm around their own phones, now expensive cameras and nothing else.

Ava rubs her hands over her buzzed head. Mack realizes Ava has become *Ava,* not buzzed Ava. She's the main Ava in Mack's worldview. When Mack woke up—before Ava—Ava's head was on her shoulder, tucked in. The soft tickle of Ava's shorn head reminded Mack of a puppy. To her shock and mild dismay, she had been sad when Ava startled awake and away from her shoulder.

"Did you sleep?" Ava's question is weighted with more intensity than it should be.

Mack nods. She can sleep anywhere. She was asleep when he finally ended it. She didn't hear. The police had been there for hours before she woke up and emerged from her hiding spot. Sleep has always been her great escape, her great comfort. The nightmares are saved for her waking hours.

"I don't sleep in public." Ava looks around, twitchy. "Not on airplanes, or buses, or anywhere where I don't know who's around me, where I don't feel safe." She had been faking her nap yesterday, using the time to listen in on the conversations around herself and evaluate the competition.

Mack had felt safe when she woke up with Ava on her shoulder. Wasn't that safe? "It was a long day," Mack says, her voice whisper-soft.

"I've gone four days without sleep while traveling." Ava's jaw clenches and unclenches. She looks up at the front of the bus, where the driver and their hostess are both missing. Then she reaches for her bag, checks around the floor. "Where's your water bottle from last night?"

Mack checks her bag. Her water bottle is gone. She shakes her head, some of Ava's uneasiness wearing off on her.

"Hey!" Ava shouts, standing up. "Did everyone fall asleep last night? Anyone stay awake?" Heads shake. "Does anyone know where we are?"

"I can answer that!" Their hostess climbs aboard, her smile as bright as the morning sun.

Ava sits back down, scowling. "Fourteen people and no one stayed awake."

"Maybe you felt safe?" Mack whispers. Her shoulder is cold where Ava's head no longer rests.

"Do *you* feel safe?"

Mack looks out the window. She had, for those few seconds between sleeping and waking. And it had been the first time in a very long time. But the feeling is gone now, and it wasn't shared, which makes it all sadder.

"Welcome to the town of Asterion! It's a bit of a technological wonder," their hostess says, giggling to herself. "An all-natural cell-free zone! There's a particular type of mineral everywhere here—they used to mine it. It interferes so strongly with cell signals that the companies stopped trying. So I'm afraid for the duration of the competition you will be without cell service."

"Wi-Fi?" Rebecca asks, the actress acting as de facto leader.

"We have some good old-fashioned pay phones. You're welcome to use them this morning as we prep before going into the competition zone. Twenty-five cents, but long distance is more so you may need to call collect."

"Who has change these days?" Rosiee voices everyone's thought as she twists one of her heavy silver bracelets.

"Why have us download an app if we can't even use it?" beautiful Ava grumbles.

Logan perks up at the mention of the app. The app is by Frye Technologies, the Silicon Valley giant he shares a last name with. It's part of why he wants to go into making apps. He feels connected already, like he's destined to share that success.

But the woman waves dismissively. "Oh! The app. I forgot about that. It's for after the competition, so don't delete it. Gathering information, feedback, blah blah. Not my department. And I am sorry about the lack of service—I know how you young people like your phones!—but it's actually one of the features that drew us to Asterion. You'll remember your NDAs. Ox Extreme Sports is quite serious about those. They're still in developmental stages on the tournament, so they need to control the flow of information. They're considering selling it as a reality show."

Half the bus citizens perk up, like dogs on a scent. Half sink down, like those same dogs after years of abuse.

"But of course nothing is decided yet. We reserve all rights. Now, I'm sure you're hungry. The Star Diner is ready and waiting. While we're there, I'll brief you on today's schedule."

Mack slouches in her seat. She doesn't have any cash.

"I can cover you," Ava says. Apparently Ava still sees her more than she wants to be seen.

LeGrand clears his throat. His voice is incongruously deep for such a baby face, and the way he talks makes it clear he both knows how deep his voice is and is ashamed of it. "I was—um—I was told all meals would be provided?"

"Oh, of course, dear." Their hostess's lipstick has migrated to her front teeth, making her smile look bloody. "Breakfast is on us! And all your meals during the competition will be on-site. Now that you're here, the only thing you have to worry about is not being found."

LeGrand wilts with relief. Mack is glad, too. She doesn't want to start on an empty stomach, and she doesn't want to owe anyone anything. Especially not Ava.

"Come out, come out, wherever you are!" one of the men trills in falsetto.

Mack's stomach turns. She might not be able to eat after all.

A computer. A tiny apartment in a run-down city. Nobody to talk to and nothing to do for the rest of her life but get by. That's all she needs. She can do this. She has to.

They file out of the bus. As they go, their hostess hands them each a nicely bound, laminated packet. "What's your name?" Rebecca asks her, settling further into her role as leader. She has that quality, that extra bit of charisma, that sets her apart. It makes everyone look closer, trying to figure out if she really is prettier than she seems. She *acts* pretty. Maybe that's it.

Beautiful Ava shifts closer to her, then steps away, then steps closer. She looks back and makes eye contact with Mack. Rolls her eyes like they're both in on some sarcastic observation.

Mack has no idea what it is.

Their hostess laughs at Rebecca's question. "I'm Linda! I was going to introduce myself last night, but you all fell asleep so fast, I didn't want to wake you."

Ava makes a small, doubtful noise. Mack deliberately moves away from her, to the back of the group. LeGrand's there. He stares down at his packet with an alarmed expression. Mack opens her own.

Legalese. She skims the terms. Limits of liability. A repeat of the nondisclosure agreement. Permission to be filmed. Release of rights to their own images. Agreements to do interviews and press and promo after the fact, if the company so chooses.

Mack will sign whatever she needs to. And then she'll take the money and run. There's no way her history won't be used for something like that. But with $50,000, she can disappear. She skips past the dozen or so legal pages to the itinerary and schedule. The Star Diner is listed for the morning, along with instructions. Which are all in the packet. Oh, *god*. They're going to have to sit there while Linda reads the entire packet aloud to them.

A rush of air-conditioned cool reaches out to claim them as they enter the diner. Out of his gas station but never out of his comfort zone when helping other people, Brandon holds the door for everyone, smiling and nodding at each of them, though most don't notice. Rosiee, the woman with all the jewelry, smiles at him. His grin gets big and sloppy. It's still that big and sloppy when Mack slinks past him. He frowns slightly, trying to figure her out. But LeGrand brings up the end of the line, and Brandon lets the door close, sealing them in the frigid diner with the AC and the permanent scent of bacon. Later that night, when Mack changes, she'll still smell it, permeating her bra.

Mack chooses a table in the middle and tucks her bag under her feet. No one else brought their stuff in except the walking toothpaste commercial, who is clutching her purse as though it's a life preserver. But then, odds are no one else has everything they own in a single duffel bag.

A man with thick forearms, fuzzy with dark gray hair that's missing from his head, comes out from the kitchen, wiping his hands on a greasy apron. "Hey-oh, look at this crew! Let me guess: You want gluten-free options. How about a cruelty-free, free-range piece of avocado toast? The avocados were raised in a hippie commune and sung to sleep every night, and they were never allowed to be friends with a single piece of gluten." He laughs at his own joke.

Rebecca raises her hand politely. "Actually, I have food allergies, and—"

The man waves dismissively. "Imaginary. Your generation, honestly. In my day, you know how many kids were allergic to peanuts? None! Now everyone is so sensitive. Sensitive to this, sensitive to that. Grow a pair and learn how to eat like an adult!" He delivers it all with the cadence of a well-practiced speech.

Rebecca's smile doesn't shift, and she hasn't lowered her hand. "I could literally die if I eat tree nuts or shellfish, or anything that has come into contact with them."

"And yet here you are! Still not dead!"

"Gary," Linda says in a singsong tone. "We know about Rebecca's allergies. A separate breakfast has been prepared. Remember? Ask Ray."

Gary lets out a dismissive burst of air from his incongruously full and red lips. "Right. Fine. Anyone else need special care for their special bowels? Hmm? I know it's hard to leave Mommy's basement and come out into the real world."

"*Gary.*"

He raises his hands, grinning. "I kid, I kid. These young folks can take a joke, right?"

"For the record, I live in my parents' garage, not their basement," Jaden mugs. Gary laughs, clapping him on the shoulder.

"I like this one. Would you feel the muscles on this guy? Wow!" Gary squeezes Jaden's shoulder, then nods. "I know who my money's on."

"You're allowed to bet?" beautiful Ava asks.

"No," Linda snaps. She takes a deep breath, and her smile goes back into place. "No, but some people in the town will naturally take an interest. It's the biggest thing to happen here in years. Now, will you please take their orders so we can get down to business?"

Gary grumbles. "We built an international chain from the ground up, a global dining phenomenon, but sure, yeah, I'll take orders like a little waitress." His scowl is carved into his face, but he gets to work.

"Hey, who's Ray Callas?" Brandon chirps, looking up from where he's reading a framed magazine article about the small-town diner that took over the world. Another older man pauses where he was coming out of the kitchen.

"Me," he says.

"My dad's last name is Callas. What a coincidence! Maybe we're related." Brandon beams, eager and genuinely excited by the connection, but Ray shakes his head.

"No." Without further comment, Ray helps Gary distribute glasses of water and well-loved menus.

Mack orders pancakes and eggs and bacon and sausage and toast and fruit and orange juice. Gary raises a bushy eyebrow. "You got an appetite." He leans closer. "You a boy or a girl? How am I supposed to tell with this?" He gestures at her neutral haircut and her baggy clothes.

"Maybe people don't owe you their gender," Ava says, slinging herself into the chair next to Mack.

"Oh god, save me from lesbians with opinions. Did you ever think you just needed to find the right man?" Gary's smile is both predatory and aggressive. "You know, back in my day we didn't *decide* we didn't need gender or marriage or procreation. We accepted how God made us without forcing our opinions on everyone around us. We also got jobs and worked honest days and moved out of our parents' houses before we were forty."

"Cool story, man," Ava says. "Tell me about how you walked uphill to school both ways, twenty miles in the snow, and how going to school didn't put you in six-figure debt, and how your first house cost less than a car, and then I'll tell you a story about how your generation fucked mine over."

Something hard and cold shifts in his smile, and his manner of speech changes from the well-worn regurgitations of what he's read on Facebook. "You're going out early. I can tell. You should respect your elders. I'm a veteran."

"Me, too." Ava leans back in her chair, yawning. "I'll have the same breakfast, only with a chocolate milkshake instead of orange juice."

Linda clears her throat. Gary snatches their menus and moves on. Linda pauses at their table, putting a gentle hand on each of their shoulders. "Don't mind Gary. He means well. We're all very glad you're here."

"Gary reminds me of my grandpa," Ava says as soon as Linda leaves. "I hated my grandpa."

To Mack's surprise, beautiful Ava joins their table. She seems agitated, constantly glancing over at Rebecca's full table. LeGrand sits by himself at the counter, frowning over the packet. He's been staring at the same page the entire time. The tall, gangly guy with a friendly face offers to help Ray in the back, but Ray waves him off. Gangly joins their table, too. He sits straight, an eager smile on his face.

"Hey! I'm Brandon. Are you guys excited?" he asks. Now Mack knows his name, too. Brandon, Ava, beautiful Ava, LeGrand. She decides that's enough names to learn. None of them matter anyway.

"For breakfast?" Ava asks.

Brandon laughs. "No. I mean, I'm excited for breakfast. I work graveyard. I haven't had a real diner breakfast in years! But no. For the game. It's gonna be fun, right?"

Beautiful Ava smiles, holding it carefully. She's sitting with perfect posture and keeps looking around the room. Scanning the walls, and then the corners where the walls meet the ceiling.

"What are you looking for?" Mack asks, unable to help herself.

The way beautiful Ava scans everything makes her nervous, like there's something she should be looking for, too.

"Cameras. Surely they'd want this footage, too?"

Mack flinches, joining suit. But she doesn't see anything that looks like a camera. "We haven't signed everything in the packet yet," Ava points out.

Beautiful Ava relaxes, her posture falling. She eyes Brandon critically. His features are blandly pleasant. Not handsome, not ugly. Skinny face, crooked teeth, small, kind eyes. There's nothing threatening in him. She decides to respond to his question, since no one else has. But keep it friendly, not flirty. He's not a good alliance. "Yeah, I think this is gonna be super fun!"

Mack and Ava don't comment. It would feel like a lie to Mack to act excited. But she feels a little bad at the expectation on Brandon's face, so she offers him a quick nod.

"I think it's gonna be awful," Ava says, reaching down to shift her right leg's position.

Brandon laughs like it's a joke, and Ava lets him.

As breakfast is served, Linda does exactly as suspected and proceeds to read the entire packet aloud to them. The only kindness is that she skips the legal documents in front. No one ever reads those anyway.

As soon as Linda begins reading the itinerary, LeGrand closes his with a relieved sigh and leans forward, listening intently. Mack doesn't. She's already committed all the relevant information to memory. The rest is just details.

Fourteen competitors.

Seven days.

A thirty-minute hiding window given at the start of each day— which is dawn.

Gameplay continues until dusk.

At dusk, everyone leaves their hiding spots and returns to base camp for their evening meal and sleeping.

"Will there be cabins? What are the room situations?" Isabella asks. She's subletting an apartment from a friend of a friend and has two roommates, so it's bound to be a step up from the modified closet masquerading as a bedroom that they gave her. She actually has to go *through* a bathroom to get to her room, so if one of her roommates is in the shower or on the toilet, she's locked away from or inside of her own bedroom until they finish.

"Oh," Linda says, pursing her lips. "It's more of a camping scenario. There are toilets and showers, of course. And a covered pavilion with cots and bedding. It's much easier than transporting you to and from the site every day. This gives you a lot more downtime."

"Cots?" Isabella was wrong. It's not a step up. How is she going to keep herself looking presentable the whole time? She *needs* a job out of this. "We're sleeping outside?"

"Part of the game, I'm afraid."

"What about eating during the day?" Rebecca asks. She envies people who don't have to consider every single thing they ever eat.

"There will be supplies. You can take them into the park with you."

"The park?" Ava sits up straight. This is the first detail they've been given about where they'll be hiding.

Linda slaps a hand over her mouth. "Whoopsie! No more about that! But you'll have supplies to choose from every morning."

"What about when we have to pee?" Rebecca continues. "Will there be breaks during the day?"

Linda clears her throat. "As I said, there will be supplies. Jars with lids included."

"Sucks to be a girl." Jaden and Logan fist-bump and laugh.

"We really can't take bathroom breaks?" Rosiee asks, nervously twisting her silver bracelet. She has a history of UTIs and has no desire to do anything that might trigger another one.

"I'm afraid from dawn until dusk the game is active. If you are found for any reason—medical emergency, bathroom emergency, food run, anything—that's that. No exceptions."

Mack tries not to smile as the majority of the room shifts nervously, whispering to each other. The careful blonde from the shelter was right. Mack's practically been training for this for years now. She's never been lucky—or she's the luckiest unlucky girl alive, depending on your viewpoint—but maybe, just maybe, that's changed.

"Mackenzie Black?" The muscled guy looks up, searching the room. Mack doesn't respond. Her plate is nearly empty. "Why do I know that name?"

She should have read the back of the packet. All their names are listed. Shit. She doesn't need this complication.

The toothpaste commercial stands up. Linda is outside, making final arrangements with a couple of men and a supply truck. Gary, thankfully, is back in the kitchen. "We should do introductions! I didn't get to talk to everyone while we were waiting yesterday. I'm Rebecca Andrews. I'm an actress. I like long walks on the beach and ridiculous competitions. Though I'll admit I'm disappointed that we don't have more diversity in the group to reflect our beautiful country's"—she reaches for a word, but ends up repeating—"uh, diversity." She's obviously disappointed in herself for not being more eloquent.

Ava and Rosiee, the only people in the room who aren't white or white-passing, share a long-suffering look, but neither engages. Mack doesn't blame them. It's not like Rebecca would give up her spot here so someone "diverse" could have a chance.

A guy stands up next, wearing a polo shirt with an embroidered company logo and khaki pants. He looks like he should be holding a clipboard. "Christian Berry. Solar panel salesman, so let me know if you have a house and I'll hook you up." He watches the room hopefully, but no one speaks up.

It goes down the line. Some try to add a clever line or two like the toothpaste commercial. Some give only their first and last name. A slouchy guy with a beanie and a hoodie on despite the heat gives a single name.

"Atrius like the insurance?" the clipboard guy asks.

"No, like the—" He sighs. "Yeah. I named myself after health insurance. It's social commentary. I can't get insurance, so I be-came insurance."

Ava laughs. Atrius looks at her gratefully.

A sallow guy with deep-set eyes—Mack remembers he spent the whole afternoon huddled over a notebook but didn't seem to write anything—scowls, folding his arms. "I don't know what the point of this is. We aren't friends. We're all here to beat each other. I don't care what any of your names are, or what you do, or your hopes and dreams."

"Aw, Ian, don't be like that." Brandon smiles. "This can be fun, too, right?"

"I'm with Ian." Ava shrugs. "I wish y'all the best, but I also hope you lose. I'm Ava, by the way."

"The *other* Ava," beautiful Ava corrects. "*I'm* Ava, and—"

The guy with the muscles leans back, folding his arms. "I'm Jaden Harrell—"

"Like that dickhead Brent Harrell?" Ava interrupts.

"Who is that?" Jaden frowns, biceps twitching.

"The Supreme Court justice? The one who assaulted women in college and makes decisions for the whole country now?"

Jaden shrugs, obviously annoyed at Ava for interrupting and also for knowing something he didn't. He tenses, the equivalent of a rooster puffing up his feathers to look bigger in the face of a threat. "Who the fuck cares? Anyway, yeah, I'm Jaden. But who is Mackenzie Black?"

"Mack?" Beautiful Ava looks at her. "That's you, right?"

Mack's food is gone. She stands and walks out of the diner. The heat greets her like an old friend, wrapping her in its embrace. Linda waves brightly but doesn't come over. She's checking things off a list from her folder. Mack's duffel is a reassuring weight drag-ging on her shoulder.

The street is lined with summer-lush trees, each shaped as though it were modeling the ideal form of a small-town tree. The street is paved perfectly black, and the sidewalks meander like creeks around the islands of the trees. Each building facade is maintained and clean. Bright shutters, cheerful paint, decorative windows. It feels like a movie. Mack half suspects that if she went down an alley, there would be no buildings behind the storefronts, wooden beams propping them up, elaborate sets of lights, tables for craft services.

"It's a vibrant community," the bus driver says. He's middle-aged but seems older, leaning against a nearby tree, eating a sandwich as though he's sorry about it. "A good town. A safe town. No crime. Everyone is employed. Lots of businesses that create jobs all over the country. The world, even."

"Can I get back on the bus?" Mack asks.

He nods. He's still staring down at his sandwich, not looking at her. "Worth fighting for. Places like this. They're special. Rare. Traditions, you know?"

She doesn't. She gets on the bus.

"What state are we even in?" Jaden asks as he climbs off the bus.

Linda taps the side of her nose. "If you don't know, I'm not telling you! The location needs to be kept secret. We may want to use it again, and we can't do that if future competitors can Google for an advantage before the game even begins. It was in your NDA."

"Right, yeah." He stretches deliberately. Mack has never seen someone who wants to be looked at as much as he does. Not even beautiful Ava or the toothpaste commercial can compete. Everyone files out after him. They've driven a couple of blocks and stopped in front of an elegant, if vaguely out of place, building. In contrast to the idealized Americana feel of the main street, this building is pure white. Greek columns frame the front. A gravel walkway is lined with topiary and fountains with no one outside to enjoy them. Just like the main street. For all Mack can tell, they're the only people in the whole town. Though she could have sworn she saw some faces peering out of windows at them as they drove past various businesses.

"What is this place?" the writer asks, frowning.

"A spa!" Linda holds out her hands, beaming. Several of the women and a few of the men clap excitedly. Mack feels dread. Ava sighs in annoyance. LeGrand takes a step back toward the bus.

"I'll wait here," he says, but the door is closed.

"Nonsense! This is a gift. The next week is going to be difficult. Let us pamper you first."

"When are we going to meet the Ox Extreme Sports people?" the intern asks. (Mack wonders what someone would have to be like to introduce themselves as "currently an intern but ready for the next challenge!" in the middle of a diner with a bunch of clearly under- and unemployed people.) She's wearing a blazer over pinstripe slacks. "Are they inside?"

"No, dear. Come on. They're ready for you, and we don't want to waste any time!"

"Then why are we going to a spa?" Ava mutters.

Mack wants to hang by the bus with LeGrand. But Linda swings back around and takes LeGrand by the elbow, steering him inside. Apparently this, like Mack's fateful shelter meeting, is mandatory.

The floor is black marble, so polished they can see themselves in it. The walls and the furniture are pristine white. The kind of white that screams *Don't touch me* to people like Mack. The kind of white that purrs *You deserve me* to people like Rebecca.

Directly across from the grand entry door, framed in gilt gold, is a larger-than-life oil portrait. A young man in a uniform that's probably from one of the world wars, though Mack couldn't say which, stares out at them. The edges of the portrait are dark, but he's surrounded by light, almost haloed by it. His gaze is determined, a noble lift to his chin as he surveys them. One hand holds a small leather book over his heart.

"Who's he?" beautiful Ava asks, pausing in front of the painting.

Linda's smile is tugged into place, but her eyes narrow reflexively as she looks at the portrait. "The town founder. Of sorts. Silly to say one person founded a town when it was very much a group effort. He certainly didn't do it alone! Now, boys, you go to the right, and girls, you follow me."

They're separated. Men in one wing, women in another. A bath stretches the length of the building. High-set windows let in light that seems alive in the shifting steam. The prettiest women are the most loath to disrobe. Ava strips without hesitating. Her right leg is a Jackson Pollock painting of damage, abstract and misshapen with scars. She slides down into the pool with a sigh.

"Okay, I changed my mind, this isn't a waste of time." She grins, then dunks herself. Water streams off her head as she emerges.

The rest eventually follow, though they do so from behind the cover of towels for as long as possible. Beautiful Ava leaves her towel tied tightly around herself in the water. She eyes the corners for cameras. Finds none. Is not reassured.

Rebecca swims elegant, leisurely laps.

Beautiful Ava is *disappointed,* and disappointed in herself for being disappointed. She's a feminist. She doesn't want to pit herself against other women, even in her own mind. But she can already see how the season will be framed if it ever becomes television. Rebecca will be the lead. Beautiful Ava will be "the other hot one," the throwaway one. Maybe she can start a romance with one of the men. That should bump her up, narratively. Brandon is the easiest target but not cinematic enough. Jaden is a good bet. She's branding herself as a fitness model, and he's a CrossFit instructor. It's a good combination. She'd rather spend time with Mack—something about her is soothing. Or sweetheart Brandon. She'd like him if she let herself. But she'll pursue Jaden.

She doesn't know if it will be a show. None of them do. The packets are very fuzzy in that regard. But if there's the chance, she'll treat it like it will happen. And she'll make sure she's the love interest, not the villain. Or the *other* Ava.

She's jealous of Brandon for being excited, for viewing this as an adventure and not an opportunity. She's so sick of trying to turn everything into an opportunity, trying to exploit every hobby, every interest, every talent, even her own fucking face and body in a desperate attempt to make enough money. The last time they spoke—a year ago, maybe?—her father accused her of being lazy, of not working, but the truth is, like everyone her age she knows, she's *always* working. She's just not making a living doing any of it. Yet.

Mack has found the farthest corner. She dunks herself, lets her hair soak, lets her whole self soak for as long as she can, until her lungs are bursting and spots dance in front of her eyes. And then she waits another full thirty seconds before tipping her head so her nose and mouth are above the water. The steam is so thick that if you didn't know she was there, you would never know she was there.

Isabella sits on the steps, arms crossed, impatient. If the organizers aren't here, this does her no good. A coiled tension in her stomach that no amount of warm, buoyant water can undo tells her that *none* of this will do her any good. She stands first, needing to get out of the steam and the heat and the relentless pressure. An attendant hurries forward with a plush white robe and guides her to the next room.

Rosiee hangs on the side of the pool, resting her chin on her arms as her legs float. She toys with the pile of silver she took off. She doesn't care about the clothes, but she feels naked without her jewelry. She's shaped herself into every piece she wears. This ring when she told her mother to go to hell and resolved to never speak to her again. This cuff bracelet with the last reserves of her silver the night before she ran out on Mitch. This delicate heart necklace with a sharp point in memory of her sharp-witted grandmother, the only person who ever believed in her. Who is she without that belief hanging around her neck?

Who will she be when this competition is over and she has to face reality again? She sinks lower in the water, squints her eyes so all she sees is light glinting off silver. A new piece takes form in her mind. One shaped by triumph. One shaped by strength.

Sydney wants to chat, but everyone else is so damn blissed out.

She should think of a great prank to do. This many strangers, naked together? But the water is too hot, and the steam makes her lightheaded, and even if she did think of a good prank, Linda took their phones at the door.

Pranks are stupid. She knows they are.

She's going to be twenty-seven next week, and she's been obsessing over where the threshold is when she's no longer in her midtwenties, but in her *late* twenties with nothing to show for any of it. She spends all of her free time watching teenagers on social media so she can mimic their movements, their mannerisms, their speech. Sometimes she's terrified the FBI will look at her viewing history and ask why she has such an intense interest in underage girls. Now she's in a room with women her age and she has no idea how to talk to any of them, how to have an actual conversation without a script.

God, she hates herself so much. It's too quiet in here. She can't take it for another second. She stands and smiles. "So fun!" she chirps, before the attendant leads her to the next room.

LeGrand refuses to take off his clothes, or be in a room where anyone else does. He sits out in the lobby and waits. Beneath the portrait is a white couch—so obviously untouched by any child ever that it makes him miss Almera with a physical pain. The world is huge and scary and confusing, and he doesn't understand how he got here. He wants to go home, to load Almera in the wheelbarrow, to push her as fast as he can until she squeals with laughter.

The rest of the men are in a sauna. It's miserable, but each pretends to relish it. Except Brandon. Brandon really does love it. He leans back, breathing deeply, letting his body relax. He's in a sauna! Last week he had to clean up after someone was sick—both ends— all over the gas station bathroom at three A.M. And today, he's in a fancy-pants spa. "Isn't this amazing?" he asks.

Atrius's fingernails are black, painted to hide the spray paint that's always under them. He picks at the chipping polish idly. This is boring.

Jaden and Logan talk sports. It's a relief, having common ground. No one talks about the game awaiting them.

Christian, like Isabella, still hopes they'll meet the organizers. Linda has dropped a few hints—this is going to be an annual event—and he wants in. He can imagine living in this beautiful town. Marrying someone. Rosiee pops briefly into his mind, a fantasy of backyard BBQs and anonymously adorable children filling itself in around her. Someone once told him that mixed-race kids are the cutest and he's never been able to stop thinking about it. He's not sure if that makes him racist. But he'll be a good dad, a good husband. He'll take Linda's job. And he'll never have to go door to door again. He'll burn a clipboard in that BBQ, ceremoniously.

Ian breaks first. He rushes out, taking grateful gasps of cool air. He tells himself this whole thing is an experience. A study. He'll use it all in his writing. His head swims as an older woman gently guides him into the next room.

Cold showers are offered. Hot showers are offered. Decadent platters of food. Salt scrubs. Massages. LeGrand stays on the couch. Mack stays in the pool until everyone else has moved on. As she walks to the showers through a cloud of perfume left in Rebecca's wake, she has an idea.

She scrubs but uses no products. Refuses the massage—after so many years of being untouched, she worries she might freak out or cry—and the accompanying scented oils. Her deodorant is unscented. She smiles to herself as she sits alone, separate, in her robe. She's going to be invisible in every way possible.

In the end, twelve contestants get massages. They wear beaded masks, so they can't see that the older woman massaging them cries silently the whole time. She wishes the other two had allowed her to perform this kindness. It's the only thing she can offer them, the final gift of gratitude for what they're going to do.

"Holy *shit,*" the prank girl says, accurately summing up how they all feel as the bus pulls to a stop in front of giant wrought iron gates. The last rays of daylight are streaming nearly horizontal through the trees to suffuse the whole scene with verdant intensity.

Above the gates, a faded and chipped sign bids them WELCOME TO THE AMAZEMENT PARK. Rusted circles that once held bulbs surround each word, with streaks of dark red trailing down like tears. But the old sign doesn't go at all with the gate. Where the sign is amusement-park garish, left to rot, the gate itself feels older but perfectly maintained. There are symbols worked into scrolling metalwork, a pattern. Mack can almost make sense of it, can almost—but no. Her eyes glance off the points of the gate, unable to focus on what's there. It's like they want to look anywhere else.

She's tired, though.

Everyone is pressed against the windows, trying to pierce the dense wall of trees surrounding them. Almost lost in the green is a ten-foot-tall fence made of metal cables, complete with razor wire at the top. It screams *Keep out*. But it doesn't bother Mack, who breathes a sigh of relief. The game isn't inside. Doubtless there will be buildings, but she doesn't have to hide *inside*. Her fear—not her worst fear, because after what happened to her family she doesn't have one of those anymore—was that they'd be in a house. This? This is different. She'll be okay. She can handle this.

She has to.

Linda keeps her back to the park. She doesn't look out the windows. "We'll go directly into your base camp. Please remember that it is only for use from sundown to sunup. There are no free spaces, no time-outs. If the sun is up, the game is on."

"Can we go into the park tonight? Explore?" Ava asks.

"You'll remember the extensive liability waiver you all signed. The park is abandoned and has been for decades. Some of the structures are unsafe. There are gaps in the walkways, uneven concrete. Lots of places to trip and fall if you don't have enough light. It's definitely not ADA compliant." Her smile is sickly sweet. Ava stiffens. Mack twitches with discomfort at the false concern. She suspects Ava is the most physically capable person here, but she shrinks into herself instead of saying as much.

Linda claps her hands together once, emphatically. "Besides, no one gets an advantage. You'll all start at the same time. You'll police each other to make certain no one sneaks off in the night." She winks. "What an adventure!"

"So let's go!" Jaden says.

The bus driver's hands are clenched around the steering wheel. "Sun's still up."

"Nah, man, it's—"

"I will *not* open the gates until the sun is down."

"That's okay," Brandon says, trying to cut the odd tension left in the wake of the bus driver's emphatic response. "Can you tell us about the park?"

Mack leans back, tuning out Linda's chirpy summary of a family fun amusement park that ran for a couple of decades in the middle of the last century. Linda's not going to give them any useful details. She's made that clear. And they're keeping them out of the park while they can see well enough to gain some sort of advantage.

Ava slides into the seat next to Mack. She points out the window. "That's a person, right?" What Mack had taken for a rock is actually a statue. There's a hint of a head, the barest form of a human. And, at the base, one perfect dismembered white hand, pointing back the way they came. Mack nods toward it.

"Well, that's not creepy at all." Ava sits back. "One week in a crumbling, probably dangerous old theme park. Still not the worst summer vacation I've ever had."

"Me, neither," Mack whispers.

"Did you see the other Ava getting cozy with Jaden? Think people are going to form alliances?"

A glance reveals beautiful Ava sitting closer than necessary to Mr. Muscles himself. Mack shrugs. "Only one winner. What good would a partnership do?"

Ava nods thoughtfully. "True. So if I need help in there . . ."

Mack shrugs again.

"Fair enough. But . . ." Ava puts a hand over her heart, her face shifting in exaggerated earnestness. "If you need help, Mack, I promise, I'll feel *real* bad for you when you get out."

Mack snorts a laugh. Ava, satisfied, watches through half-hooded eyes as the sun finally sets and the driver gets out to open the gates. The hinges squeak, the only sound in the heavy summer evening. The rest of the park looks weathered, but the fence is well maintained, though again it doesn't match the significantly older gate.

"On our own in the game, fine," Ava whispers. "But look. I know I'm paranoid; I still think they drugged us. And if *that* shit goes down again, I have your back. Will you have mine?"

Mack nods. It's an easy promise to make. She doesn't anticipate having to break it.

The driver gets back in and slowly steers the bus into the park. The road is bumpy and cracked. Several times he has to carefully maneuver them around debris too hard to make out in the quickly deepening dark. It looks like this road isn't part of the original park design—several of the pathway walls have been demolished, still sitting in rocky piles where the road was widened. The driver takes a few turns that seem random. Between his agonizingly slow speed and the winding road, it's hard to say how far they've actually gone when they arrive at last.

"This is your stop," Linda says. "I'll stay with you until the start time in the morning. I will not be back until sunset."

"Who gets us out?" the intern asks.

Linda laughs. "Certainly not me! Can you imagine, a woman my age clambering around in kitten heels. It's all part of the game. You'll find out."

"Not me," the guy sitting next to the prank girl blusters, standing. "I don't intend to find out at all."

The writer rolls his eyes. "Bully for you."

"No way that dude makes it past the first two days," Ava says, her observation covered by the noise of everyone gathering their things and getting off the bus.

"Which one?" Mack asks, as if she knows their names anyway.

"Both. All, actually. I don't like the odds of any of the dudes."

"What about LeGrand?"

Ava turns to evaluate him, still haunting the very back of the bus. "LeGrand? Really? I see him standing in the middle of a pathway, looking lost."

Mack shoulders her bag. "He seems like he knows how to hide."

"Takes one to know one, huh?" Ava's smile is wry. "You're my dark horse. Even when you're next to me, I get the feeling you're not really there."

"Come out, come out, wherever you are!" Jaden shouts from outside the bus.

Mack flinches, pushing her shoulder against her ear. The sound of footsteps. The sound of a knife being dragged against wood. The sound of her sister's gasps, wet and burbling. Mack shouldn't have told Ava she'd have her back if the worst happens. Mack already knows that she won't.

Even without four walls, the camp is a step up from the shelter. The cots are neat, the blankets soft, and a table filled with food and water means Mack can have whatever she wants whenever she wants—and take it with her, too. But judging by the complaints and disbelief of many of her fellow competitors, the circumstances are far from what they'd been anticipating after the spa.

"This is great." Brandon drops his bag onto the cot next to Mack's. "I haven't ever been camping! Just fishing. When my dad used to visit, he'd take me to the Snake River. I'd come home with, like, whole constellations of mosquito bites, but I loved it."

Mack doesn't know what she's supposed to say. So she says nothing.

Brandon doesn't seem to mind. "Is it okay if I take this one next to you?" he asks.

Mack nods. He lies back with his hands behind his head, staring up at the metal pavilion roof overhead. Brandon is benign. She doesn't mind his presence, and she'll never think about him again once he's eliminated.

Linda gestures to the pavilion around them. It's the only interior part of the park that looks newish. A cement floor under a corrugated metal roof, and a structure with bathrooms and showers. Overhead lights create pools of orange around them that bleed the color from everyone and don't extend past the edge of the concrete. Next to the supply tables, there's a mini fridge and a few machines Mack can't guess the purpose of. "This is home base for the next seven days," Linda says. "There's no rain in the forecast and the temperature should be quite pleasant at night."

"Can't we sleep off-site and be bused in?" the prank girl asks. Mack wonders if she should think of her as the prank *woman,* but . . . it hardly seems to justify the adult designation.

"No, the organizers feel that would be too disruptive. The game is intended to be fully immersive."

"Where are we supposed to charge our phones?" The guy with the prank girl holds his out, a black brick in his hand.

"Logan," Brandon repeats softly to himself as a reminder. Someone's trying to learn names, at least.

Linda shakes her head. She pats the bulky red and black machine that comes up to her knees. "The generator is for the lights and the fridge. There are no adapters that will allow you to plug in a phone."

"What about taking photos? Video?" The prank girl clutches her dead phone to her chest.

"We retain all rights to images and video content from the game. Even if you could use your phones, it would be a violation of your contract to keep or distribute anything."

That seems to end the official inquiries. Conversations, bright or hushed depending on the speakers, rise and fall on the warm night air as cots are claimed. LeGrand drags his as far from the nearest women as he can, then curls up on it, fully clothed, his back to the group.

Ava eyes the water bottles dubiously. Mack walks over and takes one, chugging it. Then she opens another and chugs that, too. She'll deliberately dehydrate herself during the days, so she needs to drink as much as she can tonight. She'll have to wake up to pee, but that's an acceptable trade-off.

Ava watches her, puzzled. Mack grabs a few protein bars, then takes an armful of whatever she can reach. She'll eat as much as she can tonight, too, and graze lightly tomorrow. She's used to not eating between breakfast and dinner.

"Hey!" the prank girl says when she sees how much food Mack is carrying back to her cot.

"We'll restock you every day," Linda says. "You don't need to plan for anything beyond tomorrow."

Mack puts four days' worth of protein bars into her bag. She'll take another four days' worth tomorrow, and another the day after that, and another and another until she's eliminated or she wins. She goes back to the table. There are a few random supplies. Some sunscreen—she opens it and sniffs, then rejects it for being scented. Bug repellent is bypassed for the same reason. There are several empty mason jars. She takes two, along with some wet wipes and a pack of tissues.

Ava's eyes widen with understanding. "Right." She begins copying Mack. Mack wishes she could have prepped in private, but there will be no privacy until the game starts.

"What if we start our periods?" Ava calls out. Linda flinches, looking at the men as though embarrassed at the very idea.

"That will be . . . unfortunate." The way she says it is much too serious. Her eyes get sad. Mack wonders if Linda—surely menopausal for actual decades at this point—has forgotten what periods are like. They suck, but they happen. Linda clears her throat. "There are supplies in the bathroom."

"I'm not due to start my period for at least two more weeks," Jaden says in falsetto.

Ava pats him on the shoulder. Cuffs him, more like. "My man, I've passed blood clots with more stamina than you."

Mack laughs. Oh, she hopes Ava gets out quickly. She likes her way too much.

Jaden, red in the face, reflexively pushes his well-sculpted chest out. He's doing it for the wrong audience. Mack turns back to the table, finishing her supply run. Ava takes a few water bottles, grudgingly, and follows Mack back to her cot. But Brandon already has the one next door. Mack is glad as Ava keeps going to find somewhere else to sleep. It'll be easier when Ava's gone. She finishes eating and curls up under her blanket.

"Who's gonna stay up to make sure no one wanders off?" the intern asks.

"I'll sit vigil tonight," Linda says, stroking the intern's hair in a motherly way. Maybe they bonded over a shared love of pantsuits. "This is the only night I'll spend with you, but you can all sleep well knowing I'm keeping watch."

Mack doesn't care. She closes her eyes. She has to be ready, and physically is the only way she can prepare. Tomorrow she'll be alone, hiding, with only her thoughts. And nothing she can do will prepare her for that.

DAY ONE

MACK DOUBLE-CHECKS HER PACK. She's leaving half her clothes on her cot—which pains her—but she needs room for her supplies.

Jaden and another guy are stretching. Beautiful Ava joins them. Then half the camp is stretching like they're at the starting line of a race.

It's a decent theory. Whoever's looking for them might start near the camp and range out from there. But it's such an obvious strategy, Mack suspects near the camp is as likely to be safe as anywhere else. Now that she can see more of their surroundings, the whole thing feels absurd. How could they find anyone in this mess? Trees arch overhead; the paths around them crowd and teem with undergrowth turned to overgrowth. All the walkways are lined with either impassable shrubbery or walls high enough they block sight lines. It's still dark, but even if it wasn't, she couldn't see ten feet past their camp clearing. From the drive in, she assumes the rest of the park is the same.

"You gonna run?" Brandon asks, face flushed with excitement. Mack shakes her head.

"Cool. I think I'm going to. Good luck!" He holds out his hand, his smile guileless. Maybe Mack *will* miss him. She takes his hand and shakes.

"You, too." She does wish him good luck. She just wishes herself better luck.

Linda is sitting on an ATV. It's humorously incongruous with her jewel-toned pantsuit. There are tears in her eyes as she looks over the group. Then she frowns, as though considering something. "There's a twist you should know about," she says. Everyone freezes, waiting for this new information. "If you find a book—small, leather-bound—you get a bonus for bringing it to me."

"What's the bonus?" Ava asks, at the same time Jaden shouts, "Where is it?"

Linda's eyes flash with something like annoyance, but her tone comes out singsong sweet. "If I told you where it is, finding it would hardly be a challenge." She claps her hands, something she does whenever she's shifting the conversation. "It's time to start! Good luck! And . . . go!" She revs her ATV and peels out.

Linda didn't answer the question about what the bonus was, and Mack's sure it wasn't in the packet anywhere. Seems like an odd addition at this point in the game. Without a good reason to look for it, Mack resolves to forget about it. Actively trying to find something while someone is trying to find her? Not worth the risk.

As she listens to Linda's ATV engine fade into the distance, Mack wonders if the seekers—that seems to be the title the other competitors have settled on for those looking for them—will have ATVs. If so, she'll be able to track their movements by the noise.

She turns away from the exhaust lingering like perfume. Everyone is gone, except Ava, who's on the opposite side of the camp. Ava nods, then walks into the trees. Mack does the same in the other direction.

Come out, come out, wherever you are.

She shudders against the prickle of cold dread on the back of her neck.

In the predawn haze, everything looks lazy and soft. But the intense, wild plant life, riddled with thorns, quickly dissuades her of the notion of simply pushing into the hedges and hiding there.

She lets the vague remnants of a weed-choked path lead her away from the camp.

The clock is ticking. She can feel it with every beat of her heart. But she doesn't rush. Shapes loom in the darkness. What she thought was a huge tree ahead of her is revealed to be a statue, swallowed by ivy. The topiary trees have shifted like nightmares, taking something known and distorting it until the familiar becomes monstrous.

She looks away from an agonized, swollen head screaming leafy terror at the sky. The branches are tight and small. Even if she could climb, she couldn't hide. And something about these trees bothers her, haunts her. They seem sick in a way she can't articulate. She wants nothing to do with them.

The path meanders in an almost aggressive manner. It doesn't function like a path should. Instead of guiding to a destination, it seems determined to confuse. There are no straight lines. Everything curves, making it impossible to see more than a few yards ahead at a time. There are stone walls bordering most of the offshoot paths, which seems like an odd choice for a theme park—they block easy routes to destinations. She follows new directions at random. In the invisible distance—it's hard to gauge how far away with no landmarks and such dense growth—someone swears.

Up ahead, there's a break in the trees. She's seen nothing promising, so she heads for the clearing. A series of small, sagging buildings along a more open central walkway greet her. In the nearest shack, a man is sitting at a rotted piano, his back to her.

He doesn't move.

Neither does she.

After it starts to hurt, she releases her breath and creeps forward. Where a face should be, she finds blank, chipped emptiness. A statue. Maybe in its glory days a statue of a clown sitting at a piano filled people with delight, but seriously, what the fuck.

The thought that she could sit on the statue's lap and be hidden

unless someone looked closer briefly crosses her mind. But she'd
have to stay in its faceless embrace all day. Its hands, once gloved,
have rotted with mold and dark spots. They look like claws, or
bones.

She turns away. This must have been the games section. Midway? Is that what those parts of a fair or amusement park are
called? She's not sure. Booths jostle for position, shouldering up to
one another. A few are collapsed, the structures standing next to
them looming like triumphant bullies. The ones that are still intact
have counters, shelves, dim interiors. It would make sense to hide
inside.

She looks up, instead.

From a nearby shack, a plague of once-cheerful rubber ducks
hangs in nets from a half-caved-in ceiling. *Maddie.* A memory hits
like a bullet, almost making Mack stagger backward with the force
of it.

Maddie (at three? maybe four? Mack can't remember and doesn't
dwell on the spike of pain and guilt that not being able to remember causes) had a bundle of yellow yarn that she tied into an impossible knot as big as her own fist, declared was a duck named
Poopsie, and dragged everywhere—including the bath, where it
disintegrated and clogged the drain. While Mack silently watched
and Maddie wailed, their mom had quietly, furiously fished it out
string by string, sweating the closer it got to when their father
would get home.

Poopsie. Mack hasn't thought of Poopsie since she had to give
Maddie her own stuffed rabbit to keep her from crying herself to
sleep over the loss of the imaginary duck. But here she is, playing
hide-and-go-fucking-seek, and there is a shack filled with rubber
ducks.

Mack doesn't believe in signs, and even if she did, Maddie has
no reason to send her a helpful one. The opposite, really. But she's
nearly out of time, so Mack climbs onto the counter, then grabs
the edge of the roof. She scrambles up. Just as she suspected, the
roof is concave, slowly pushed down by the elements. The wood

is spongy. It creaks, but it's only mildly alarming, not dangerous. If it caves in, she might be impaled, but she wouldn't break any bones. Mack puts her pack down and then lies flat in the depression in the center of the sinking roof. From her vantage point she can see only the raised borders of the roof around her and the clear pale light of the dawn sky. Which means no one from the ground can see her.

Maddie taught her to hide in unexpected sight lines. And look where that got them.

Shaking it off—but not literally, as the roof creaks in protest with every movement—Mack pulls out a single protein bar and preemptively unwraps it. No water. If she has to, she'll pee her pants. She has extra clothes she can change into before returning to the camp. If she can even find camp again. Her path here was all trees and twists, no landmarks. She should have paid better attention.

The sky blooms blue. The game has started.

Mack closes her eyes, and waits.

The sun creeps along, as the sun is wont to do. The occasional insect wanders across Mack's legs, as insects are wont to do. Mack does nothing, as Mack is wont to do.

The waiting is dull and hot. With agonizingly slow movements, she pulls out a spare shirt and puts it over her face to block the sun. Her mouth is dry, her back uncomfortable against the uneven surface.

It's fine.

She's careful not to fall asleep, but exists in a heavy sort of limbo, almost like meditating. One of her foster families had a daughter who was into meditation. She taught Mack. They'd find Mack at all hours, sitting, eyes closed, perfectly still. "I'm pretending I'm dead," she'd say. "I like it." They didn't. They passed her along soon after.

The oppressive heat builds. She's glad she wore long sleeves and long pants to protect her skin, even though the shirt over her face is stifling. She almost doesn't hear it over her own soft breaths. But—

A padding of feet. Not quite the right rhythm for a person. And then—even harder to hear over the new pounding in her chest—a sort of sniffling, snuffling noise. Are there animals in the park?

The sigh that follows sounds less animal, though. Soft, plodding steps continue on.

If it was an animal, it sounded like it walked on two feet. And if it was a seeker, Mack is disturbed. She expected ATVs. Boisterous shouts. Not near-silent searching. It makes her feel . . . hunted.

She's not. She can leave at any time. Get up and walk out the gate. No one cares. She's not hiding because she has to. She's hiding because it's the one skill that's ever done anything for her.

"Fuck you, Dad," she whispers. And she waits.

The carousel looks like something out of a horror movie. Not a high-budget one, either. One of the cheap, off-brand films doomed to languish in the depths of Netflix and the $2 bargain DVD bin at Walmart. The chipped and decaying horses are less gruesome and more pathetic. A once-jaunty sign is hanging loosely from one corner, slowly shifting in the wind. OFF TO THE RACES! it says, all the paint gone so it's wood on wood, the letters raised. No one is racing here anymore. If anything, Rosiee wants to race away.

But she's running low on time. Should she look for the book? No way could she find a single object in this nightmare landscape. She twists her silver rings nervously, aware of how close to dawn it is. Maybe she shouldn't hide in such an obvious landmark, but nothing in the damn park feels obvious. No wonder it shut down. Imagine coming here with kids! The whole day would be spent trying to find something, anything, in the mess of greenery. Maybe it used to be more organized.

She climbs onto the carousel. The platform is rusted and falling apart. One of the poles holding a horse has snapped, and as she twists to avoid a fallen chunk of wood, the metal scrapes her arm, drawing blood. "Shit," she hisses, covering it with her hand.

Food, bathroom, first-aid runs—all will get her out. She'll be fine. A few drops of blood fall, squeezed out between her fingers. Is a single day enough time for infection to set in? Probably. She keeps going. Her steps are a careful dance around further injury as she makes her way to the center. Two panels around the closed interior of the ride have come loose. She slides between them, careful of her arm. She used to have curves—god, she loved her curves, the weight of her boobs, the soft comfort of her belly— but she's lost too many pounds from stress and poverty. She squeezes in between the big metal gears that once ran the carousel. There's just enough space to sit, and she can't see outside. Tiny knife cuts of light pierce the space from above. Good enough.

She pours some water on her arm. It's bleeding, but it's not terrible. Won't need stitches or anything. She wishes she had a strip of cloth to wrap around it. Thinking of wrapping herself up in things sends her mind away, though.

Sometimes when things got bad—worse, really, since they were always bad—with Mitch, she'd sit in the back of the closet and imagine herself small. Not skinnier, but actually small, like a child. And then she'd curl up, wrapped in her grandmother's shawl, and stop being herself for a few precious moments.

After she left, he sent her photos of that shawl. Then, when she didn't respond, he sent her a video of it burning along with all her photos.

She clutches the pendant around her neck, accidentally getting blood on it. She makes her own memories now, out of silver, out of metal. Strong and beautiful and only her own.

Christian laughs when he sees the roller coaster in the center of a large, relatively clear space. He doesn't actually do rooftop solar installations, but he's gone on enough service calls to have no fear of ladders or heights.

The roller coaster is a wooden skeleton, not even the biggest one in the park, but he doesn't know that. A few sections have collapsed in on themselves. He picks the most stable-looking portion and climbs up the latticework of the exterior. A few sweaty and splintered minutes later, he hits the top.

He did not think this through.

There's nothing up here but rotting track. Even if he lies flat, he'll still be visible from the ground. And he can't see any better options from this vantage point. The trees are greedy for the sky, obscuring everything. He can make out a few areas where there might be some sort of buildings, a distant Ferris wheel, and a couple of other ride things breaking through the trees, but there's no way he'll make it to any of them in time.

Down a tremendous swooping dip, a single cart is still on the track. Taking a deep breath, he aims for it. He doesn't realize until he's halfway there that it's completely possible for him to die doing this. But he needs to make it far enough in the competition to impress the company. A broken neck will not impress anyone. Especially not Rosiee. Whispering promises of a cushy job, already picking out furniture for the biggest house in the town (without solar panels, fuck his monthly energy bills), which he'll share with Rosiee and their two kids and a dog, he makes it to the cart and climbs in.

And laughs in surprise. On the side of the cart, stamped into the metal, is his mother's maiden name. STRATTON ENGINEERING, it says. What are the odds? He never met her family—they disowned her when she ran off with his father. It wasn't a romantic story. It was a story of slowly being ground down, worn thin, aged before his eyes. He was always sure she regretted her choice—regretted him—regretted giving up what she came from. She died of breast cancer three years ago. He read once that stress can lodge in the body, can fester and multiply, a cancer of the spirit that contributes to a cancer of the body. So in a way, her choice to abandon money and comfort for his sucky, loser dad actually killed her, didn't it?

It feels like a sign, seeing the name *Stratton* here. Like this is his chance back into the world she left behind. The one he's going to make for himself, and his wife, and his kids. He smiles and settles in, kept company by an imaginary Rosiee while the real one bleeds and sweats and worries in the middle of an engine.

Logan has always been afraid of clowns. A few years ago, there was the double whammy of the new *It* movies plus the random clown sightings in forests, and the recurring nightmare he'd thought was left behind in childhood popped back up. He didn't sleep well for weeks. He'd never admit his phobia to anyone—can barely admit it to himself—but really, is it that stupid? It's a more rational fear than, say, sharks. It's 100 percent guaranteed that a shark can't get you if you don't go into the ocean. But clowns? Apparently they hang out in forests now.

Logan thinks of all of this as he stares at the giant clown head. What its original purpose was, he can't say. Its nose has fallen off, and only one eye has kept its paint. But the clown's gaping mouth is a doorway, framed by cracking red lips and browned teeth. He can't figure out what it led to, because the building behind it is gone. (There was never a building. It was the entrance to a tent featuring a magic show parents forced their kids to endure so they could sit in the shade for a few blessed minutes, rest their feet from trying to figure out where the next ride was. Logan would be relieved to know the clown itself was false advertising.)

"Buck up, buttercup," Logan whispers to himself. What better way to conquer a fear than to go into the very belly of the beast—or in this case, the mouth of the clown. Logan climbs in, finding a perfect body-shaped space between the teeth and the tongue.

See? Clowns can't hurt him. This clown will help him. It'll be a funny story to tell his employees someday, when he's part of Frye Technologies. Or, better, when he *owns* Frye Technologies. He won't even have to change the name when he takes over. Imagining his future—glossing over what app, *exactly,* will somehow lead to this chain of events—is like drinking a warm glass of milk, bland and soothing and soporific.

Logan, once plagued by nightmares of clowns, falls asleep in one. Much like the clown, Logan needs a new nose, or at least major sinus surgery. His snores saw through the air, amplified by the cavernous clown mouth he sleeps in.

By two P.M., Isabella has had enough.

It's hot. She needs to pee. She hasn't heard a single noise all day. The whole thing feels like a practical joke. Like that Sydney woman planned it. Oh, *god*. What if she did? What if when she told them all about her prank show, it was dramatic irony for her audience?

It can't be that. No YouTuber could afford this. Unless she was only pretending to be a YouTuber. Isabella's heart races, her breaths getting fast and shallow. She closes her eyes, regains control. No. Ox Extreme Sports has to be real.

She has a lot of notes for them, though. She'll present them smartly. Articulately. Mixed with praise and an action plan for how to improve and market their brand through this stupid competition. She doesn't want to win, anyway. She wants a fucking job. She wants these miserable fuckers who can afford to run a $50,000 children's game to give her a salary and benefits.

She pushes free of the clump of topiary she had shoved herself into. Her suit jacket snags and she can feel the pulled thread down to her very bones. She can't afford to replace this. It's her best interview outfit.

Humiliated and angry, Isabella refuses to stoop any lower. She will *not* pee in the bushes. Her pumps are almost silent as she winds her way back toward the camp, mentally practicing the speech that will get her a job with these fucktrumpets. *Maybe,* she thinks, carefully timing the smile that will soften her words, *the efficacy of offering a $50,000 prize for a competition that wasn't advertised or broadcast is worth reviewing.*

After thirty minutes of walking and composing, she's sure her speech will come across as both polished and unpracticed as soon as she can get in front of someone from the company. But she's made a mistake. There are no landmarks to look for. The trees are so tall and crowded that, combined with pathway walls, they obscure everything. And she's been walking way too long now.

She turns at a towering hedge, hoping it borders something worth getting to, and follows it. There's an offshoot that looks less overgrown. She follows that. By the time she takes her fourth turn, trying to course-correct, she's blistered and ready to cry out of exhaustion and frustration. This is the stupidest fucking game ever.

She takes off her jacket and her shoes and sits in the middle of the path. Her bladder is so full it's making her ovaries hurt. She's not going to convince anyone to hire her in this state. Hell, right now she'd take a restroom over a job offer without hesitation.

Then she hears soft padding. Approaching.

"Thank God," she says, wiping under her eyes and standing. "You found me." She turns to greet her savior.

The sun setting has never felt so momentous. Mack watches, enthralled, as blue fades to purple and then soft indigo. She hasn't seen a sunset in so long—it wasn't worth giving up her bed at the shelter for. But tonight she wonders if maybe it was, after all.

Even though Linda said sunset, Mack doesn't move until she's counted ten stars. Her whole body protests almost as loudly as the roof beneath her. Everything creaks and groans. She crawls carefully off, then drops to the ground. There's a painfully tight knot in her back she'll never be able to reach, and she has to pee so bad she knows it will hurt. But she made it without wetting herself, which is no small victory.

It's going to take her forever to find the camp again, so she squats behind the piano building and waters the weeds there. When she looks up, relief almost as powerful as an empty bladder hits her. A spotlight is shining straight into the sky, calling her back to the camp.

Even with the beacon, it takes her nearly an hour to wind her way there. No path is straight. They loop and twist and curve, doubling back constantly. She pays as much attention as she can, chugging water and devouring protein bars. She's happy with her spot. She'll try to find it again tomorrow. And she'll try not to think of Maddie, or Poopsie, or anything other than hiding.

To her surprise, even with her slow pace, she's the third person back. Linda waves at her from the spotlight. Jaden, he of the sculpted muscles, and beautiful Ava are at the food table, heads close together, deep in discussion. They jolt apart when Mack walks up.

"I've never been so bored or missed my phone more. Worst day of my life, and six more to go!" beautiful Ava chirps, rolling her eyes to contradict her cheery tone.

Mack drains a couple of water bottles, then takes an apple and heads to the showers. If drinking water was nice, standing under even this lukewarm stream is divine. She stays in as long as possible, rinsing everything, wiping away the strain of the day.

Six more days. Six more days is nothing.

When she finally comes out, ten of the competitors are back. Everyone is sunburned, sweaty, bug-bitten, and cranky. Except Brandon, of course.

"That was wild!" he says, carrying a full plate back to his cot. "I don't think I've held still for that long in my whole life. I found this weird old roller coaster, shaped like a circle—or a cylinder, I guess? Is that a 3D circle? No, that's a sphere. Anyway, it goes down in a ring around and around and around the frame. Called the Cyclone. Pretty cool! It seemed a little obvious, but how could I pass that up? So I climbed the frame—I thought for sure it was going to break—and set up shop near the top. Man. I wish I could have ridden it down at the end of the day. How great would it be if everything was still running?"

Mack wants to tell him that he shouldn't share information. But he's happy and unconcerned, so why bother?

He sees her eyeing a cookie and passes it to her without being asked. "Did you look for the book? I don't know how anyone could find it out there. Are you going to hide in the same place tomorrow, or pick a new spot?"

Ava plops down on the end of Mack's cot. She's sweat-stained and dirty and frankly glorious, as refreshing to see as the water was to drink. "I don't think it matters, strategically," Ava says. "This place has to be a mile, mile and a half across at least. I walked the perimeter fence to get back here. It's the only cleared-out space. Honestly, I'll be amazed if they found anyone at all. It's not like there's a limited number of places to check and they can just cross them off."

Brandon hands his last cookie to Ava. "I think I'll find somewhere new tomorrow, anyway. Make it more exciting!"

She grins. "Yeah, fourteen hours of silence and stillness. Loads of ways to make that exciting. I'm glad you two aren't out yet, though."

Mack fights against the instinctive relief and happiness she felt when the other woman returned. Ava's serious competition. Mack should be disappointed she's still in. She leans away from the other woman and takes stock of who remains.

The writer, clutching his notebook and looking exhausted. Everyone who returns eyes him for a moment until they realize it's just his notebook, not whatever bonus book Linda mentioned.

LeGrand, already off in his corner.

The sad-eyed woman—Ruby? Rosiee? Maybe Mack should learn their names now that people are going to start getting out—toying with her silver jewelry and sporting a bandage on her arm.

Jaden and beautiful Ava, back in secret conversation.

The toothpaste commercial, talking with a chipper Linda. "Can we get more information on that book?" she asks.

Linda laughs. "No, no. Just keep an eye out for it."

"What about the bonus?" Ava shouts.

"You'll know it when you get it!"

"Fuck that, then," Ava mutters dismissively. Mack feels the same, and suspects most of the others do, too. What's the point in looking for a bonus with no hint as to what the bonus is?

The prank girl, so sunburned she's almost purple, winces into camp. "Has anyone seen Logan?" she asks, holding a cold water bottle against her face. The clipboard guy reappears from the bathroom, adding himself to the lineup. Mack honestly can't think of which one Logan was, but probably the bland-looking dude in the backward baseball cap always sitting next to the prank girl. Either him or the slouchy guy with the beanie and the black fingernails, but Mack can't imagine the prank girl worrying about him. The only other person missing is the intern who went into the park in pumps and a pantsuit. No surprise there.

"No Logan, no Isabella. No Atrius." Ava frowns thoughtfully. "Hey, Linda! Who's out?"

Linda doesn't hesitate. "Logan and Isabella."

"Who's Isabella?" Brandon asks, then grimaces in embarrassment over not being able to remember her.

Ava answers. "Blazer. Looked like she was going to a job interview instead of playing hide-and-go-seek in a creepy-ass rust jungle."

"I was going to make an app with Logan," the prank girl says. She sounds like she's on the verge of tears. "When are they coming to say goodbye?"

"They're gone, Sydney," Linda says.

"Wait, really?" Beautiful Ava is aghast. "No goodbyes? No ceremony, or interview?"

"They were found. They're out. Two per day, that's how the game works."

Mack frowns. They hadn't been told that detail before. It seems important. Why, if only two people per day get out, did they have to keep hiding if two had already been found?

Ava seems to be wondering the same thing. She opens her mouth, but Linda neatly cuts her off by emphatically clapping her hands together once. "Now, if you need anything, leave a note on the table. An alarm will give you your thirty-minute warning in the morning. I'll see you—" She pauses, then tries to smile. Mack wonders if she's sad over Isabella getting out, since they might have bonded over an affinity for pantsuits. "I'll see most of you tomorrow night. Sleep well."

With a roar of her ATV, Linda disappears into the night.

"Fuck, that's cold," Jaden says.

"Maybe it's like *The Bachelor,* and you only get goodbyes if you make it further so the audience is invested in you," the toothpaste commercial says.

"What audience?" beautiful Ava mutters, still looking at the pavilion roof as though she might have missed a camera.

The prank girl—Sydney, Linda called her—slumps on her cot. The cot next to her, and another in the middle, have been stripped of belongings. "I didn't even get his number."

"I'm sure you can get it from Linda next time she's here." The toothpaste commercial sits next to her, putting an arm around her shoulder.

Sydney winces at the contact. "I'm taking all the sunscreen tomorrow."

Everyone splits up, getting ready for bed. Even though she spent the whole day lying still, Mack is exhausted. She tries to reach the sore spot on her back, but it's impossible.

"I can get that," Ava says. She pauses with her hands outstretched. "If you want." Ava has come from the shower. She smells like water on clean skin. Mack wants to say no, needs to say no, but her head betrays her by nodding. Ava gets to work and then Mack couldn't say no even if she tried.

"God, Mack, I've never met anyone so tense, and I've been on bomb disposal squads." Ava laughs softly. Her hands are not soft. They're strong and searching, finding the tenderest places.

"Hey," beautiful Ava says, joining them. Mack instantly loathes her presence, wanting her to leave. But Ava doesn't stop massaging as beautiful Ava lowers her voice. "Did you guys see any cameras?"

"What?" Mack peels her eyes open. Beautiful Ava leans closer.

"Cameras. Did you see any? Because they said this might be a show. But none of us have been filmed or interviewed, and I haven't seen a single camera out there."

"Maybe they're hidden," Ava says. "Or maybe the seekers have them. GoPros or whatever."

"Yeah, I thought of that. But then what role would we even have? It doesn't make sense to frame a show that way. You'd focus on the people vying for the prize, not the people trying to find them. Maybe you could do both, but you'd definitely have to film the hiders."

Ava stops kneading. They both look to Mack for an opinion.

"Dry run," she offers. "Seeing if the mechanics of the game work." She hopes if she can get this conversation over, Ava will touch her again.

"I guess," beautiful Ava says, frowning. "Seems like an expensive test run if they aren't even practicing shots or forming a narrative."

"That we can see," Mack corrects.

"Yeah. I guess. Keep your eyes peeled for cameras tomorrow, okay?"

"We'll tell you. Unless you get out," Ava says, cheerfully.

Beautiful Ava glares. "I'm not getting out."

Brandon returns from the bathrooms, and beautiful Ava stands. Mack, now gloriously loose and comfortable and pretty certain Ava won't be doing any more, just wants to go to sleep.

"Yo, anyone else realize Atrius isn't back yet?" The clipboard guy peers into the darkness. He's changed into a fresh polo shirt, bold blue with some sort of company logo over his heart. "That's cheating. He's probably looking for the book thing, or scoping the best spots."

A few competitors voice grumbling agreement.

"Like he can even see anything out there," Ava counters. "Besides, it's not hard to find good hiding spots."

"Tell that to Logan." Sydney walks over to the spotlight and shuts it off.

"Hey," the toothpaste commercial says. "How will he find us?"

"I don't really care. He wants to stay out for an advantage? Let him stay out all night." Sydney stomps back to her cot.

Ava stands, stretching.

"Thank you," Mack says, the words like an offering placed on the altar of an unknown god. She doesn't know what else to do, how to respond to kindness. "I can get you?" She's never massaged anyone. But she doesn't like being in debt, doesn't like the way she already misses Ava's hands on her. She can't owe someone she's so inclined to like.

"Nah, you look beat. Get some rest. Another day of perfect stillness ahead of you." Ava's grin is strained. Mack realizes how tired the other woman looks.

"You sleep at all?"

"Don't feel safe," Ava says as she walks to her own cot.

Mack wakes in the middle of the night. She tiptoes silently to the bathroom. Hushed voices catch her attention on her way back to bed. Two figures sit on the edge of the camp. At first she suspects beautiful Ava and Jaden. Then she realizes the man is crying silently.

"It's okay," Ava—Mack's Ava—murmurs. "I'll sit with you until morning."

Mack can't tell who the man is. But the way he's curled around himself tells a story Mack is familiar with.

"You shouldn't," he says. LeGrand.

"Got nothing better to do."

Mack feels a tug from the center of her chest. LeGrand is in pain. She wants to keep vigil with him. With Ava.

She goes back to her cot.

DAY TWO

MACK BEATS THE ALARM. She leaves yesterday's clothes folded under her cot and snags an extra blanket from the supply table. It's lightweight, dark color. Perfect.

"Hey, are you allowed to use props?" Jaden asks.

The clipboard guy sits up, rubbing his eyes blearily. "That doesn't seem fair."

"Nothing in the rules against it." The jewelry woman shifts, her pretty heart necklace falling free of her tank top. She slowly puts on all her rings and bracelets, like suiting up with armor. Checks her bandage. It's seeped a bit, but not too much. "Besides, one blanket is hardly an advantage."

Mack feels bad now for not remembering what her name is.

"We don't know that," Jaden says.

"Then take one, too," Ava snaps. Her eyes are red, bruised hollows beneath them. She hasn't slept at all. "Don't give Mack shit."

"Speaking of shit." Jaden nods to Atrius, who's at the table, eating, beanie pulled low. "Where were you last night?"

Atrius shrugs. "Exploring."

"That's cheating!"

Atrius grins. "Sorry, I mean, I got lost. Someone turned off the spotlight."

"Yeah, fuck you." Sydney brushes her hair with vicious force. "If you win, I'll file a formal complaint."

Atrius's grin warms something in Mack. He so genuinely doesn't care. She heads to the table—blanket in her bag—and nibbles, picking her supplies for the day. Atrius's hands and arms are covered in a fine mist of dried paint.

He notices her gaze. "Leaving my mark on the competition."

"And if they don't use this site again?"

"I do it for the sake of doing it." It sounds rehearsed. Mack is disappointed. She suspects he wants an audience as much as Sydney and beautiful Ava, just in a different way.

"Okay," she says.

"It's a maze," he blurts, spinning a can of spray paint and shoving it into the back pocket of his sagging pants.

"Your art?" Mack wants out of this conversation as soon as the question leaves her mouth, wishes she hadn't asked.

He frowns, then pauses thoughtfully. "The art is a maze. The maze is art. Hmm." He wanders away, back into the park.

"The alarm didn't go off yet!" Sydney shouts after him. Muttering to herself, Sydney grabs the whole aerosol can of sunscreen and disappears into the predawn dark.

Rosiee has her eyes closed and appears to be repeating directions to herself. Mack suspects she's heading for the same spot she hid in yesterday. Makes sense. Mack is, too. She isn't in a rush, though, reasonably confident she can find her spot again. She uses the bathroom, then double-checks her bag.

LeGrand walks past Ava. Neither says anything, but she nods. And, to Mack's surprise, he nods back. He seems confused and tentative, even scared, as he mumbles, "Good luck," before ducking into the bathroom.

Ava looks half dead. She won't make it at this rate. Before she can stop herself, Mack walks up to her. "Do you feel safe with me?"

"What?" Ava's eyebrows draw together. They're black, like her eyelashes, emphatically framing her dark eyes.

"Could you sleep if I had your back?"

Ava's face shifts through several subtle emotions. Her smile is weary and wary, but somehow brighter than the fast-approaching dawn. "Yeah, I think I could."

"Come on."

Mack leads Ava away from the emptying camp. It's stupid. She shouldn't do it. But there are still so many competitors, so what can it hurt? Ava isn't a miser with kindness. Mack is. Today, though, she can still afford to be generous. Today she will repay Ava with sleep, so they can be even. That's all. She just wants to be out of Ava's debt.

After one panic-inducing false turn, Mack finds the right path. They come out of the trees to the midway section.

"Shit!" Ava shouts, grabbing Mack and putting herself between Mack and the threat she sees up ahead. Mack eases out of Ava's protective grasp and walks forward, tapping the piano player on his plaster head. Interesting that Ava's first response wasn't to hide, but to protect Mack from attack. Maybe Mack isn't the only one who brought more than a duffel bag's worth of trauma with her into the park.

"Charming," Ava mutters. She follows Mack to the ducky building. This is good, though. With Ava here, Mack doesn't have time to think about yarn and baths and sisters. Mack helps boost Ava, then climbs up after. The depression is big enough for them both, but only just.

As the sky changes, they settle in, shoulder to shoulder, hip to hip. Mack puts her backpack beneath Ava's head.

"Fair warning," Mack says. "I will wake you if you snore, and I will also piss my pants if I have to."

"I'll do the same. Piss your pants, I mean. Not mine."

Mack smothers the laugh with her hands. She's laughed more at Ava's words the last two days than she has in months, maybe years.

"Did you do that yesterday?" Ava whispers. "You're hardcore."

"No, I made it. Peed behind the piano player's building over there."

"Can you imagine Rebecca peeing herself to avoid being caught?"

"The one who looks like a toothpaste commercial? Can't imagine, and don't want to."

"Yeah, not really my kink, either." Ava snorts. "Toothpaste commercial. She really does, doesn't she."

The sun is almost up. "Get some sleep," Mack whispers. "Only silence now."

Ava shifts so her head rests against Mack's shoulder. No accident this time. Mack lets out one long sigh, and then the sun is up and day two—already more complicated thanks to her own confusing impulses—begins.

It's been seven months. That's all LeGrand can think as he climbs a tree. Anyone watching would be surprised at how adept the soft, doughy-looking, very tall boy—because even at twenty, LeGrand is undeniably still a boy—is at scaling a tree that looks impossible to climb. He's had a lot of experience, though.

As he tucks himself into the green, he wonders: *Is Almera dead? Has she died yet?* Because her cough was so bad this time, and it's been seven months since he was banished. But it could be seven years, and it wouldn't matter. He'll never know. And he'll never be able to help her. Trying to help is what got him here in the first place, and he genuinely does not—cannot—understand what he is doing or why. Nothing in the world makes sense. Everything they taught him about the evils out here is wrong, but nothing feels right, either.

He closes his eyes and pushes his forehead against the rough bark of the tree. Pretends like he is home. Like he accepted that Almera would be saved no matter what, and that it didn't matter what she went through in her mortal life, because her calling and election was made sure. Like her cough hadn't gotten so bad this time he could no longer stand to sit next to her, holding her hand, watching her lips turn blue as she gasped for air. Like he got to celebrate her thirteenth birthday last month by blowing bubbles for her and listening to her delighted laugh. Like he climbed this tree for a moment, to get a break, and his mother and his aunts and his dozens of siblings are all there, busy with the washing and baking and sewing. Like when he climbs down, his sister will screech and laugh and he'll carry her on his back through the compound so she doesn't have to crawl.

But no. None of that is real, or can ever be real again. He can't even think of her laugh, the brightest, most joyful thing in the world, without hurting because he kept his bubble formula a secret, worried that the prophet would ban it. Now what makes her laugh? Now who carries her so she can see other parts of the compound besides her bed? Now who figures out what she needs, since she can't tell anyone?

She must think he abandoned her, like he abandoned God and all their teachings. He did it for her, and she'll never know, and none of it mattered anyway.

It's been seven months. Seven months is an eternity. After all, God created the world in seven days, and LeGrand destroyed his own in seven hours.

Brandon half dozes, tucked into a car in the middle of a dim, musty fake tunnel. Shiny material drifts from wooden hearts. A menacing swan with one broken wing guards him, and cherubs—somehow still garishly painted after all these years—hang overhead. There were two choices this morning: Lovers' Hideaway or Underworld Inferno, but the other building had a big scary devil hanging over the entrance so he picked the hideaway, which also fits nicely for the game.

He can't decide which he likes best: the hiding, which is exciting even if it is kind of boring, or hanging out with everyone after. He hopes they'll keep in touch when the game is over. Maybe even come visit him. Or he could visit them! He really likes Ava, even if her buzzed hair intimidates him. He suspects she's a lesbian, which is super cool. He's never been friends with a lesbian before. He doesn't think they have any in Idaho. And Mack is quiet but he likes her, and he's sure she likes him. Jaden and Christian seem too much like the big-city kids in Boise who have dads and summer cabins on the Snake River and steal things from the gas station even though they have money. But the other Ava, well, he can barely talk to her, she's so pretty. Rebecca, too. And Rosiee. He likes them all. Except Jaden and Christian. But that's unfair of him, because he doesn't even know them.

Tonight he'll try to talk to them, too. Poor sunburned Sydney—hopefully she feels better—and the sullen guy, Ian, and the cheater guy, Atrius. Depending on who's out. Maybe he can get everyone playing a game or something now that they've had a couple of days to settle in. He beams back at the grinning cherubs. God, this is the greatest thing that's ever happened to him.

Jaden was careful. He'd have to be even more careful if he was going to pull this off. He wanted it to be someone else—the creepy quiet girl with the blanket, or the stupid gay chick who thinks she's so tough, or Atrius, preferably. But he found Sydney, so Sydney it is.

He watches from the shelter of a building that once served as a restroom and now serves as a breeding ground for spiders. Sydney climbs up a service ladder and crawls out across one of the arms into a miniature airplane suspended in the air. She has more guts than he expected. She sprays herself copiously with sunscreen, and then tucks herself into the airplane, invisible.

He settles in to give the seekers enough time to get this deep into the park.

Sometime after the sun has hit its zenith and is creeping toward the western horizon, Mack hears it again.

She slowly pulls the blanket off her face, careful not to disturb Ava. She can't afford Ava startling and making the roof creak.

Close by, the snuffling. A wet, hungry breath. A sound like something pawing at the ground. Mack can't be sure, but it seems like it's coming from where she peed behind the clown shack yesterday. Her skin prickles with relief that she didn't pee right by her own building.

The noise—a huff, then soft padding around and around—makes her want to scream with terror and tension. *She's being hunted.*

She can tell herself otherwise, but she knows how it feels to be stalked as prey. *He's dead, he's dead, he can never find her.* Something else has taken up his task.

It brushes up against the side of her building, sending a tremor through the whole thing straight up to the roof. Straight through her bones. She opens her mouth to whimper, to cry, to release this terrible tension and let it find her, let it be over.

A hand closes around her own, tight, anchoring her there. The blanket is drawn back over her face, centimeter by centimeter, sealing her in the hot dark with Ava. Ava, who woke up without a sound. Ava, who is with her.

Come out, come out, wherever you are, he croons in her memory. She squeezes Ava's hand hard, too hard, but Ava doesn't move. A single rubber duck on the ground beneath them makes an agonized, slow death squeak.

And then a distant scream of rusted metal sounds through the air like a siren. Great bounding steps take off in the direction of the noise.

Mack lets out a shuddering breath of relief. Ava shifts, slowly, carefully, and Mack puts her head on the other woman's shoulder. It's stifling beneath the blanket, but she has no doubt Ava still feels the tears that leak from Mack's eyes onto her shirt.

"It's just a game," Mack whispers. But she knows it wasn't the idea of losing that filled her with existential terror. It was the idea of being found.

And then dying.

"You son of a bitch!" Sydney shouts as she watches Jaden run into the trees, away from the noise he'd made to draw the seekers to her. If she gets out, she's taking that prick with her. She scrambles out of her airplane, almost breaks her neck climbing down. Racing after him, she shoves through the branches. Her sunscreen falls out of her pocket with a clang.

She screams as her hair catches on a branch, yanking her backward. The trees around her go silent. And then she hears a heavy footstep. And another. Something about the slow, deliberate pace drains all her anger and replaces it with fear. She sinks down into a crouch, closing her eyes, reduced to a child's logic. If she can't see them, they can't see her.

She's wrong, of course.

Mack and Ava stay on the roof for a few minutes after the spotlight announces an end to the day. Their hands tremble as they down water and shove granola bars in their mouths.

Ava nudges Mack with her shoulder. "Thanks. I'm sore and starving and afraid I'm gonna get a kidney infection, but I'm not tired anymore."

Mack can't say the truth—that without Ava's hand anchoring her, she would have lost it. So she pretends it was a normal day, as normal as a day spent hiding in an abandoned theme park can be. "No biggie."

They help each other down. Mack goes straight to the piano clown's building. She wants—needs—to see footprints. Normal, boring shoe prints. Even animal prints. The ground seems disturbed, but she can't really remember what state it was in the day before. And in the dim moonlight, she can only be sure there are no obvious shoe prints.

"We should hide somewhere new tomorrow," Ava says. Just like that, she's paired them. They're a team. Mack should argue—should say no, but . . .

"Any ideas?"

Ava nods and they walk back toward camp. "I think climbing is our best bet again. There's an old bumper car area. The trellis above it looks steady enough to hold us. It's totally overgrown with ivy, so if we lie flat, we should be invisible from the ground."

She pauses. "And we could peek through if we heard something again."

"See what it is," Mack whispers.

"Who it is," Ava corrects. But she doesn't sound as confident as Mack wants her to. They stop on the edge of camp. "Hey, Linda!" Ava waves the woman down. She's setting the last of her supply refills on the table.

"Yes, dear?" Linda looks exhausted. Even her lipstick has bled out into the fine wrinkles around her lips, making them look blurry and indistinct.

"Are there wild animals in here?"

Linda blinks several times. "There is some local fauna that might have made it past the fence. But nothing large or dangerous."

"Maybe like wild pigs?"

Linda lets out a surprised laugh. "I've never seen a wild pig. But in a park this size, who can say?"

"How many seekers are looking for us?"

Linda shakes her head, that smile bleeding out of the lines just like her lipstick. "Does it matter? Caught is still caught." She hurries away to pull supplies from the four-wheeler before they can ask more about the seekers, or who got out that day.

"It matters a lot," Ava mutters, looking to Mack. Mack shrugs. It matters, and it doesn't. One seeker or one hundred seekers—it won't change how she plays the game.

Could have been a pig they heard. A big one. Or it could have been one of their mysterious seekers. Back at the camp, the terror that she was being hunted feels more like PTSD than something real. Still, Ava doesn't leave her side. They sit together, eating, unwilling to shower yet. It feels important to watch as everyone comes back. To see who's still in the game.

Jaden and beautiful Ava come back together.

Clipboard Christian after them.

Then the writer, Ian.

LeGrand.

Rebecca, the walking toothpaste commercial.

"Brandon, Atrius, Sydney, Rosiee," Ava lists, ticking off who still hasn't come back. Mack catches herself holding her breath, straining to see into the darkness. She shouldn't care who gets out. All it means is she didn't. But she wants to thank Rosiee for sticking up for her this morning. And Brandon's smile will ease some of the lingering fear and panic in her chest. He's the happiest to be here. She wants to have that close by. Try to borrow some of his warmth.

Somewhere in the night, she hears the soft but unmistakable hiss of a can of spray paint. "Atrius is still in," she says. She's ambivalent about that, except it means one of two people she actually likes is out. Or both.

Brandon lopes into the camp, grinning. "Oh man, today was wild. Or boring. I can't tell which."

"Sydney and Rosiee," Ava says.

Linda nods, distracted. She keeps fiddling with the food placement on the table. "Well, good night, then." She hurries away. Mack wonders why Linda doesn't stay like she did the first night, or why it's only Linda who interacts with them. She seems like an odd representative for a sporting goods company.

Brandon begins piling firewood into a stone pit outside the pavilion area. "Does anyone mind a fire? If they don't give us goodbyes, we should celebrate each other, at least. I found a bag of marshmallows!"

Beautiful Ava joins him. After a few false starts, they get the wood to catch. They all gather around the fire. Even the antisocial writer and LeGrand sit nearby. Rebecca giggles, showing all her straight white teeth, as her marshmallow slides off her stick and into the fire.

"Colgate or Crest?" Ava whispers to Mack, and Mack tries to hide her snorting laugh.

"Should we do a game?" Brandon asks.

"Two truths and a lie!" beautiful Ava immediately declares.

"God, no." Ava stands and heads to the shower. Mack wants to,

too, but following Ava into the showers feels too intimate. She'll
wait until Ava's done.

Jaden leans forward so his face is illuminated, gold and gleam-
ing. "Let's do scary stories. I'll go first. Have any of you heard of
the infamous Hide-and-Seek Massacre?"

The fire is so hot on Mack's face, her back is cold. She can feel
the night there, all the darkness pausing, leaning in to listen like
everyone around the fire. This isn't real. None of it is real.

"You're making that up," beautiful Ava says, scowling.

"I'm not. My ex-girlfriend was obsessed with true-crime pod-
casts."

"What's a podcast?" LeGrand asks, his voice soft.

"Where did you even come from, Mars? Shut up and let me tell
the story."

He tells it almost right.

So this guy. Has a wife, two daughters, another on the way. Can't
keep a job long-term for the life of him. Real chip on his shoulder.
Drunk. Mean.

(He made the best pancakes, light and fluffy with little chocolate chip faces.)

His latest firing is the last straw for the wife. She tells him if he
can't swallow his pride and keep a job, she's leaving. Moving back
in with her parents.

(Grandma and Grandpa's house was always too warm, the air
dry and scratchy. It made her sneeze. Once she got a bloody nose
there that lasted so long they almost took her to the emergency
room.)

So the guy tells his wife he has a new job. Invites everyone in
the family over to celebrate. The adults are all sitting in the family
room. He tells his daughters they're going to play hide-and-seek,
and to go hide until he finds them.

(It was their favorite game. They hadn't played it with him in
so long. Everyone seemed happier. More relaxed. It felt like . . .

maybe they were safe. Mack laughed too loud, chased Maddie around in circles. When he told them again to go hide, there was that warning edge to his voice, so they did.)

As soon as he finished counting—

(Speculation. No one could know exactly when it happened.)

—he took a knife and slit the throat of his father-in-law. Stabbed his mother-in-law in the chest. And then, after his wife had watched her parents die, he stabbed her in the stomach. The screaming made the younger daughter come out of her hiding spot. He killed her. Carved her right up. Then he started looking for the last daughter. But he messed up. His wife wasn't dead, just dying. She crawled out of the house, but she only made it to the porch before finally dying. So the dad spends the night—the whole night—looking for his remaining daughter. Finally, at dawn, a jogger sees the dead woman on the porch and calls the police. When he hears the sirens, the dad cuts his own throat and bleeds out on the floor, not five feet away from the little girl's hiding place. The police were on the scene for two hours before she finally came out and asked if the game was over. The lucky survivor.

(It wasn't luck. And Maddie didn't come out because of the screams. They both knew to stay put when Mom and Dad were screaming. No, Maddie got found. Mack saw that part. She only heard the rest.)

"Why would you tell us that?" Rebecca wraps her arms around herself. "That's terrible."

LeGrand is rocking back and forth. The sullen writer is fiddling with his notebook. Mack is silent. She should have gone to the showers with Ava.

Jaden leans back, folding his arms. "I told you so you'd all understand how intensely fucked up it is that the sole survivor of the Hide-and-Seek Massacre is competing in a hide-and-seek tournament. Isn't that right, Mackenzie Black? I knew I had heard that name somewhere."

As everyone exclaims at once, Mack stands and goes to her cot. She's ready for bed.

She can hear beautiful Ava and Rebecca and even the writer guy pestering Jaden with questions. Clipboard and Brandon murmur. The voices rise as Ava comes out of the shower. She'll know, too. They'll all know.

At least it will make the competition simple again.

Someone kneels next to her cot. Brandon drops an armful of her preferred supplies into her bag. "I hope you win," he whispers.

She doesn't hope anything anymore. When she closes her eyes, she's back in that space. Curled up. Staring down at Maddie, who stares up at her with teary accusation in her eyes.

Atrius doesn't mind the dark. It's when he usually works, anyway. But here's what he's wondering: He's spent two days on the move, painting and tagging and trying to get a handle on the layout of this place. And he hasn't seen anyone in the park with them. He climbed all the way up the Ferris wheel today, and the view proved what he suspected: It *is* a maze. Which makes him wonder if the game is less about not being found and more about doing the finding. Linda said that weird thing about a book. What if that's the *actual* goal? It's hide-and-go-seek, after all. Maybe that's the twist— they have to do both.

He's running low on paint, but he marks his path as he goes through the maze. He saw a building—white, with pillars like the spa—in the exact center. He'll get there. First.

Eventually, though, he gets too tired and hungry. He's close, he knows he is. He'll find the building and the book tomorrow. His paint, like bread crumbs in the moonlight, will lead him back here.

Eyes on the ground, he doesn't see the child's shoe, but he does notice the sensible pumps discarded under a bush. Weird.

He gets back to camp to find a dying fire. Jaden's cot has two occupants. That's not the only weird sleeping arrangement, though.

The spooky chick with eyes too big for her face is sleeping on her cot, but curled on the ground next to it is the military chick.

The whiny writer's notebook has fallen off his cot. Atrius picks it up to make sure it's not the book he's looking for. But no. Just a notebook. And more than that, it's blank. Ian's been pretending to write this whole time.

Bored, Atrius showers and eats and then takes an empty cot for a couple of hours of sleep. He's going to get to the house in the morning.

DAY THREE

ATRIUS LEAVES BEFORE DAWN.
He finds the temple.
And it finds him.

Mack is surprised when she wakes up in the morning to find Ava sleeping on the ground next to her cot. It's still the soft predawn light, enough time to get to a good spot. A new spot. She won't use yesterday's again, not after that snuffling sound. That searching. She tries to cobble together an image of the person it was, but it's never a person her brain settles on, and she recoils from the monstrous shape longing to form itself if she'll only look right at it.

She won't. She's good at closing her eyes and her ears and pretending away the horror.

She's so distracted that she doesn't notice that Ava is coming with her until she steps out of the camp and onto one of the trails that litter the park. Ava walks quickly, gait uneven and confident.

"Come on," Ava says, as though she didn't learn last night that Mack is tainted, broken, haunted. "I saw this place the first day. It'll be perfect. We'll be hidden, but we can see the ground if we want to. If we hear something again."

It's not lost on Mack that Ava said some*thing*, not someone. Maybe her imagination is having a hard time filling in the blanks, too.

Mack wants to ask about it, wants to ask why Ava is still with her, but more troubling than either of those is the sheer relief Mack feels with Ava at her side. She shouldn't feel relief. She shouldn't feel anything. And she shouldn't have to fight the impulse to reach out and take Ava's hand in her own as they walk down this path together.

Mack deliberately shuffles so their steps aren't quite so in sync.

But it's too late to hunt for a better solo hiding place. That's why she stays with Ava, she tells herself. Just this last day. And then she'll be alone again, and it will be better. And if it's not better, well, at least it will be safer. For which of them, Mack isn't sure.

Ava leads them through twists and tangles of shrubbery, skirting around a few old rides and leaning structures that definitely don't seem safe. She points to a wide, squat tower with several slides circling it. All the slides have huge gaps, places where entire sections have fallen, and each slide spits the rider out onto a different path. "Hid there the first day. It was a bitch to climb. It's called a helter-skelter, like the Beatles song."

"They were singing about a slide?" Mack asks, baffled. "Isn't that the song that the Manson family claimed inspired their murders?" She flinches. She shouldn't have brought up murders. It's an opening to a path into Mack's past, and Ava will take it. This is why she never talks, why Ava is dangerous as more than just competition. Mack drifts to the side. She'll walk away. Easy.

Ava links her arm through Mack's, snagging her and keeping her moving forward. "Weird, right? Though to be fair, those slides definitely look murdery." As easy as that, Ava closes the opening, leaving Mack's past safely sealed away as they walk in silence.

At last, they get to what looks like a flat concrete pond. Like everything, it's a ruin of its former self, its smooth surface now pitted and cracked, green stabbing its way upward to the sun, slowly but surely reclaiming everything. There's a shade structure built over the rusted uniformity of the bumper cars, and though it sags in the middle like Mack's roof did, it seems solid enough. Better than that, it's latticed metal thickly embroidered with ivy. Ava's right. If they're up there, they'll be able to see down, but no one will be able to see up.

If something comes again, rooting with that horrible wet sniffing noise, padding softly with feet that sound like no feet Mack has ever heard, it'll be a simple matter of turning their heads and pressing their eyes to a gap in the ivy.

Or not. She could choose not to look. She could fill her head with imagining what's causing those sounds, live with it every day and every night for the rest of her life, but never know for sure. She has experience with that, at least.

Mack boosts Ava up first, and as Ava disappears over the top of the structure, Mack has a moment where her stomach drops. Ava could leave her. Settle in safely, forcing Mack to scramble to find a new hiding place.

If she were smart, she would do exactly that. Mack is half turned, already resigned, when Ava's face pops over the edge. "Seems stable enough." She holds out a hand.

Mack takes it.

Ava is right. The structure groans in complaint, and they'll have to be careful to stay as still as possible, but it doesn't feel like collapse is imminent. They settle close to the edge, where it's supported the most. This spot is better than Mack's, anyway, with massive overhanging trees providing relief from the impending assault of the sun. They might not have to cover themselves with the blanket at all.

Mack sets up carefully, meticulously, anything she might need in easy reach. She didn't shower last night, not after the bonfire, and she regrets it as she can smell a hint of her body and the smoke, but above the ground like this with a healthy breeze she doubts any human could smell it.

Ava settles in next to her, so close their bodies have barely a rumor of space between them. As the sun cracks the horizon, breaking open the tedium of the day ahead of them, Ava whispers, "If Jaden doesn't get out today, I'll beat the shit out of him tonight."

It's not a comment on Mack, or her past. It's not a question, or a demand. It's an offer. An intimacy. Ava has her back.

Mack shifts slightly away.

It's still predawn when Rebecca finds the old carousel. There's something unnerving about the whimsical animals, once brightly painted, now chipped and faded to the wood beneath. She knows it's wood—she knows it—but with the twin ruin of rot and sun bleach, her brain tells her she's looking at bones, tortured and impaled in place forever, gruesome horrors of life.

Actually, she kind of loves it. It looks like a movie set. She can *feel* the camera behind her, taking in the view with her, letting the audience reach their own conclusions about what waits in the middle of the carousel, lurking in the shadows. *Don't go in,* she almost hears them saying.

The hairs on the back of her neck rise, and she rubs her arms, though the slight early morning chill is already evaporating. No. Not a horror movie. Doubtless with her food allergies, a horror movie would find some really terrible, traumatic way of killing her. As if she hasn't imagined asphyxiating nearly every day her entire life. As if her allergies are a plot gimmick and not a very real, constant source of everything from inconvenience to incredible pain and fear.

Not horror. A rom-com. She's inherited a dilapidated old amusement park from a distant uncle. No. An estranged parent, so there are more emotional complications. This is her first tour, and she's aghast at the state of it. What's she supposed to do with a broken-down amusement park? Never mind that her fondest childhood memories took place here, the last time she spent a happy summer with her father. (Mother? Father. Paternal estrangement is less painful than maternal estrangement. At least for audiences. She finds both plenty painful, herself. But back to the movie.)

Now she's going to turn around and run right into a man in a flannel shirt. Jeans that fit snuggly on a perfect ass. Sturdy boots, needed-to-shave-three-days-ago stubble, gruff voice, vibrant eyes. A contractor! Hired by her father before he passed! But why would she invest more in the park? Unless it means spending time with those vibrant eyes . . .

A stray breeze groans through the carousel, like the last breath pushed from dead lungs. No. This is not a rom-com set. This is a zombie movie set.

Focus, Rebecca. She steps into the carousel. It looks like the panels in the center are split apart. If she tries, she can squeeze inside. Bonus to not having her C-cups yet. Those would definitely get in the way.

But as she puts her first leg in, she looks down and sees a dull glint of silver. She knows that necklace. It looked so pretty on Rosiee. She had envied what a specific, clear sense of self Rosiee conveyed with her heavy silver jewelry. She crouches down and picks up the necklace. The clasp is broken.

Rebecca looks closer. There's a black mark on the clasp. Sticky, and actually not quite black. Very dark red. If Rosiee's necklace caught and dug in hard enough to draw blood, surely Rosiee would have noticed.

Rebecca slowly withdraws her leg. Looks closer at the opening.

There's a scrap of cloth, torn. She recognizes it from Rosiee's shirt. A few steps backward, bumping into one of the skeletal horses, grinning sightlessly at her. There, a boot. How hard would Rosiee have to be struggling to lose a boot? It isn't like it's a pump, or a slip-on. There are deep gouges in the boot, too, scrapes where it must have been dragged against the ground. Trying to find purchase.

Rebecca stumbles off the carousel platform, heart racing, eyes searching wildly. This is not a rom-com.

This is not a rom-com.

The sun cuts across the treetops, flooding the carousel with light. There are dark smears of what could be rust. Oil. Black water. Blood.

"Fuck this zombie shit," Rebecca whispers. "Hey!" she shouts, hitting the nearest path. "Hey! Help! I need help! I think something bad happened to Rosiee! If anyone is watching, I don't care if I'm out! Something is wrong! Something is seriously wrong!"

She runs into the hedges, pushing through toward the camp. With her shrill cries fading and muffled by the eager green, it's as though the carousel has never been disturbed. All except for the glints of silver left behind, winking a code in the sunlight no one is there to decipher.

Mack feels the tension as Ava hears it, too. Whether the person shouting is near or far is hard to tell, with the structures and the trees and the general chaos of the park breaking up the sounds, flinging them haphazardly through the air.

Ava shifts and pushes her eye to the ivy. Mack does the same, only because she can't bear not to.

They don't see anything.

"Sounds like Rebecca," Ava whispers.

Mack hisses in response. Someone got set up to lose yesterday. That had to be what the ringing metal was. This is probably another trick.

The shouting cuts off abruptly, and Mack nearly lets out a sigh of relief, but it catches in her ribs, static and terrible, as a single scream careens through the park, echoing and being torn apart as it looks for purchase in their ears. In any ears.

Ava moves. Mack's hand shoots out, grabbing her arm.

"No," she whispers. "It's a trick."

Footsteps, then. An awkward, uncoordinated run. LeGrand hurries past them in the direction of the screams. He's an idiot.

He's not an idiot. Mack knows it. She knows the difference between a horror movie scream, a scream meant to *imitate* human agony, and the real thing.

She turns and sees a single tear trace down Ava's face before Ava squeezes her eyes closed and turns her head so she can't see down anymore. Ava knows the difference, too. "Jaden," Ava whispers, reassuring herself or Mack or neither of them. "I'll bet it's him, setting everyone up."

They both stay where they are, trapped in the prison of silence left in the wake of an unanswered scream.

The sheer, mindless boredom of the passage of the sun, written on their bodies in dappled secrets, feels like it's mocking the panic and fear the beginning of the day offered. Mack has nothing to do but wait, wonder, and replay the scream over and over in her head until it blends and bleeds into the other screams that have been a constant soundtrack in her life.

Until she can convince herself that she was hearing what she wanted to. What she didn't want to. Whichever. It wasn't a real scream. She's primed to expect terror, to hear pain. That's all.

Ava is silent and still next to her, and whatever her thoughts are wrestling with, Mack is not privy to them. She's glad for it, too. She'd rather be alone in her own head. She shifts, infinitesimal movements so as not to shake the trellis or make the ivy whisper betrayal. Pressing an eye against a gap in the leaves, she stares down at the park.

She isn't looking for anything, not hoping for anything, utterly incurious. But a neon slash catches her attention. Everything else in the park is time-faded, sun-bleached, rust-rotted, mold-claimed. This strip of paint is like a blinking Vegas sign.

Atrius. She follows the line of it, and at the edge of her vision she sees another, this one formed like an arrow. A path. A path to what, though? What was Atrius doing? Trying to keep track of where he was going or where he had been? Trying to lure them into a trap? Or just being an asshole with a can of spray paint, marking his presence on a place utterly indifferent to it? Why anyone would want to leave traces of themselves everywhere they went is beyond Mack.

But then it clicks. *It's a maze,* he'd said, and she assumed he was being a pretentious artist. But he was telling her about the park itself. She turns her head to whisper her revelation to Ava, but Ava's eyes are squeezed shut, and even this close, she seems impossibly far away. So Mack does what she does best:

Nothing.

At last, the sun sets. Mack lets Ava climb down first, leaning precariously far over the edge to keep one of Ava's hands to steady her. Then she follows. They don't talk on the way back to camp, but Ava moves with an urgency she didn't have yesterday. She's nervous. She wants to know what happened.

Mack decides she would rather not. She deliberately slows her pace, lets Ava leave her behind. But to her frustration, Ava keeps slowing, looking over her shoulder.

"Come on, Mack," she huffs. "I want to pee in a toilet."

Mack can't argue with that, so she rejoins Ava, letting her eyes track the trail Atrius left. The neon is holding on to the last glow of twilight.

Mack wonders what would happen if she followed it. If she let herself be swallowed by the night, by the maze. Would the arrows point her deeper and deeper into the park until she never returned? Or would they disappear, leaving her alone, aimless, directionless? Lost.

It doesn't feel like a bleak option. It feels familiar.

They reach camp after a solid twenty minutes of walking toward the spotlight. Ava has an uncanny sense of direction, which is useful for now, but overall bad news for Mack. She has to remember that. Ava isn't her friend, she's her competition. The money seems nebulous; even the nature of the competition somehow burned away as the sun crawled overhead. It feels like Mack has always been here, like she will always be here. The idea that there's an end point, a goal, is gossamer floating on the air, sparkling and ephemeral.

Is any of it real? Is she still up in the rafters, staring down at the shelter?

Is she still up in the pantry, staring down at the pool of darkness seeping slowly across the floor?

She reaches out and lets her fingertips brush the back of Ava's shirt. She presses her fingertips against her own heart. The only breathing noises she hears are her own. Not the wet, gasping breaths of a dying life.

Mack closes her eyes. Her head aches. She might have heat stroke in spite of the shade. Doesn't matter.

Ava strides into camp toward the sullen writer and Brandon, the only two back so far, and ignores the bathrooms in contradiction to what she said earlier.

The table is absolutely laden with food and water. Four or five times as much as was there before. Why?

Doesn't matter. Bathroom. Mack nearly cries at the pain of relief.

When Mack comes out, Ava is standing on the edge of camp, her arms folded, her eyes narrowed. "They didn't hear anything," she says, as though Mack asked. Mack did not ask. Mack will not ask.

"Do you think something is really wrong?" Brandon joins Ava, his kind freckled nose wrinkled in concern. "Maybe she got hurt. It would have been Rebecca, right?"

"Or the other Ava," Ava says.

"I am not the other Ava," a voice snaps from the darkness. "You're the other Ava." Beautiful Ava staggers into the camp and flings herself at the table, chugging a water bottle so fast it drips down her throat. Her eye makeup has drifted downward, leaving dark hollows beneath her eyes. Lines of either sweat or tears have created a strangely striped effect through her foundation. Jaden prowls in after her, sweaty and dirty and struggling to maintain his cooler-than-thou expressions.

"What did you do to her?" Ava folds her arms over her chest. It accentuates her not-negligible biceps, whether she intends it to or not.

Mack wanders away. She doesn't need to know. She doesn't want to know. She wants to sleep.

Jaden smiles.

"Listen, asshole, if Rebecca doesn't come back tonight—"

"Wait, Rebecca?" beautiful Ava interrupts. "I thought we were talking about Sydney."

"You're helping him?" Ava says, shaking her head in disgust.

"Why would we be talking about Sydney?" Brandon asks, innocently confused.

"Because they were the ones who got her out," Ava says.

Jaden shrugs, a smug mask descending over his face. "All's fair, et cetera et cetera." The way he enunciates *et cetera* sets Mack's teeth on edge. It sets Ava's fists on clench, as well. "I would think you'd know at least about the war part," Jaden continues, "if not the love part."

Ava laughs. It takes Jaden by surprise, cracking his deliberately posed face. Then she moves so fast toward him that he stumbles back, bumping into the table. "Stay the fuck out of my way or you'll wish we never met."

Jaden tries to recover with a laugh, but it's as empty as beautiful Ava's discarded water bottle. "Too late for that."

Ava turns to Mack, but Mack is already heading for the showers. She's not on Ava's side. She's not on anyone's side. She forgot, today. She can't forget again.

Ava's still prowling the perimeter. Everyone's back except Atrius, LeGrand, and Rebecca. The writer—Ian, who Ava honestly cannot believe is still in—has his notebook out, nervously eating. Christian is less chatty today, sunburned and cross. Jaden and Ava Two have retreated to the corner of the covered area, dragging cots next to each other. Their laughter is forced, performative, their chatter unnecessarily low to emphasize that they don't want to be overheard. As if Ava would ever care about anything they were saying.

"Do you think three people got out today?" Brandon asks, clearing his throat nervously. He looks shyly over at Mack. "I'm glad you're still in." She doesn't respond, and he feels guilty for what he knows about her now. He wishes he didn't know, because it makes him sad, and it also makes him a little scared, and he doesn't like feeling either of those things.

A twig snaps. Even Mack, determined not to care, turns and watches like a fishing line is caught behind her eyes, tying her to whatever is coming.

LeGrand shuffles into camp.

"Did you find her?" Ava demands. She doesn't even have time to be glad that it was Atrius who got out and not LeGrand. She has to know what happened.

LeGrand shakes his head. His hands tremble as he takes a water bottle. He says nothing else, because he doesn't have anything else to say. He doesn't ask how she knows he was looking. He looked, and he didn't find, and he's pretty sure that's not how this game is supposed to work at all.

Mack wonders who LeGrand is, why he is the way he is. She doesn't know him, but she knows that when someone screams, LeGrand runs toward it. And she doesn't. What else would anyone ever need in order to weigh their worth?

"No Rebecca, and no Atrius," Ava says. She frowns. "And no fancy white lady to summarize the day for us or tell us who got out."

Does no one else keep such desperate track of food? Mack can't believe they don't notice. There's enough for the rest of the game. Linda dropped off food and turned on the spotlight and then left. She isn't coming back.

"Linda never said she'd be here every day." Ian snaps his note-book shut, irate. Why are they pretending like it matters to them who got out? As long as it was someone else, isn't it a good thing? He hates them for taking the game seriously. It's all so sophomoric, so pointless. But he peed in a jar today rather than risk leaving the shelter of a collapsed wall he found to hide in. So he hates them, and he hates himself, too, and he hates the people running the game. There's a lot of hate to go around. He plays with his fancy silver lighter, a present to himself after getting his MFA, flicking it open and closed. "Do you really need Linda to tell you the obvious? Two people a day. Two people not back. Atrius and Rebecca are out. I don't understand why you're upset. You didn't care yesterday."

"I cared," Christian mutters. The specter of his lost imagined future with Rosiee hovers over his shoulder. He can't recast it with anyone left. Rebecca's gone and she wasn't his type anyway. Beautiful Ava is obviously with Jaden—he can't compete with that—and he's pretty sure the other two don't like men. He tries to be open-minded about stuff like that, but it rankles him. There's nothing wrong with him. He's a catch. It's not his fault something got wired wrong in them and they can't see it.

Maybe there will be a party afterward. He imagines himself the winner. Reunited with Rosiee, who got out early enough that she won't even be jealous because she knows she never had a chance. She'll only be happy for him, happy that the best person won. And then . . .

He's too tired to finish it. He lies back on his cot.

"It's obvious Jaden and Ava Two have been sabotaging other players," Ava says without preamble, standing in front of Brandon, Mack, and LeGrand. Her voice is calm but not hushed. She doesn't care if the other Ava and Jaden hear her. "And whatever they say, someone fucked with Rebecca in a serious way today."

"Excuse me?" beautiful Ava says, indignant.

"So we get them out." Ava shrugs.

"You know we can hear you," Jaden says, standing to expand his plumage to be as threatening as he can manage. Ava knows exactly who he is, exactly the type, exactly what will happen if he is ever faced with actual terror. Actual pain.

"I know," she says. "And I want you to know how few fucks I give about that. I'm going to get you out. I know it, you know it, carry on."

Jaden rolls his eyes and shakes his head. He hates that bitch. She thinks she's so tough, with her buzzed head and her creepy muscles. Girls shouldn't have muscles like that. She only has one work-ing leg, for fuck's sake. Does she really think she could beat him in any way that mattered?

"Whatever," he says, but it comes out slightly too high. He wishes he could have a do-over. Say something tougher, cooler. But it doesn't matter. It was his Ava's idea, but he's the one who got Sydney out. He doesn't know what happened to Rebecca, but let them think that was him, too. Let them enter the park paranoid and determined to beat him. It'll make them sloppy, and he'll win. He's going to win, he can feel it. He's the only winner here.

"I'm on your team, Ava," Brandon says, pointing to the correct one. He doesn't like the tension, but he likes Ava. He's never liked Jaden. Jaden is the type who moves through the world asking oth-ers to challenge him, daring them to call him on his garbage, knowing most of them never will.

This time, with strong Ava on his side, Brandon can call him on it. It's exciting, being part of a team. Maybe this is why other guys like sports so much.

LeGrand nods, silent. He spent the whole afternoon in the open, looking for Rebecca, and he didn't see or hear anything. No one searching. And no Rebecca, either. He has a bad feeling. But he's had a bad feeling since he was kicked out of home. The entire world is one big, bad feeling.

He knows Ava is a sinner, dirty, wrong, but he also feels like Ava would have helped him back home. Would have made the same choice he did. If Ava's lost, so is he, and, well, at least she's the kind of lost who stays up with you when you're crying at night.

"Get each other out for all I care," Ian mutters, pulling a pillow over his head. "Just do it fast."

Christian holds up his hands. "I'm Sweden."

"Switzerland," the other Ava says, unaware that even the lowly solar panel salesman thinks of her as the *other* Ava. It would make her furious if she knew.

"What?" Christian asks.

"It's Switzerland that's neutral, not Sweden."

"Thanks, Professor." Christian tries to make it flirty—maybe he does have a shot with her—but she looks away, biting one of her manicured nails. She doesn't look happy.

She isn't. Jaden seemed like the best choice. But looking at the other Ava, strong and angry and flanked by the only nice guys here, she wonders. No, she doesn't wonder. She knows. She's dated a dozen Jadens, and they're all the same, and it always ends the same way. He'll betray her out there, on a day close to the end, when he can't get anyone else out.

She knows it. She can feel it coming. But leaving him now wouldn't change that. So she laughs. "It's a game, remember, guys?"

"Mack, you're on our team, right?" Brandon asks, hopeful.

Mack lies on her side, curls around her own emptiness, and falls into sleep like stepping off a ledge.

Beautiful Ava wasn't quite right that first day, but she can be forgiven for not seeing what she was certainly not meant to see.

There *are* cameras. One in the building in the center of the park, though no one ever watches that feed unless they absolutely have to. One on each of the towers, but starting tomorrow the fence will be on and the towers will be manned, so the cameras are redundant. There's another one trained on the camp site, grainy green night vision capturing the argument. Linda was correct in assuming she shouldn't go back today. They'll realize soon enough what's happening. Maybe some of them already feel it, but they're still clinging to the hope that they don't *know* something is wrong.

And then there's the point where no amount of pretending can hide them from the truth. It's an ugly, desperate, messy time, and she prefers to watch from a distance from here on out.

She puckers her thin, deeply lined lips as she reapplies her lipstick to get ready for the meeting. Only a few more days. She lowers the volume on the screen, lets their arguments become white noise. She can be grateful for them, spend this time as witness in honor of what they are doing, without having to actually listen.

This is the only camera feed she ever looks at. She's the one who brought in the contestants—she still thinks of them as contestants, because it's an easier word to say and swallow and digest—and so she will watch as they disappear. But there's no reason to be gruesome about it. The other cameras are not for her.

Her face is as good as it's going to get. She's old, and she hates that they have these meetings at night. But she understands it, too. Night is calmer. Night is safe. The tension during the day—knowing what's out there, what's happening—makes the meetings too fraught.

She climbs into her car and steers it like a boat through the river of darkness to the spa. She's the first to arrive. Of course she is. She unlocks the door, marching straight to the conference room, right past Tommy Callas's smug portrait and the empty safe it hides.

She takes her seat next to the head of the table, glaring at the empty chairs. *Her* family made the gate. *Her* mother created the Amazement Park. And *Linda* figured out how to keep things working after it closed. How to run this stupid game. But by all means, save those spots for the Callas heirs.

As though summoned by her resentment, Ray and his cousin Gary amble in. Ray sets a carafe of coffee in the center of the table, the scent dark and bitter. Linda wrinkles her nose. Who drinks coffee at this time of night? The least they could have done is bring something nice. But the least they could do is more than they ever actually do.

Ray and Gary take their seats at the head of the table. "Chuck's coming," Ray grunts.

Linda musters up some sort of smile to flash in response. "Good," she says, biting off the word. By all means. Another Callas. She glances at the chair next to herself, the one reserved for another Nicely representative. It'll stay empty. Her daughter hasn't returned her calls in months.

The others fill in. Weepy Karen Stratton, the only family volunteer for spa duty, sets up several iPads in front of empty chairs for the Frye, Pulsipher, and Young representatives. Linda catches herself grinding her teeth, remembers what the dentist said about wearing away what little enamel she has left on her remaining teeth. Puts on a smile instead.

"Shall we begin?" she says, as Chuck usurps the Nicely seat next to her, a vision of things to come.

"Why do they get to call in?" Chuck nods toward the iPads.

"Couldn't make it," Leon Frye says from his screen, smiling broadly. "But my team tells me the app is working exactly as it should."

"Great, yeah, you have a team to make an app and a genealogy database. Meanwhile, the rest of us have to stay here and do everything ourselves," Chuck mutters darkly. He's in his forties, his firm jaw already softened with age, his hairline abandoning his forehead just like his hopes for a bigger life outside of Asterion abandoned him when he was inducted into the inner circle.

"And be the heir to an international diner chain fortune," Linda chirps brightly. She always calls it a diner, not a restaurant, no matter how many times Ray and Gary correct her. "Besides, Asterion is your home. Our home."

"Yeah." Chuck leans back, folding his arms. She can't believe they think he can take over her role. He's hardly been groomed for leadership. He spends every summer on a yacht, every winter in Aspen, anything to pretend like he's not forever tied here, anything to avoid his responsibilities. "I'm just saying, it feels like some of the families do a lot more of the work."

Linda's hands twitch into strangling claws, so she moves them onto her lap where they can't be seen. Chuck drove a *bus*. One bus! Meanwhile, she found the contestants, coordinated the invitations, handled all the logistics, even risked going into the park during the season!

Rulon Pulsipher stares over his glasses, his own webcam at an awkward angle so even though he's on an iPad on the table, it feels like he's looking down at them. "Do you really want to itemize contributions?" His voice is heavy with malice and meaning. They all know he has the freedom he does because of his (frankly repulsive) actions to create assurances for Asterion's future pool of potential contestants.

"I have a question," Karen says, raising her hand. It fills Linda with disgust. They're not in a kindergarten class. Karen needs to grow up. She's never done anything, though. She keeps her garden and redecorates her house every few years, living off the rest of their hard work after her *one* task was accomplished twenty years ago. "Why did you tell the contestants to look for a book?"

Linda feels the question like an icy blast, freezing her in place. "What do you mean?" she asks, stalling, panic filling her brain with the black-and-white snow from the end of a programming day.

"On the first morning, you told them to look for a book as a bonus. What was that about?"

Linda laughs, hoping it sounds tired and dismissive, not forced. "I can't believe you actually watch the feed." But Karen doesn't say anything, so Linda continues. "I always try to throw in something extra, to keep them scrambling. To keep them focused on the game. It makes things more exciting for them. Draws out their hope longer. Last time I told them three golden 'immunity' coins were hidden around the park." She crosses her gnarled fingers that Karen wasn't watching the live feed seven years ago to know that Linda did no such thing. She told them to look for a book then, too.

"Hmm." Karen nods, but she doesn't seem convinced. Of course that bitch would be the one to ask, since it's her own mother's fault. She can't know that Tommy's book is missing, though. She would have said something by now.

Linda needs to change the subject, and quickly. "Is the guard rotation set?" she asks, even though she's the one who made the schedule.

Chuck lets out another mumbled groan, but this time in assent. The men start talking about updates to the rifle collection, which gets them talking about guns and ammo and weapons development and Frye's investment in a new congressperson on some sort of defense committee.

Linda pours coffee for everyone around the table, relieved that everything is back to normal. Usually she'd be livid that they hijacked her meeting to talk about things other than their solemn duties and how things are progressing in the park, but she's relieved today. When the season is over—four more days—she'll figure out how to replace the book.

Or maybe she won't. Karen's own daughter isn't old enough to go through the rite of passage of reading Tommy's careful translations, the method by which all this came into being. Linda will probably be dead before she is. And then they can deal with the mess without her, see how they like it.

She deliberately spills coffee on Chuck's chair, so he has to move. He doesn't deserve to sit in a Nicely seat. Callas or not, this isn't his town. The running of a perfect season isn't his responsibility, or his burden, or his privilege. It's *Linda's*.

DAY FOUR

I T'S THE SPIDER THAT MAKES UP MACK'S MIND.

Ava, Brandon, and LeGrand are gathered by the overflowing table, making a plan for the day. Beautiful Ava and Jaden are on the other end of the camp, carrying on a whispered conversation in harsh tones. Ian and Christian are hovering near their cots, debating whether they feel left out enough to overcome their inherent ambivalence about each other.

A solitary spider drops from the ceiling of the pavilion, nearly invisible in the low orange lights, right in Mack's path. It hangs, legs caressing its strand, between her and the others.

Maddie hated spiders. She'd scream bloody murder whenever she found one. But Mack didn't like killing spiders—the way they shrank in on themselves, legs curling up, sinister beauty reduced to small, tangled waste—so she'd have to painstakingly capture them, carry them outside, and release them. It got to the point where, as soon as Mack heard Maddie shriek, she'd immediately go for a glass jar and a sheet of paper.

But the time Maddie screamed when it mattered was just like the scream yesterday. Mack stayed hidden, and her sister was reduced to small, tangled waste.

Mack looks at the spider, looks past it to Ava, and then slips into the trees. Alone. It's better that Ava know now that Mack can't be counted on. Shouldn't be trusted. Last night, again, Ava slept next to her as though that were any guarantee of safety. After what Ava saw on the trellis—how easily Mack simply stayed put rather than trying to help—how could she sleep?

Doesn't matter. Mack's not a mystical person by any means, but she's going to win. It feels inevitable. It's not a triumphant feeling, though. It's heavy and monstrous.

Familiar.

At least this time, her sin is passive abandonment, not active betrayal.

"What do you think, man? Want an alliance or whatever?" Christian warily eyes where the hot ones are debating whether it's better to head into the park first or second and the weird ones are calmly gathering supplies.

Ian is in neither of those groups, and doesn't want to be. He definitely doesn't want to be. He's told himself so several times as he tears apart his bag for the fiftieth time. He can't find his pen. How can he write without his pen? All this inspiration, and he can't even—the back of his neck is already sticky with sweat, and he can feel several bug bites, not to mention a blistering sunburn on one patch of arm that he missed with the sunblock yesterday, and no, he is not feeling inspired, he is feeling drained and exhausted and annoyed and where the *hell* is his pen?

All this inspiration, and he can't even write because he doesn't have his pen. That's what's holding him back. It has to be what's holding him back, because if there's not some magical formula for writing, some mystical combination of the right objects and mood and setting and music, that means there's no way for him to find the right way to do it. That means all there is to writing is just . . . writing. And it's hard. It's so hard. He hasn't finished a piece since he graduated. What if he never does again?

"So?" Christian prods.

"Do you really think you're going to win?" Ian asks, staring up with slightly more malice than he intended. Christian's not going to win, and neither is Ian. He never wins anything, not ever.

Why did he agree to this? That stupid DNA ancestry test he took, hoping for some unknown connection to a culture he could tap into. To something that would infuse him with purpose, with story. Instead all he got was a random woman, second cousin or one-eighth cousin fourteen times removed or whatever, reaching out to him and telling him about this contest. Why had he thought it could be good? When was anything ever good in his life?

Christian lets out an angry huff and stomps away into the early morning darkness. Just as well. Ian doesn't have any desire for an ally, any will to play whatever game the others have decided to turn this into. Wasn't it a stupid enough game on its own without making it *more* complicated? They're playing hide-and-go-seek, for god's sake.

Despondent, penless, and knowing that even if he did have the pen he wouldn't write today, Ian abandons his heavy bag and wanders out of camp into the overarching shrubbery. He walks aimlessly, shoulders hunched, hands shoved into his pockets. How can he be chilled and sweaty at the same time? He hates it here. He hates it everywhere.

If he were someone else, doubtless he could have found a story in all this, but he doesn't want to be one of those cheap genre writers, vomiting out word garbage for the tasteless masses. He has an MFA. He wants to make art. He wants to write things that *matter*. He wants to give interviews in a masculine, casual, big-money study, surrounded by classics—none of his own books, of course, because he wouldn't need to do anything as gauche as show them off. Obviously whoever interviewed him would note the lack of ostentatious self-advertising. He wouldn't need to promote himself. The work would be enough. There would be a photo of him, unsmiling, staring boldly at the camera, which would make his face handsome somehow. And he'd have a pipe that he'd smoke during the interview without apology, lit by his sleek, expensive lighter.

Dammit. He left his lighter in his bag.

His wood-paneled study disappears, slapped from his mind with an errant branch to the face.

Swearing and sweating, Ian passes the entrance to a cavernous building with demented cupids hanging—literally, in one case, swinging by its neck—from the faded, rusting sign. LOVERS' HIDE-AWAY. Whatever the attraction was, it's all indoors. Probably used to be a water ride, which brings to mind mildew and rot and mold. He imagines it infiltrating his lungs, settling in, populating his body with millions of tiny mold spores shot like arrows from Cupid's bow. Hard pass.

A little farther down the twisting path he's on, he sees a building that fits his mood. The opening gapes beneath a massive demon. Once it was probably covered in plaster, but the rain has gradually melted it away so only the metal skeleton remains: a horned skull, a barrel chest, skeletal wings. Still not as creepy as the cherubs, really. A love tunnel and a hell tunnel so close to each other. Probably better if they were combined.

That's a clever thought. Or at least there's a clever thought somewhere in there, if only Ian had his fucking pen to write it down.

He pauses at the ticket booth. Prices listed on the side were stamped into a metal plate, so he can still make them out. Someone had a sense of humor. Park-goers had to purchase a sin in order to enter—Lust, Envy, Greed, Sloth, Gluttony, Pride, Wrath. Oddly, someone has scratched in ASTERION beneath those. Isn't that the name of the town?

His interest is piqued, and he's running out of time, so Ian steps beneath the demon and enters the building. He's made the same error he hoped to avoid with the love tunnel. Half of the roof here has caved in; the ride also used an artificial river to move boats along a path. Of course, that's long since dried up, leaving only mildew and a depression in the middle of the pathway. Mildew and depression: both familiar states for Ian.

Another good joke, and no way to write it down or share it.

The hell ride reminds him of something, and he feels a rush of embarrassment that arrives before his realization why this place fills him with humiliation. Then he remembers: Gorky. Maksim

Gorky. Ian had gotten weirdly obsessed with the Russian dissident writer during undergrad. At parties his go-to line was to quote Gorky and his thoughts on the repulsiveness of American excess. He tried it so many times, and he never got a single date. The last time he used it, the girl he was talking to actually knew who Gorky was. He thought he had finally met a good match, until the girl laughed and said, "Yeah, he was hot, that's how he got away with being such a pretentious asshole. How do you think you're going to get away with it?"

Ian shoves down the reflexive, residual shame. Gorky had written about Coney Island, hadn't he? He had! How did Ian not think of it until now? Gorky had a way of shoving more over-the-top emotional descriptions into a single paragraph than most people did in an entire piece. He wasn't a pretentious asshole, he was a genius. He had gone to Coney Island and hated every moment of it and written beautifully about how awful it was. There was something about a monkey, something about a banal hell ride like this one, something about infant incubators. Initially Ian had imagined those as a weird ride designed like strollers for adults, but it turned out it was a building that was literally built to house premature babies in incubators. Amusement parks used to be a lot weirder. Maybe they even had one of those here, but it doesn't seem quite old enough.

He tries to think of what else Gorky wrote. He had underlined so much of that essay. But Ian can't remember any specifics other than Gorky only truly being happy while imagining the whole place on fire.

Maybe Ian *can* find inspiration here. If Gorky, Russian dissident genius, could write soul-searingly beautiful hatred about Coney fucking Island, Ian can write about the Amazement Park. But if he wants to do that, he needs more time here.

He pulls out his phone. He turned it off as soon as it was clear there was no reception, so it's not dead. Powering it up, he turns on the flashlight. The sun still hasn't risen, and he needs a better idea of what this building offers before picking a hiding spot. He doesn't doubt whoever is looking for them will cheat with lights, so he can't trust simple darkness to hide him. Plus, with the caved-in roof, who knows how bright it might get.

He sweeps the light back and forth. There are a few rotting boats pushed up against a wall, one capsized in the center of the dried-up river. He could crawl under it, maybe, but the idea of being that close to the mildew smell makes him gag. Maybe there's a back room. A closet. Anything. His flashlight catches a set of teeth, and he jumps back, heart racing.

The teeth don't move. They can't move. They're painted on. Annoyed with his panic-induced itchy pit sweat, he stalks forward to face his artistic foe. This wall, farthest from the caved-in ceiling and protected from the elements, has been painted. He doesn't think it's part of the original design. It doesn't make sense, as it couldn't be seen from the boats.

There are a bunch of men and women in white clothes, surrounding a fire. The next image is men and women, sitting on thrones on top of a rocky hill.

No. Not a rocky hill. A hill made of bodies. Charming. The next image is more men and women, this time in red, all in a circle. Seven of each. Ian pauses. Seven men and seven women. He trails the flashlight along the wall to the next scene. It looks like a maze as seen from above, and in the center, black paint so thick it actually tricks his eyes into thinking there's a hole in the wall.

The next image is the teeth. The ones he saw before. But he was wrong—they aren't teeth, because they're all going the same direction, pointing upward, long and curving and sharp. What's behind them is indistinct, blurry, either on purpose or with age. But lovingly painted beneath it, with so much detail it's almost respectful, are fourteen skulls.

Fourteen. Again.

He doesn't like that number. Or these images. Who painted them here? Why go to all the trouble of painting creepy murals in a decades-old abandoned amusement park attraction on the off chance someone tries to hide in here and sees them?

Chekhov's mural. If a monster appears in a mural in the first act, it must necessarily eat someone in the final act. Chekhov was another Russian. Why couldn't Ian's ancestry have been Russian? He could be on a soul-discovery trip to Moscow right now instead of stuck in an abandoned amusement park.

This is stupid. It's all so stupid. Ian keeps whispering that word to himself—stupid *stupid* stupid—in an effort to combat the dread that keeps finding new depths for his stomach to drop to. He doesn't like this. Not this room, this building, this park, this contest. He turns to leave but trips on old cans of paint left here. They must have been used to paint the mural.

He goes back to the black hole at the center of the maze picture, shines his light right on it. And . . . he was right. It *is* a hole! Someone left this here deliberately, added it after the fact. Which means it's part of the game. Which means . . .

He takes a deep breath and reaches inside the hole, ready to have his arm bitten off or mangled or something. But his fingers come down on something dusty and rectangular. He knows a book when he feels it.

"Ha!" he shouts, then cringes as it echoes off the walls and ceiling. "Ha," he repeats in a much softer voice. He found the book. He found the fucking book. But it's too late to hurry back to the camp. He settles in the darkest corner of the building, beneath a pile of the roof materials that will shield him from view if anyone comes inside, and examines his prize.

The cover is old, the leather cracked and worn. The pages inside feel brittle, and he can't quite believe they've managed to survive the elements. As he opens the book, several pages fall free, and he sets them carefully in his lap.

His triumph surges as he reads a blue ballpoint inscription on the front inside cover of the old book.

She must have known I was against her, because she threw me in here with the beast. But she didn't know I had the book with me already. Maybe they are all in on it, though. I stay hidden for fear of

*both them and the beast. One and the same, really. It doesn't matter.
I'm out of time to find a solution in these pages, to find an ending to
this nightmare. I cannot stop it, and I will be consumed.*

*I deserve it. We all do. I'm sorry. May you do what I could not.
And if you are reading this, Linda, I hope you rot in hell. I'll be
waiting there for you.*

Linda! So this *is* the book. Of course it's the book, and Ian's
going to get the bonus. He hopes it's cash, but he'll even take an
advantage. Maybe he really can win this thing.

Eager, Ian turns the pages. The writing changes immediately,
old and faded, spidery flourishes neater than any modern writer
could do. It's all Greek to him—literally. He's pretty sure, at least.
Someone has made detailed translation notes in the margins. Ian
flips through, faster and faster. There, a diagram that matches the
patterns and symbols he saw on the entrance gate. There, plans for
a building. It sort of looks like a miniature temple, with more diagrams of symbols and patterns. And then, at the end, more Greek,
pages of it, pages and pages.

Ian doesn't like this book. It's not funny, or cheeky, or inspiring,
or frankly helpful. Is he supposed to do something with it? Is there
a further task besides finding it?

Ian should read the transcription. He should. Maybe there are
clues.

But this doesn't feel like a prop. This isn't something thrown
together by a sporting goods company. He knows books—they're
the only thing he knows, really—and this book is *old*. Ancient. It
doesn't belong in a stupid hide-and-seek game. He pauses on the
last drawing, a depiction of something monstrous, something that
doesn't belong *anywhere*.

Shuddering, he turns to the papers that fell free from the book.
Maybe those are the clues.

He reads, and he wishes he hadn't.

The means by which we intend to make the sacrifice and the methods we discovered are detailed in Tommy's book, but they do not matter right now.

We only want our families to understand: We have lived through the great war, and we fear others looming on the horizon, and we refuse to watch our children suffer and want and struggle and die the way we watched our brothers and sisters and parents. If making this choice means we protect our town and our children—our blood, our people—and ensures that our lines carry on stronger, our names marching forward, growing and building and becoming our dreams made real, then we are satisfied that our sacrifice is worthwhile. Who wouldn't sacrifice all for their children?

Know this: We are making the deal, and we do not know what the cost is, but we will pay it and send our love to you down the generations.

We leave Hobart Keck as witness, and in charge of administration. Individual notes from couples to follow; please see that our children receive them, and take care of our little ones as you would your own, knowing what we have done.

Solemnly,
Tommy and Mary Callas
George and Alice Pulsipher
Orville and Ethel Nicely
Willie and Ruth Stratton
Joel and Mary Young
Robert and Rose Harrell
Samuel and Irene Frye

JULY 10, 1925

We finished Tommy's temple last week and the gate this morning, built and placed and sealed and protected as detailed by Tommy's careful notes, though I cannot see the sense in any of this. They designated me the witness and I don't know what they intend me to witness other than fourteen desperate fools go into the woods and make themselves silly with chanting and spells.

Still, Tommy is my brother, if not by blood then by choice, so I'll do as they ask and write it all down and at the end when they're red-faced and humiliated I'll have whiskey waiting.

JULY 13, 1925

Tomorrow is the day. I've strict instructions not to interfere, no matter what I see or hear or how long it lasts.

The little ones have been divvied up among relatives. Mary, who has shed buckets of tears over little Tommy Junior and his weak lungs, did not so much as cry, which makes me suspect they do not think this will work, and if it does, they do not think the cost will be so high. Today they are bathing together, purifying themselves, and I can't look at any of them without laughing, so I'm going to sit in the corner pretending to take down serious notes for their posterity.

Tommy is never going to live this down. I'll see to it. We'll be old men and I'll ask if he's preparing to summon an ancient power every time he goes in a pool.

JULY 14, 1925

Well, I've sent them into the forest and closed the gate behind them. Seven days, they told me. Maybe they want a holiday away from their children. Easier ways to do it than creating an elaborate ceremony based on secret writings found in a burned-out church in the middle of no-man's-land.

I've set myself up a nice camp near the gate. I don't mind sleeping outside when no one is shelling or gassing me. I'll drink coffee and sleep under the stars for a week, and when they trudge out, I'll only mock them a little.

But I cannot fail to remark on this: They took a cow with them. Why did they take a cow? Tommy shook his head and told me not to think about it as they walked past, leading a cow.

I can think about nothing else, now. Why did they take a cow?

JULY 15, 1925

I cannot—
I have to gather my thoughts but my fingers are trembling
There was a noise.
No not a noise the opposite of a noise like the ringing absence when a shell has gone off nearby and all sounds are cut off and you don't know if they'll ever return or if you'll forever exist in this ringing pulsing void cut off from the world around you

JULY 16, 1925

There was a noise. I will call it a noise. And then pressure, unbearable pressure that made me think I would faint or die. When it finally released, my ears were bleeding.

I can attribute the noise and the pressure and my ears to memories, to an incoming storm, to anything, really. I will not let their damned nonsense and superstition infect me. I am angry with Tommy. And Mary. She should have more sense than this. The rest of them I barely know, but I am angry with the lot of them.

JULY 17, 1925

The gate is bothering me. It's just a gate. It's surrounded by trees. There's no fence it connects to. Just a gate, standing alone in the forest.

Why can I not bring myself to touch it?

I moved my campsite further down the dirt path. I can still see the gate. The whiskey is nearly gone, and I want to go into town for more, but I promised Tommy I would stay. After this, I think I will take my own holiday, far away from Tommy and this gate.

JULY 18, 1925

This morning as the sun crested the horizon I heard screaming. I was about to run into the trees at the screams, but then the laughing started.

I have killed men with my hands. I have taken shelter behind corpses to shield myself from bullets and shrapnel. I have seen all the horrors that war has to offer, and I have never been more frightened than I was of that laughter.

I am a coward. I do not care. If it had only been the screaming, I would have gone in. But I did not want to see what could make someone laugh like that.

I did not go in I will not go in I am staying on this side of the gate. If something terrible has happened, well, it has already happened and I have not interfered I have done what Tommy asked me to. I will stay out the full week here.

Then I will punch Tommy right in the face and leave.

JULY 22, 1925

If I had known what they were really asking me to do the burden they were putting on me the ghosts they were shackling me with the horror they were leaving me to wade through I would have told them no. I would have known they were asking me to sacrifice right alongside them.

God damn you, Tommy. God damn you all.

But I suppose he already has.

I am tired. I will finish my account tomorrow.

JULY 25, 1925

I have had all the whiskey in my house, and all the whiskey in Tommy's house for good measure. It is not enough.

I waited until the eighth morning, because I am a coward. I could have gone in the seventh night, but my soul recoiled at the very idea of crossing the threshold of that gate under cover of darkness. The gate had become an unpassable barrier in my mind, the only thing between me and whatever was happening in those trees.

Screaming. Weeping.

Laughing.

On the eighth morning, I unlocked the gate and stepped over the line into Tommy's new no-man's-land. I expected it to feel different—for my ears to pop and bleed once more, for my skin to crawl, for something to tell me what had happened here before I had to see it for myself—really, for an excuse to turn and flee.

But it was just trees like any other trees, slowly humming to life with birds and bugs and the creeping natural things of the world that either did not know or did not care about whatever was awaiting me.

I think of him, that person, that Hobart, walking slowly toward his goal, unaware of what he would find. Maybe if I had turned around, maybe if I had let myself keep the gate closed, maybe then I could have

But no. Tommy was my brother. I had to know. I owed it to him. Or I thought I did. Now I know the burden they placed on me absolved me of all debts, and put them in a debt they could never repay to me, a debt they never intended to repay because I was not included in their blasphemous ~~accursed god damned shit~~ ~~shit~~ ~~shit~~ ~~god damn you Tommy god damn you~~

I went into the woods. I walked softly as though hunting or being hunted. I made my way to the center, where they had cleared a circle of trees around Tommy's temple, where a great bonfire had burned that first night.

I found the cow, or what was left of her, rotting and putrid, the whole stomach of her blasted outward through some means I could not understand. It was worse than anything I had imagined the poor cow being used for, and I vomited and braced myself to see the fates of the fourteen people if this was the fate of the cow.

There was evidence of the bonfire. A ring of rocks, ashes, the lingering scent of smoke.

And there was some evidence that people had been here. Footprints, some gouges in the dirt. A neat row of fourteen pairs of shoes. Some of their clothes, folded next to the shoes, others torn and discarded. The camp told a tale of order descending into chaos, and it was a tale I did not want to read.

But the part of the story I most wanted to see was nowhere to be found. There was no evidence of Tommy, no evidence of Mary, no evidence of the Pulsiphers or the Nicelys or the Strattons or that moon-faced idiot Robert who had no right to be married to lovely Rose, or any of them. Any of the fourteen people who had entered these woods. They were gone. There was a folded bunch of papers on top of Tommy's book and I took them and tucked them into my pocket. I didn't want to open them there. I still do not.

There was a smell. And it was not the cow; the wind was wrong for that. I have been in trenches. I have crawled through mud churned with the gore of the living turned dead. I know the smell of death. It was everywhere.

Part of me wanted to believe this was a grand jape, a joke to end all jokes, myself the butt. That Tommy and the others were hiding in the temple, or had slipped out and around me and were safe and warm in their houses, waiting to laugh at me upon my return.

But I could not deny the smell of death, and the knowledge that Tommy and the other thirteen fools were never coming back.

The temple waited. I trembled, I shook, I am not ashamed to say I wept. But at last I set foot inside and found nothing—or so I thought. It was empty, the floor bare save the patterns Tommy meticulously laid into the black-and-white stonework. Even though it was empty, I felt no relief. No release. Because of that smell.

And then I noticed it. The gentle inhale and exhale, the steady pace of sleeping breath.

Something was there, and I could not see it. Something slept, breathing deeply, soft wet exhalations. My eyes insisted nothing was there, but I could hear it, I could smell it. I ran then, from the temple and the woods, then shut and locked the gate behind myself, haunted and hunted.

Tommy and Mary and the rest are gone. Whatever they did, they left something behind.

JULY 30, 1925

I hate them. I hate them all.

AUGUST 15, 1925

Following I have transcribed the instructions he left for me. I don't have his book, the one he found and brought here, the one he took his terrible instructions from. His brother took it and I was too shell-shocked to stop him. I am only sorry I don't have it so I cannot burn it. I am only sorry I did not take my knife and gut Tommy as he tried to walk into the trees. I am only sorry I ever met him, ever knew him, ever loved him. He gets to be dead and I have to live with what he did, what he made.

The burden is mine now. Tommy saw to that. He must have hated me, I think. Or he did not know, he did not suspect, he did not realize. But I cannot be generous to him or his memory. Not after what he has done.

I will watch at the gate. I will stand sentinel to the horror they left behind. And every moment for the rest of my life I will be haunted by the sound of that breathing, wet and slow and waiting, and breathe out my own hatred for my friend and his thirteen fools.

No, I will not bear this alone. Their children will know, and carry this burden, and remember what their parents did for them. To them.

To us all.

JULY 21, 1925

Instructions left by Tommy Callas on behalf of the Callas, Pulsipher, Nicely, Stratton, Young, Harrell, and Frye families, to be followed exactly:

We have paid the price and secured our prize. It is not what we expected, but we have faith god we must have faith we have to have faith faith is all that is left to us we have faith that the transaction will be honored. Prosperity and protection on all our blood from this moment onward through all generations of time.

We have paid this first price and when the last of us has been consumed, it will be me, I have witnessed them all except my beloved Mary and myself we are all that are left and Mary sits as though already consumed, here but gone from me all the same, I have loved her and it led us here so I must have faith I will have faith.

When I am consumed it will sleep and it will protect us and we will have given you what our parents could not give us what our country could not, we will have secured your fates and prosperity.

Prosper.

Prosper.

It is your right. It is paid for.

Set a watch. When it wakes if it wakes it will need to be fed. This deal has been sealed with our blood and will continue with our blood. Feed it and prosper and feel our love. My Mary was a woman built from love burning with it fueled by it and now she has burned out.

Set the watch.

<u>Do not leave the gate open.</u>

<u>Do not let it go hungry.</u>

Do not forget that we love you and you deserve this gift.

It awakens. Our time is over. We will be consumed for our children and our children's children and our children's children's children.

The price is paid willingly and with faith for the future that the future will hold the faith with us and we will endure through you I have faith I have faith I have faith I have faith but oh god there are stars beyond its maw and they are stars I do not know and my Mary has gone to them and now I will too.

Farewell.

JULY 15, 1926

They did not believe me, did not want to believe me, these brothers and sisters and children, until we entered the temple and the screaming started. It is not a monster for me, and yet it is my monster. I am not covered by Tommy's <u>blessings,</u> but I still suffer the cost.

We have set a guard. May the monster sleep forever in its sepulchral temple, and may the fourteen fools who brought it here never find peace.

JULY 15, 1930

It sleeps, I drink, the nation starves but we do not.

JULY 15, 1932

It is awake. We did nothing, nothing changed, there was no new ceremony, and yet it is awake. And Tommy said it must eat.

JULY 22, 1932

I had thought the worst moment of my life was behind me, but there were so many more moments to come. In the end, I stood at the temple, weeping, begging for release, and still I saw nothing, and it did not take me.

We were not prepared. We offered a cow and it ate the two men, Frye's brothers, who brought it in. After that we drew straws. We marched the unlucky ones to their death, two by two. Two a day for seven days and in the end we could not march them we had to drag them. I had to drag them, because I am not damned as they are, I am damned all on my own.

Seven years. They bought us only seven years. Six months for each life given. Is it worth it, Tommy? What has your <u>faith</u> inflicted on us all?

I am executioner now.

Seven years to prepare. We will do better next time. We must.

JULY 22, 1939

The doctor says if I do not stop drinking, I will kill myself. There are faster ways to be consumed by oblivion, I said, but not for me. Not for me. Oblivion does not want me.

Our gamble did not work.

We tried the first day with Rose Harrell's sister's maid Doreen, but it left her untouched and prowled to the gate.

In a panic, we threw in Rose's own sister and Orville's brother. We could not let it get out. Doreen saw them devoured into nothingness, but it does not matter. Who would believe her? Invisible monsters devouring people whole in the woods. Imagine.

Imagine.

Fourteen years after the original fourteen sacrifices. Their families are the police now, and the senators, and the judges. There will be no consequences. We let Doreen flee, because she does not matter, which is why it is so maddening that she could not be the sacrifice.

It answers the question, though. Only the blood that brought it into being can sustain it.

We had bought a day with our hasty sacrifices, and sent out word. Every family submitted two names, sealed in envelopes—except Rose's and Orville's families, which only had to give one now. They did not submit their own names, of course. Their parents and siblings had sacrificed for them—not so they could be sacrifices, but so they could flourish. But the monster had to be fed.

Twelve distant relations, bastard offspring, feeble cousins, shameful secrets hidden no longer. Two by two they were invited into the homes they had never been welcomed into, and two by two they were escorted to the temple. By me, since I cannot be consumed.

It is too much. Surely there is a death faster than the bottle and more willing than the monster. I go to find it. Let Asterion keep its own cursed vigil. I seek the peace of hell, content that even hell is too good for Tommy Callas and we will never be reunited.

God damn Asterion and everything it touches forever. Amen.

IAN TURNS OFF HIS FLASHLIGHT APP and carefully places the loose papers back into the book, as though they'll know if he doesn't treat them well. As though he's being watched.

The meticulously translated writing, the diagrams, the last terrible drawing. It makes sense now, and he doesn't want it to.

He likes to be a skeptic. Wrapping himself in cynicism is the easiest way to protect his heart as he moves through a world utterly indifferent to him and his dreams. Part of him is embarrassed—knows how humiliated he'll be later, looking back on this—but the rest of him does not care.

Ian runs straight out of the building, back along the winding, curved pathways toward where the camp is. He gets there as dawn breaks, out of breath but finally certain of what he wants to do: Get the hell out of here. Maybe the bonus for finding this book is a cash prize. Maybe not. Doesn't matter.

He shoves the accursed book into his waiting bag, throws his things together, makes one last sweep for his stupid motherfucking pen. He even checks Jaden's things, because he wouldn't put it past that asshole to have taken it. But it's not there. It's not anywhere.

A loud crack echoes through the air, and he jumps, spinning wildly, but there's nothing there.

Whatever. Time to go. He doesn't want all the prize money, anyway. Money would ruin his creativity. Make him too comfortable. Artists need to suffer, right? Gorky would approve of this choice.

He lets out a strangled laugh at the absurdity of his fear, the certainty of it. The knowledge he wants to deny but just can't that something here is very, very wrong. It's tempting to lie down on his cot, pull the blanket over his head, and go back to sleep. Let them find him there.

But no. He's going to use the road they drove in on and walk to the gate, hand the book over to Linda, and never think about any of this, ever again. He's giving up. He doesn't want to play anymore. But he has to leave *now*. If he lies down on this cot, he'll marinate in his own doubts and sweat, talk himself out of his feelings. Better to lose in the open. To be laughed at and understand his own ridiculousness, his own weakness. To be able to look back not with terror but only with shame.

He understands shame. Shame is comfortable.

As he slings his bag over his shoulder, he hears it. At first his brain dismisses the wet, snuffling noise, but there's something wrong with it. Birds in undergrowth make oversize noises. Whatever is approaching makes almost no noise at all, except that breathing. Nothing small has ever breathed like that.

Ian remembers that terrible black hole, and the image of the horns illuminated in the darkness. He remembers Hobart's description of sleeping, invisible breaths. He remembers the drawing in the back of the book, and terror freezes him. His whole body is a held breath.

Something crashes through the bushes into the other side of the camp, blood soaked with crazed eyes.

"What the hell?" Ian shouts.

Mack takes too long. She's distracted. None of the spots seem good enough. Time is slipping away from her, and the approach of dawn fills her with surprised panic.

It's Ava's fault. Mack can't afford distractions, thoughts, feelings. A carousel ahead catches her eye. Surely there's somewhere unexpected to hide there. She shouldn't—it was too direct a path from the camp, making it an obvious hiding spot. But she's out of time. Mack hurries over to it.

She sees immediately what it took Rebecca too long to notice. The silver. The boot. The signs of violent struggle.

The opening in the center of the carousel gapes, patient and cold like a mausoleum. Waiting to swallow her, to put her where she belongs. Where she should have been all these years anyway. It doesn't matter how quiet she is, how invisible, how small. How little she lets herself want.

Death missed her that night, and now it misses her, and really, doesn't she miss it, too?

Mack steps gingerly onto the carousel platform, picks up each piece of Rosiee's artful silver. The cold darkness inside the center pulses, waiting to embrace her.

She remembers the warm darkness beneath the blanket. Ava's hand grabbing her own, helping her stay silent. Helping her stay hidden. *Wanting* her to stay hidden. Stay safe.

Dawn is breaking, and she turns away from the terrible ending waiting for her here. One of Atrius's neon arrows is illuminated on the back of an old food stall. *That way,* it points. That way to what?

Anywhere is better than here.

Mack follows it.

Christian didn't mean to hit the edges of the park. It's impossible to tell which direction he's actually going. He thought he was heading east, inward, but now that the sun is coming up, he sees that he got turned around somehow, actually went west and found the border. He's greeted by the massive metal cable fence, the only new—or at least well-maintained—thing he's seen besides their camp.

There's a sort of tower by the fence, not technically outside the boundaries since it's part of the fence. If Christian can climb it, he'll have a good view of the whole park. He might even be able to see where everyone else is hiding, and then Ian will regret not accepting an alliance. They'll all regret it. But he'll be a good winner. He'll congratulate everyone else, and Ox Sports will be so impressed with him, they'll offer him Linda's job on the spot.

The after-party is going to be amazing. No one said anything about an after-party, but Christian can already taste the champagne, can imagine the dress Rosiee will be wearing.

Humming happily to himself, he doesn't notice the low ambient hum in the air. One hand on the fence is all it takes. He's thrown backward, one second lasting an eternity as the current cycles through his body in an endless, brilliant white loop.

He passes out, or he doesn't. Time passes, or it doesn't. Electric. The fence is electric. Why is the fence electric? He wants to laugh. He always thought selling solar panels would kill him. Maybe electricity really *was* out to get him.

Tears trace down his face with relief as he stares upward. There's someone in the tower. They saw what happened. The person leans over, staring down at him, too far for Christian to really see the face.

And then the person retreats into the shade of the tower. Why aren't they helping him? Maybe they're calling for help. But after a few minutes when he finally has enough control of his body to move again, no one has come. They haven't called down to ask if he needs help, if he's okay.

Why is the fence electric? There aren't any warning signs. Forget winning the competition, Christian is going to *sue* them. Get his money that way. Start his own company. Pissed off and shaky, Christian examines the tower. It looks like a guard tower, now that he thinks about it.

Maybe he didn't really see someone in it. Maybe it was his brain, sparking from the electric shock, sending random images. It's risky, he knows it, but he reaches out and touches the bottom of the tower, anyway.

Not electrified.

"I'm gonna throw that son of a bitch right out of it," Christian mutters to himself as he begins climbing. He's a good climber, and even with the lingering muscular twitches, he's halfway before he has to stop and rest. He looks up.

He was right. There's a person in the tower.

Before his brain can process what the person is holding, the shot rings out. Christian drops to the ground, and the pain of the fall can't claim a spot in his brain with the hole in his shoulder demanding all his attention.

Shot.

He's been *shot*.

He stands up, staggering, hand pressed against the bullet wound. There's no space for anger, for questions, for anything other than the need to run. He staggers back into the park, an animal keen of terror and pain coming out of his mouth.

Christian pushes straight through, ignoring the paths. The paths all lie. He stumbles and careens but somehow aims better than he had this morning. If he can get back to camp, if he can get there, there will be help. He'll be okay.

He'll be okay, because he has to be okay.

He has to be.

At last, he breaks free of the grasping branches and finds himself face-to-face with a terrified and shocked Ian.

"What the hell?" Ian shouts.

Christian falls. Ian crouches over him, saying something that Christian can't understand. A shadow appears behind Ian. It blocks the sun, and Christian is hit with a sudden clarity that electricity would have been a better way to go, after all.

The sun goes down, blanketing the world in a darkness that does little to soften it. The spotlight doesn't turn on. Ava, LeGrand, and Brandon use Ava's sense of direction and make it back first.

"Holy shit," Ava breathes out like a prayer. Her heart races, trying to flee its fragile cage of bone and flesh. She throws the spotlight switch, illuminating the way, then turns and watches the path behind them, waiting. Hoping. Refusing to look at the overturned table, the scattered cots, the blood.

The blood.

"Come on, Mack," Ava whispers. "Please."

Ava, not feeling at all beautiful, is exhausted. She can sense the resentment radiating off of Jaden as they trudge back toward the camp, like the Axe Body Spray of aggression, stinging her nose and making her heart skitter with anxiety. Their plans today—to follow the others and figure out a way to set them up like Jaden did with Sydney—didn't result in anything. Instead, they ended up out of time to find their own good spot. The trunks of one of the tortured topiaries had grown around a hollow center, and they squeezed inside. In another circumstance, maybe it would have been romantic. Hot, even.

It *had* been hot, but not the good kind. She's sick of Jaden, sick of the way he walks a step ahead of her always, sick of the way he didn't even go far enough away for her not to hear and smell him peeing as soon as it was dark enough to climb out of the tree. Sick of him for not waiting for her to pee before they started back.

Sick of herself for choosing him.

She'd had other options. She could have stayed friends with Mack and the other Ava. She could have reached out to sweetheart Brandon, or even annoying Christian. Not LeGrand, still. He gives her the creeps. But she made her bed—cot, in this case—and now she has to sleep in it. She chose what was familiar because familiarity felt comfortable, but this *comfortable* has no comfort.

Lost in her own misery, she doesn't even notice the state of the camp. Doesn't have a chance to, though, with the other Ava launching herself in a snarling whirl of fists at Jaden.

"What the fuck did you do?" the other Ava demands, Jaden already on the ground, arms up to protect his face as the other Ava straddles him, pinning him down.

"Get off him!" Ava tries to tug them apart, but Brandon, sweet Brandon, takes her firmly by the elbow and turns her around.

"Oh," Ava breathes.

It looks like a crime scene. The supplies table knocked over, contents scattered, some of it trampled and smashed. Half the cots have been flung aside. And in the center there's a dark pool. A trail of dripping accusation leads up to it, and smears of horror lead away from it.

There's a bag on the ground, and a notebook half in the pool, the pages slowly being filled for the first and last time.

The other Ava is shouting something.

"It wasn't him," Ava says, numb. "We were together the whole day. We tried to find you guys but we couldn't, and then we hid. It wasn't him. It wasn't us," she corrects, because if they're accusing Jaden, they're accusing her, too.

"Fucking bitch," Jaden spits, lowering his arms now that the other Ava has paused in her onslaught. "What are you even accusing me of? You think I murdered them to win? How exactly would I spend the cash in jail?"

"I heard something." Ava can't tear her eyes away from the pool in the center of the camp. She smells it now, a tang of iron and something fouler, older. "In the morning. I thought it was a car backfiring. But there are no cars around here."

The other Ava leans back, then stands. Jaden scrambles to his feet, face purple with rage, lip already swelling.

The other Ava doesn't seem worried about being attacked, and, flanked by both tall Brandon and silent LeGrand with his vacant eyes, she doesn't need to. Jaden points a shaking finger at them. "You're all idiots. Fucking idiots. It's a game. Don't you get that? This is part of the game! This is the twist! They want you to be convinced that it's real, or that it's dangerous, so you'll get yourselves out! God." He laughs, the sound high and harsh. "I shouldn't even tell you this. I should let you work yourselves into a frenzy and run for the gate. But apparently it needs to be said that we're playing a *game* before Iraq Barbie here goes full Rambo and murders me."

The other Ava turns to her, dark eyes showing whites all around. "You swear, you were with him the whole day."

Ava nods, her head bobbing eagerly. "And he really didn't get anyone out except Sydney."

"Shut the fuck up," Jaden says. "Don't tell them anything." He pushes past and goes into the bathrooms. They hear a shower start up.

"I swear," Ava whispers.

The other Ava nods, expressionless. She looks out into the darkness. "I heard it, too. The shot. I thought I was losing my mind."

"He's probably right. That this is part of the game."

"Maybe." The other Ava twitches, her hand going down to one of her legs. "Maybe. I might—I might be seeing a threat where there isn't one."

"It's a pretty sick game," Brandon says, frowning at the camp. "I don't mean sick like cool. I mean sick like gross. I don't like it. It's not fun anymore." He looks up, searching both Avas' faces. "What should we do?"

"I need the money," Ava blurts. "I really do."

"We all need the fucking money," the other Ava says, but it's without venom.

"Look, maybe they did mislead us. Maybe it's a meaner game than we thought it was. But what's the alternative? You think Linda brought us in here to, what, murder us two by two?" It sounds ridiculous when Ava says it. It *is* ridiculous. Jaden is right. He has to be right. This is another twist in the game. Ava frowns, struck with a sudden thought. "You were all here at camp before we were."

Brandon tilts his head, confused. The other Ava understands immediately. "You think we did this to freak you out. I wish. God, that'd be a great strategy." She takes a few steps toward the darkness pressing in around them. "Could have been Christian or Ian, making a play."

"Or Mack." Ava shrugs defensively when the other Ava cuts a narrowed look at her. "Look, all I'm saying is, what she's been through, she's probably kind of messed up."

"No one is looking," LeGrand says, his voice soft, his watery eyes drifting somewhere along the ground. She thinks his eyes are a weak sort of blue, but in the orange light, none of them have color. Not even the sticky pool in the middle. Maybe it's not darkest red turning to black. Maybe it's purple, or blue, or—

Yeah. Maybe someone melted a whole cooler full of blood-scented Popsicles. Sure. Ava shakes her head, knowing what she's seeing and smelling but still wanting to deny it, because how could it be that?

"What do you mean?" Brandon asks LeGrand.

"Out there." LeGrand shrugs, his sloped shoulders making him look smaller than he is. "No one is looking for us."

"Just because you weren't found doesn't mean no one is looking," Ava says. "You probably got lucky; they had already gotten two people out for the day. That's the pattern, right? Two a day. So if the two have already been found, you're safe."

"We're still missing three." The other Ava sits on a cot and hangs her head, rubbing the back of her neck.

Ava sits gingerly next to her, keeping vigil to see who the night returns to them. Wishing with sudden sharp longing that Jaden had gotten out today.

Beautiful Ava's made a mistake. She can't see Jaden behind them, peering out from the bathroom, eyes narrowing as he decides exactly who he's going to trick into getting out the next day.

Brandon is scared. He's not having fun anymore, not at all. He doesn't even care about the money. If it wasn't for his friends, he'd leave right now. But he doesn't want to ditch his friends.

LeGrand is resigned. They're being punished, hell is real and they're in it, they're going to die or they're not. It doesn't really matter, because, really, he's been in a color-bleached, hopeless hell ever since he was banished.

And Ava stares into the darkness, darkness in her mind and her heart, smelling phantom smoke and charred flesh as she waits to see who comes back.

DAY FIVE

THE SPOTLIGHT IS ON NOW. Someone is calling her back, waiting for her.

Mack sits, knees up, arms around them. Her cart—bucket—whatever they call the part of a Ferris wheel that people climb into to circle in defiance of gravity—sways gently in the night breeze, and she could almost fall asleep. Curl up in the bottom with the dirt and debris and sleep forever.

Atrius's arrows led her here, and they kept going, but she didn't. She thinks he solved the maze. Whether that meant he got out, or got in, she doesn't know. He's gone.

She rubs the heavy silver of one of Rosiee's rings, slipped onto her finger so she wouldn't lose it. Gone.

Mack's hungry, and she's thirsty, and she's tired. She doesn't want to go back to camp, doesn't want to see who's not there, doesn't want to think about what that might mean. It's a game, yes. A game. A game run by people, and she understands perfectly well how monstrous people can be.

But she needs to know whether Ava is still here. Even if Mack chose to leave her. She has to know.

Mack climbs down and walks to the camp.

Ava is sitting on a cot, her face hollow, beautiful Ava sitting next to her. Brandon is cleaning up the table, which, judging from the mess, got knocked over. LeGrand is on another cot. There's a dark pool in the middle of the cement that seems to exert a reverse magnetism. Everyone is pushed out away from it.

Mack doesn't like what her heart does when she sees Ava. Or Brandon and LeGrand, to a lesser extent. Because she's glad—*god, she's so glad*—that they're here. Which means it will hurt when they aren't. And she can't help them, can't protect them, can't do anything to keep them here.

Someone takes her roughly by the arm and drags her into the light. Jaden holds her hand up triumphantly. "You want to know who pulled all this shit to scare us? Maybe the person wearing Rosiee's jewelry as a trophy!"

Mack stares at Ava. Ava hasn't gotten up. She looks at Mack like Mack is a ghost, like Mack already died and doesn't know it yet.

"Found it," Mack says. "And her boot. And some blood."

"Liar." Jaden drops her hand in disgust. "Should have known a freak like you would fight dirty. Listen, if you have your old man's genes and decide to get busy with a knife, kill them first." Jaden ignores Brandon's outraged cry and stomps off to a far cot. "Are you coming?" he snaps.

Beautiful Ava stands slowly. She offers Mack the smallest of smiles. "Glad you didn't get out." Then she follows Jaden.

"Where did you find it?" Ava asks.

Mack slowly unburdens herself of the silver, which feels heavier than it should. She carefully lays the pieces on the newly righted table. A ring etched with a scrolling pattern. A cuff bracelet with a snake wrapping around it. The heart pendant, the point of the heart so finely made it's sharp, she keeps around her neck and under her shirt. "Carousel."

Ava leans, staring at her boots, rubbing her hands over her neck and her buzzed head. "I don't know. I don't know. I don't know." She says it over and over, a chant.

"We could walk out," Brandon says.

LeGrand and Mack make eye contact. They both know they can't. It's not over yet, so they can't leave. It's that simple. Mack sets down her bag and carefully sorts through the unspoiled supplies Brandon put back on the table, taking enough for three more days. The sense of safety here, of light against the night and rest against long, draining days, is gone. The camp is exposed now, the park pressing hungrily against it, all the fluttering eyes in the darkness drawn to them.

LeGrand joins her, filling his bag.

"Are you guys packing to leave?" Brandon asks, hopeful. Doubtless if they quit, he'll feel better about it, too. But Mack can't offer him that.

She shakes her head. "Not coming back to camp."

Ava stands, eyes wide, hands trembling as though she's in withdrawal from something. She clenches them into fists. "Either it's a game or it's not, it's real or it's not, either way, yeah. Yeah. Shouldn't be where they expect us to be, ever."

"Who is *they*?" Brandon asks.

"That's the question." Ava takes her bag and shoves things haphazardly inside. "If it's a game, I want Jaden out before us. And if it's not, well, we stick together. All of us," she emphasizes, looking at Mack. Is she mad that Mack didn't join them, or does she want to keep Mack where she can see her? Does she suspect that Mack did something, something bad, something to Rosiee?

It's the wrong suspicion, but it feels deserved. Everyone should suspect her, all the time. But it hurts, because she wants Ava to believe her.

No.

She wants to be free of them all. To release Ava to the night, to walk away, to sever the ties and be nothing and no one and just . . . hide. Hide and never stop hiding. Like the bird in the shelter, up in the dusty rafters, isolated and hidden and safe. She wants that life.

"I know a spot," Brandon says, obviously feeling better with a plan and friends.

"Hey," Ava shouts. "Ava Two. You can come with us, if you want."

"She doesn't," Jaden answers.

Ava gives Ava Two a few seconds, then shrugs. Her face is grim.

"Okay. Lead on, Brandon. Let's go hide." She grabs Mack's arm. "I need your help in the dark," she says, and Mack doesn't think it's true, but she walks into the bleak empty blackness of earliest morning with Ava holding her in place because she can't hide when Ava's anchoring her here.

Brandon leads them to the Lovers' Hideaway. It takes some time to find in the dark—everything in the park takes some time to find—but they make it. Farther down the path, a skinned demon hangs in eternal watch over his realm.

"What if Jaden followed us?" Brandon asks, on high alert. This was his idea, his hiding spot, and he feels responsible for everyone now. Though the game is no longer fun, it's exciting in a different sort of way. All his friends moved out and moved on after high school, and he hasn't really been close with anyone since Grammy died. Out here, in the dark, full of adrenaline and questions, he feels close to Ava, LeGrand, and even Mack.

Though she kind of scares him now, too.

"If I see that motherfucker, I'll destroy him," Ava says. Her voice is tight and strained. Brandon wonders if her leg is hurting her. He has so many questions. Not only is she the only lesbian he's ever met—if she is, he doesn't want to assume, but she has to be, right?—but she's also a veteran. He hopes they'll get close enough that he can ask what happened to her leg, and if she knows any amputees. He's always been curious about amputees, if that ghost limb syndrome thing is real. Ghost limb? Haunted limb? Something like that. Ava will know.

He wants to talk to Mack, too. To ask her about what happened to her family. But no, he doesn't want to. He wants her to decide to tell him. He wants to prove to all of them that he's worth their friendship. Maybe after this, whatever *this* ends up being, they'll keep hanging out. Maybe they'll all move to Idaho, and they can work at the gas station together, and after their shifts they can sit on the curb watching the sun rise, laughing about all the inside jokes they'll have.

First things first, though; he has to take care of all of them so they'll know what a good friend he is.

It's not fun anymore, but it's *important* now, and he likes that.

LeGrand wonders if he died. If this is outer darkness, the hell he knew he'd go to if he sinned. Or if God made an exception for him and is punishing him right now instead of waiting.

Mack meets his eyes in the dark, enough moonlight for them to see by. She gives him the slightest nod. She understands. They *are* being punished, and for the first time since he was excommunicated and banished, a thought rises to the top, burning bright and holy like a bush on the mountainside:

I don't deserve this.

And, for the first time in as long as he can remember, long before he was shoved out into this cold, baffling world, LeGrand isn't scared anymore.

He's angry.

"So, what's the plan?" Brandon asks as they huddle inside the musty interior of the Lovers' Hideaway. It's a lightless void, impossible to navigate far past the entrance. When it's closer to dawn, then they'll be able to see well enough to pick a place. But Mack already doesn't like it. Too exposed. Too many people. Too many ways to be found.

"We set up a base camp here." Ava sits on the floor, easing her bad leg out in front of herself. Mack can't see the grimace, but she can sense its outlines in the way Ava moves and the way she speaks. "No more going back to the other one, not for anything. Treat Jaden and the other Ava like enemies, because if this is a game, they are, and if it's not, they still are." She pauses, and her normally strong voice gets tentative. "Am I crazy?" she whispers. "There's something wrong here, right? Because I know I have shit—acres of shit—in my head, but . . ." She trails off.

Mack hovers near the gaping entrance, looking out into the night. Who is she to tell someone whether or not they're crazy?

And who is she to say whether what's going on here is more wrong than anything else? She knew she was being preyed on from the moment she stepped into that office at the shelter. She knew, and she came anyway, and now all she can do is all she has done:

Keep hiding.

"Mack, don't you dare," Ava hisses. Mack pauses, her feet on the warped, uneven threshold between the rotting wooden planks of the tunnel of love and the path back outside into anonymity, where the only thing she has to hide and protect is the only thing she trusts herself to.

"We are sticking together," Ava says, her words as much an anchor as her hand in Mack's had been.

LeGrand drops his pack on the floor next to Ava. "Gonna climb a tree," he says, in the same tone someone might say, *Gonna run to the store for milk*. LeGrand, somehow, is handling this better than any of them. That, or he knows what Mack knows—something was always wrong here—and isn't surprised by a potential detour into violence and death. Business as usual. "I won't go far."

Ava nods. "Good. Better vantage point. Whistle if you see anyone coming."

"Can't whistle."

"No one ever taught you to whistle?" Ava sounds sad about it.

LeGrand makes a clicking noise with his tongue. It carries well in the night air. "Good enough," Ava says, allowing him to leave. Ava stares down at her hand, her fingers curled around the shape of a phantom gun. "Brandon, look for weapons."

"Weapons?" Brandon says the word as though someone has fingers around his throat.

"Anything sharp that can function as a knife. Chunks of concrete we can hold easily in our hands. Metal bars."

"Professor Plum in the tunnel of love with a lead pipe," Mack whispers. A memory, drowned with the gurgling of lungs trying to breathe while choking on their own blood, arrives fully formed in Mack's mind, as though it were waiting to be invited.

Her mother laughs. Mack had lost that laugh, had it cut out of her as surely as if the knife had found her own throat. *Mack glares, but her mother makes faces at her until she relents and rolls her eyes at her sister's outrageous cheating. Maddie* always *cheated. At least Mack got to be her favorite piece this time, Miss Scarlet. Even though the pieces are featureless, uniform plastic, Miss Scarlet is the most beautiful on the box, so she and her sister always fight over it. There's a bowl of popcorn, and a game that means nothing, and her mother's laughter.*

That's it. That's the whole thing. She doesn't remember who won, if anyone. She doesn't remember what they did before, or after. She doesn't know where her dad was in the memory. But her mother's laugh. Mack's terrified to replay it, terrified to wear it out, wear it thin, though she wants to wrap it around herself like a blanket.

Her entire life has been *after*. But there was a before, wasn't there? Is she living in another before right now, or will she forever be stuck in an infinite after?

"But we don't really think we need weapons. Do we?" Brandon's life has been quietly, consistently sad, never blown apart or cut into by violence. The idea that reality—his reality, this reality—could take a sharp detour into terror and blood and death is so foreign to him that he cannot understand it.

It's a language Mack and Ava both speak. Which makes Ava wonder if they're interpreting it wrong, looking for meaning where there is none. Maybe something here—even though it's nothing like her time in Afghanistan—has triggered PTSD, has turned on the part of her brain that is still back there, still in the desert, still lying on the ground with her leg crushed and her heart destroyed. This *could* all be a game. Ava can't say for sure. If it is, if it isn't, she has to play for keeps.

And she's made a huge error. "*Shit*. Mutually assured destruction."

"What?" Brandon looks to Mack for clarity. Mack has none to offer.

Ava shakes her head. "We should have forced them to come with us. Jaden and Ava Two, I mean. We all hide together, we're all found together."

"Like, taken them hostage?" Brandon shakes his head. He's okay with helping Ava, happy to hide with his friends instead of alone. But he doesn't actually think something is that wrong. Definitely not wrong enough to get aggressive and hurt someone else. He probably should have stopped Ava when she was punching Jaden. He feels bad that he didn't. He might not like Jaden, but it's not right to go around beating people up. Even when you're upset. "I don't think that would work," he says, hoping Ava's not going to decide to do it right now.

"No, you're right. Logistically impossible with our current resources."

Brandon picks up a chunk of concrete, hefting it with dubious care. They've amassed a small arsenal. A few pipes. A board with rusted nails. Chunks of concrete easy enough to lift and swing like a fist. Brandon is upset about all of them. "Besides," he says, still troubled, "we don't want them with us. Two people have to get out every day."

"Why, though?" Ava asks.

"Why any of it." Mack drifts deeper into the dark confines of the tunnel of love. The moon has come out from behind clouds, and there's enough ambient light from the gaping entrance and holes in the roof that she can navigate. She doesn't like this spot, doesn't like that they brought Brandon along, wonders if LeGrand is smart enough to have slinked away into the night, away from them. Away from her.

Is Mack's instinct to always climb actually a smart hiding strategy, or is it rooted in trauma? The ghost of her sister, prompting her higher? Or Mack climbing to try to escape her? To get to a place where she doesn't have to think about Maddie, or her father, or anything. Untether herself from the earth.

Whatever the reason, it's served her so far and she's not going to stop. She eyes the curve of the ceiling, the artificial cave over them.

It was made of plaster, and huge chunks of it have fallen, revealing the beams and cheap corrugated metal roof beyond. Could she get up that high? It doesn't look like there's an easy route up. She doubts Ava could climb it. So, surprising herself, she stops looking for a route, instead searching for a place Ava can access, too.

No fair, Maddie whines in her memory of that night.

Brandon joins Mack, yanking her back to the present. "I hid in there." He points to the line of cars forever frozen halfway through the tunnel, a swan hovering menacingly, one wing spread and one cracked and fallen to the floor. The building is split in half down the middle so the track goes behind the wall, but most of that wall has fallen, revealing the whole of the pathetic loop. And revealing no good hiding spots.

"Obvious," Mack says. How did no one find him? If she were searching, this would have been one of the first places she'd hit.

"Yeah." Brandon scratches the back of his head, frowning. He doesn't seem hurt or angry she dismissed his suggestion. He looks guilty, like he feels bad that he doesn't have something better to offer. "Sorry. I don't want to let you down. I shouldn't have acted like I knew a good place."

Mack recoils emotionally. She doesn't want to reach out to him, to comfort and reassure him. To be tied by yet another point to this game, this world. But. Brandon's soft *I hope you win* lingers like a hug in the back of her mind. Like an emotional contract. "No, this works. It's better for more people. Look, there." Mack points to the section of wall over the entrance. There's a hole there that looks intentional, several feet across and two or three feet high. It's not a cave-in or a structural failure, as far as she can tell in the dark, which means there might be a crawlspace between the ceiling and the entrance to the tunnel.

She can't know that it was used to access the overhang above the entrance and change out the decorations—the delicate streamers rotted fast, like most delicate things do—but it meets Mack's requirements for unexpected sight lines. And it's hard to access, too. So anyone trying to get up to them will give them time to—

Time to what?

She doesn't know.

Brandon is cheered by it, though. "So I did pick a good spot?" he asks, hopeful and happy.

Mack resists the urge to pat him on the head. She couldn't reach, anyway. "Yeah, Brandon. You did."

All this emotion, all this *need* tugging on her. Mack is tired. She's been tired for so long now. She climbs into the access hollow. It's exactly what she hoped, perfect for their needs. Rather than going back down and telling the others, though, she curls around herself and closes her eyes.

Three more days. Is it? Is it only three more days, or is it forever left hiding, afraid of what she knows and what she doesn't know, feeling safer in the nebulous stalled space between them? Wasn't it better to still be up in the pantry, terrified of what happened, suspecting what was being done, what had been done, but still not sure?

She should have stayed up there forever.

At some point, another body crawls in and curls up next to her, facing her. She doesn't have to open her eyes to know it's Ava. Her Ava. Somehow, in this dark space that smells of dust and decay, an errant board jabbing her hip, the dread of knowing the morning will bring someone—something?—looking for them, somehow Mack is as happy as she's ever been, with Ava's fuzzy head tickling her chin, Ava's solid body an undeniable presence, Ava's hand draped on Mack's waist, holding her in place.

It makes her want to scream, this feeling, this *hope* that feels more dangerous than anything stalking them. Because the hope has already found her, already snared her, already sunk in its claws that will absolutely eviscerate her when it's ripped away.

"I killed Maddie," Mack says, without preamble.

Ava says nothing.

"That night. It was *her* hiding spot. It was the best spot in the whole house, the only one where our father had never found her. I never won the game. But she showed me a few weeks before, after I saved her from a spider in her room, to say thank you. She showed me the ledge over the pantry door, big enough for one small body, where no one would ever think to look. And that night, I took it. I took her spot. She cried and glared at me and begged me to make room, but there wasn't room, so she hid on the bottom shelf, instead. And he found her, and I watched as he dragged her out. And I was safe."

Mack's never told anyone before. Now Ava knows. She knows that Mack is alive because her sister is dead, and her sister is dead because Mack isn't. Ava knows that when the knife comes out, Mack will stay hidden and let someone else be found.

Ava nods. She keeps her arm around Mack, and she nods her head, and she doesn't say it wasn't Mack's fault, or that she's sure Maddie wouldn't blame her, or try to make Mack feel better. She just says, "I'm sorry that happened."

And something *breaks* in Mack. She gasps for air, putting her arm around Ava, pulling her closer.

"When Maria died," Ava whispers, as the darkness around them begins to soften incrementally, "I lost everything that defined my borders. I lost Maria, and I lost my friends, and my job, and my purpose. And I couldn't even be mad, because lying there in the hospital, waiting to see if I would lose my leg, too, I tried to imagine what the man who did it must have been thinking, must have been feeling. And I knew, without a doubt, if I were him, I'd do the same. So I couldn't hate him anymore, and I couldn't feel any sort of purpose anymore, and I couldn't love Maria anymore, and there was nothing holding me in. I was evaporating, becoming less and less solid until I didn't even know who I was. *If* I was. Does that make sense?"

It doesn't make sense, not to Mack, because Ava has always seemed so strong, so solid; the idea that not even Ava's body is enough to hold her in terrifies Mack.

Mack felt the opposite. She had taken herself and pushed who she had been, who she could have been, so far down, so deep, that it became super-compacted, a well of gravity pulling everything—

happiness, sadness, joy, fear—into itself so she didn't have to feel any of it. So she could walk around, go through the motions of living, a protective, cavernous shell around an impossibly heavy nuclear core.

If Ava needs borders to feel real, Mack needs the opposite. She needs to be cracked open. And Ava has done just that tonight.

Mack doesn't want it, though. It makes her heart race with panic, worrying that the cracks will let all the vile guilt and shame and terror leak out. Does she really want to remember her mother's laugh, if it means remembering everything else? If it means remembering Maddie's angry face looking up accusingly at her as she took Maddie's hiding spot? If it means remembering the glimpses she saw as the officers rushed her out of the house?

But *shouldn't* she remember those things? And the things that came before the blood and the endings? If the people we love live on in us after they die, Mack has kept them buried, and she can't think about that, can't wonder what that means about her that her father might have killed her family, but she buried them again and again, every moment of every day.

"I didn't have a choice with Maria," Ava whispers. "I don't care if you want to leave. I have a choice with you, and I'm not letting you go." Her hand twitches, catching in Mack's shirt, twisting there. And then Ava takes a deep, shuddering breath, and she releases her grip. "No. I'm sorry. You can go, if you want to. There's still time to hide alone. But Mack. Please. I'm *asking* you not to. I'm asking you to stay with me. To remind me I'm here. Because I'm scared shitless that none of this is real, or all of it is, and I don't—I can't—" Ava's voice cuts itself off.

Ava's afraid, and Mack wants to hide from it, because holding someone else's fear means opening her shell even more. Letting her own fear out.

But she has her mother's laugh again, and the way Maddie wrinkled her nose up like a pug when she was trying to look *extra* angry, and it's precious and devastating and she wants to feel it. Wants to feel anything, for the first time in years. And knowing that Ava—strong, bold Ava—needs help makes Mack feel a little less alone. She puts her hand against Ava's cheek, presses her forehead to Ava's. Wonders if the explosion of releasing all the pain and guilt at the core of her will be worth a little happiness, a little joy.

"Yeah?" Ava asks, and neither of them knows exactly what she's asking, but they don't need to.

Mack presses her lips against Ava's. It's her first kiss, and it's soft and scared and hopeful, surrounded by darkness and suffused with it.

With the dawn deadline nearing, Brandon steps outside. Mack and Ava have been up in the hiding spot for a few hours now, and he can't be *sure,* but he's pretty sure they're a thing now. Which makes him happy for them but also feeling a little left out. He doesn't want their team to pair off, to create bonds he's left out of.

At least he doesn't have to worry about that with LeGrand. Maybe LeGrand will become his best friend. It doesn't seem likely—LeGrand hasn't really been friendly, even if he hasn't been unfriendly—but there's a chance. Brandon can imagine it. Becoming roommates. Staying up late playing his secondhand Xbox. Pooling their money for new games. Inviting the girls over for pizza. Sharing the out-of-date snacks he brings home from the gas station.

"LeGrand?" he whispers into the night.

A click answers, and Brandon follows it. He knows he shouldn't be out, that maybe Jaden is looking for them, but it feels so lonely waiting in the Lovers' Hideaway by himself, counting down until it's light enough to join Ava and Mack in the good hiding spot so he doesn't feel like he's intruding. He checked it out when he helped Ava climb in. It's super cramped up there. He won't even be able to crawl; he'll have to scoot on his belly. He's not looking forward to it. He's never been afraid of heights, but he doesn't like enclosed spaces.

A building looms at the end of this path—the one with the rotting demon with skeletal wings. It's hard to make out the details of it in the night, and somehow that makes it even creepier. At least if it was light, he could see how silly, how old and fragile it was. An impression of it, with his brain filling in the details, is worse than the actual thing.

Brandon leans against the bottom of LeGrand's tree. He doesn't know whether he wants his back to the demon so he doesn't have to look at it, or to face it so he can keep an eye on it. Both options make him nervous, and make him feel silly for being nervous about an old decoration.

"Hey," he says, looking upward as a compromise. The foliage of the tree is so dense, he wouldn't know where to start with climbing it, and he can't even see the other guy. How did LeGrand manage?

"Hey," a soft voice answers.

"We're up in a sort of crawlspace in the building. Against the front wall, overlooking the entrance. So you know where to find us." If Brandon feels left out, LeGrand might, too, and he doesn't want that. In his head, LeGrand is already his roommate. LeGrand's weird, sure, but he's nice-weird. Not mean-weird, like Atrius and Ian.

Brandon instantly feels guilty for the thought, because they're out, or . . . well, they're out. That's what Brandon is okay with thinking. He understands why Ava's wigged out, why they're all scared, because he is, too, but he doesn't want to be. And he doesn't think anything bad happened. He just thinks someone here is a dick. Jaden, more than likely. It doesn't really seem like something Linda would do. She seems too . . . classy for that. Nothing to do with her age, though. She doesn't remind him at all of his grandma—Grammy had pink hair from a time she mis-dyed it and then declared *Why the hell not,* and she wore men's T-shirts and short shorts, her tanned skin soft and crinkly. There was nothing fancy about his grandma, only funny warmth and honesty. Always honesty. Brandon misses her so much. Nothing's been the same since she died, which is even sadder, because nothing has changed.

He still lives in her tiny house, still works his same job, still does all the same things, only now he does them alone.

Everyone here is so worried about money, and he doesn't have any, but he's okay, thanks to Grammy. He's going to invite them all to live with him. If they want to.

Brandon leans against the trunk of the tree and stares at the outline of the devil. He should check before he plans on LeGrand moving into Grammy's house with him. "Do you have any family?" Seems like most of them here either don't or aren't really close with theirs.

"Yes."

Brandon's heart falls a little. If LeGrand has family, he's probably not going to pack up and move to Idaho. "Cool. Brothers and sisters?" Brandon always wanted a little sister. He sometimes imagined what a good brother he'd be, sticking up for her, helping her with homework. Well, that was a stretch. He'd never been great at school. But he'd make sure she was. She'd probably be valedictorian, and he'd clap so hard. He'd start a standing ovation for her.

"Thirty-seven," LeGrand says, though he sounds strangely unsure, like there's a hint of a question mark at the end of the number.

"What?" Brandon exclaims, then catches himself and lowers his voice. "What?" he repeats at a more appropriate volume.

LeGrand doesn't elaborate.

"Wow. Okay. Well, you know where we're hiding if you're seeking." Brandon waits, hoping his stupid joke lands. He doesn't want to have to explain why it's funny because then he'll know it's not.

"Half," LeGrand says, softly.

"What?"

"A lot of them are half brothers and sisters, I guess you'd call them? Different moms. My favorite sister is named Almera."

"Cool!" Brandon says, and he absolutely means it, even though the information is weird at best. He really does think it's cool that

LeGrand has so many siblings, and that he has a favorite. "I'll bet you're her favorite, too."

"They banished me."

Brandon knows what *banished* means—he's pretty sure—but it seems weirdly formal for a family. He doesn't know how to respond. But then he lights up, because this is it. "You can come live with me. After the game, I mean. I have a house. It's small and old but pretty cool."

The silence stretches for so long that Brandon's sure he messed up. But then LeGrand says, "Okay."

"Okay. Okay! Cool. Well, see you later!" The sky is starting to lighten, so it's time to barge in on Ava and Mack. But with this boost of confidence—LeGrand is going to stay his friend!—he's ready to extend the offer to Ava and Mack, too, and then settle in for a long day of waiting and hoping that absolutely nothing happens.

Things feel less scary and weird. He has a team. Friends. And a future with them.

LeGrand watches as Brandon walks back to the building where the others are hiding, the odd cheerful spring in his step back. It had disappeared on their trip from the camp here, but apparently Brandon's optimism is revived.

LeGrand has no feelings about that one way or another. *Almera.* He hasn't said her name out loud, not since he snuck out of the compound to the closest town and tried to tell the doctor there about her. He was rushed out the door, no help, no concern, nothing.

Why didn't the doctor help him?

Why didn't *anyone* help him?

It's a numbers game, the woman from the service to guide them in adjusting to "the real world" had said with a sigh. *If they keep all the boys in the community, there aren't enough girls for them to have more than one wife. They have to make up reasons to get rid of you. You didn't do anything wrong.*

At the time, heartbroken, shell-shocked, LeGrand had felt instantly defensive. It was sin to talk about the prophet, the elders that way. He *had* done something wrong. This was his fault, not theirs.

He feels a little bad now for how much he secretly hated that woman. She really did try to help him. Including filling out the application for this exciting competition that she had heard about through a friend of a friend. All she wanted was for these poor lost boys, uneducated, functionally illiterate, raised for one world only and then abandoned into another, to have a chance.

He'll never have a chance. His father saw to that. Even now, LeGrand's mind snaps reflexively at his own familiarity. The *prophet,* it corrects. Not his father.

LeGrand settles against the trunk, eyes on the demon spreading its skeleton wings out over its domain. If LeGrand is wicked for trying to get help, then the doctor, and his *father,* and his mother, and all his aunts and cousins and siblings and the elders and the mayor of the next town who looks the other way and the police department that takes his father's money and lets him run Zion Mountain like his own private country and the state that can't be bothered to care about what's happening in its borders and everyone—everyone, *everyone*—is evil for not helping. For seeing what Almera needed and not getting it for her. And if everyone is evil, then no one is, and he won't wonder anymore if he's a sinner.

He *is* a sinner, and it doesn't matter. Whatever happens next, he's going to help whoever needs it. Just like that woman from the service. Just like Brandon, giving LeGrand a place to live for no reason other than that he somehow knew LeGrand needed it. Just like Ava, taking LeGrand into her protection, even though no one else would have.

If all the world is hell and evil is all around them, what else can they do but try to help each other?

Brandon climbs into the hiding space. Mack and Ava fit better—he knocks his head against low-hanging beams three times while trying to get settled. But some of the tension in his chest eases, because Mack—not Ava, *Mack!*—shifts to make room for him, a half-sleeping Ava rolling onto her side with her head on Mack's shoulder. Brandon tamps down the thrill of being right about them, not wanting to be awkward. He can be cool about it. They'll know he's cool about it by how he doesn't react.

Mack tentatively pats the floor on her free side, and Brandon carefully stretches out, overjoyed that they're still making literal space for him. Whatever happens, it's going to be okay. They're going to stay his friends. One of them will win, and they'll all stay together. He knows it. "You guys want to move in with me after the game?" he says, and then he rushes to clarify. "LeGrand is, too. I have a house. It's small. But it's mine. Could be ours."

Mack lets out a puff of air he's pretty sure is a laugh. "Sure," she says, and he wonders briefly if she's making fun of him, but she wouldn't do that. And she follows up with, "That would be nice." He can tell by her dreamy, soft tone that she means it.

"Yeah, why the hell not," Ava says. "Where do you live?"

"Idaho."

"Okay, maybe that's why the hell not." But Ava laughs. Not *at* him—she's inviting him to laugh with her.

So he does, and he's happy, and things aren't so bad at all. Maybe they'll even get fun again. "What should we do at the end of this day? Find another spot, or stay here?"

"It's a maze," Mack says. "The park. Atrius figured it out."

"So tonight we try to solve it?" Ava sounds intrigued. "Makes as much sense as anything else." She doesn't add that it's good for her to have a goal, a purpose. That she needs to keep them all focused. Organized. *Together.*

Ava wraps an arm around Mack's waist. Mack agreed to stay, but Ava's not taking any chances. She wants to anchor her here, to keep Mack next to her, to have someone to press against and remember her own borders. Her own realness.

Ava still thinks some fucked-up shit is going down, but she can keep Mack safe, and Mack can keep her safe, too. And they'll both keep that overgrown puppy of a human Brandon safe, and sad, lost LeGrand safe, too. A new platoon. A new family.

Mack can't decide if it's claustrophobic having Ava on one side and Brandon on the other. All this warmth and affection and companionship and, most foreign, hope for a future, utterly lacking in her life for years and now hyper-concentrated. The pressure is building in her chest, and if she opens her mouth, she doesn't know whether a laugh or a scream will come out. So she strokes Ava's soft fuzz of hair and closes her eyes and tries to simply exist.

Yes, she's not alone. But it doesn't mean she's not still hidden. It just means she has help now.

LeGrand in his tree.

Ava and Mack and Brandon in their wooden womb.

Beautiful Ava and Jaden on the other side of the park, Ava walking a few steps behind Jaden as he looks for the best place to betray her.

And, in the center of it all, shuddering wet breaths grow shallower and more erratic as dawn approaches and hunger spikes.

Jaden's not a bad guy.

He'll be the first to tell you that, and he *has* told people that, over and over, so many times that it's become something of a catchphrase. "I'm not a bad guy," he says, his arms held wide, a wryly innocent grin on his almost handsome-enough face.

One of his exes once said he looked like the guy they put in the picture frame to sell it. Blandly attractive, a filler until the frame has something that actually matters in it. *No!* her friend had exclaimed, all of them several drinks deep. *He looks like a sock model!*

He had laughed. But every time he pulled on socks or walked past a display of frames in a store, he remembered their appraisals, and it rankled him. But he wasn't a bad guy. He had nudes of that ex, and he never posted them.

That ex is on his mind as he stands back, watching the current future ex in his life examine an old roller-coaster track. It climbs until it disappears into the trees, an ivy-choked outline of what it had once been.

All Jaden wants is one, just one, woman in his life who is loyal. Who is beautiful and funny and lives for him. Who doesn't let him down. Doesn't laugh at him. Looks at him and makes him feel as special as he wants to be. Even his own mother barely waited for him to graduate high school before declaring herself retired from parenthood and moving to Florida. He once decided to see how long it would take her to call him if he didn't call her once a month. After seven months, on the verge of tears, he broke down and called her. She honestly had no idea how long it had been. She didn't miss him at all, didn't think of him when he wasn't there.

Object permanence doesn't exist where Jaden is concerned. Out of sight, out of mind.

It's been the same with every girlfriend, every woman in his life. They always hit a certain point and then can't wait to get rid of him. So now he gets rid of them first.

"We could follow the track up," Ava suggests. She doesn't want to try to find the others. *We should win on our own merit,* she had said earlier, as if sabotaging others hadn't been her idea, floated to impress Jaden and make him invest in her. And as if they could both still win. As if they don't know there's only going to be one winner.

What was she talking about with the freaks? Were they mocking him? Plotting? Did she talk him out of trying to find the other group as part of a larger play? They all know he's the biggest threat. He's going to win. No matter what they do, he's going to win.

He looks at the track. He could climb it, no problem. He's in the best shape of his life. When he was fourteen, chubby, depressed, mocked at school and ignored at home, he had discovered obstacle-course competitions. He loved watching them, but more than that, he loved the interviews. All these people who had sad lives like him, who had been unloved and lost, had turned that in on themselves and crafted perfect machines of bodies. Machines that could do incredible things. Machines that functioned so well they couldn't be sad or hurt or lonely anymore.

He tried getting on the show seven seasons in a row, and never made it past the walk-on line. What did that say, then, that he had spent so many years doing exactly what they did, exactly what they told him to, overcoming everything in his life, practicing his backstory in front of the mirror so that he would come across as *not a bad guy, not a bad guy at all,* and they had never let him on?

He flexed reflexively. He'd made it into this competition, and he'll win. And after?

A reunion with his mother. She'll be so proud of him, so sorry for all the years she wasted not being proud of him.

A reunion with that girlfriend, who'll finally know he's worth putting in a frame. A gift of socks for her bitch friend.

A reunion with that fucking competition, a celebrity guest spot, or maybe he'll turn them down. He'll be busy with his own gym, a dedicated group of worshippers coming to his church of the body, begging him to show them the path forward, to save them from themselves the same way he saved himself. They'll all look to him, and he won't give up on them, won't get tired of them, won't abandon them.

Ava's not part of that future.

"Doesn't seem stable," he says. "I wouldn't want you to get hurt."

Ava releases some of the tension in her shoulders, and as she turns, he can see her smile. See her relief at this evidence of how much he cares. He remembers how she stood back and let Iraq Barbie hit him. Imagines what she must have been saying to that pack of freaks later, imagines the way they were laughing at him.

"Come on," he says, slinging an arm around her shoulder. "I have an idea."

Ava's relieved.

Jaden wanted to try to find the others to sabotage them. And actually, Ava is pretty sure she knows exactly where they are. The second morning of the competition, she had seen Brandon go into the weird love tunnel building. Few other places to hide that many people in one spot. She'd bet money that's where they are. In a way, she *is* betting money—$50,000 worth—but betting against herself by not betraying them. Still. She regrets ever giving Jaden the idea of getting other people out.

Besides, the others offered to let her come, offered to let her into the group even after she chose someone else, and so she steered Jaden away from them.

But now that she's back in the creepy, boring park, she thinks Jaden must be right. The destruction at the camp was staged. She doesn't think it was another contestant, though. She thinks it was the game itself.

That's why she hasn't seen any cameras. It's not a traditional reality show. It's a *horror* reality show.

She watched something sort of like this, once. They took a bunch of college students to a house, told them about the grisly murders that had happened there, explained past hauntings, then led them to the most haunted spot in the woods and had them report on what they felt. Almost all of them felt something—intense cold, an inexplicable presence, overwhelming fear.

Only after everyone had shared their experiences did the filmmakers explain that the house had been built only ten years prior and there was no history of violence or hauntings or really anything, at all, there.

Most laughed it off, sheepish. A few still insisted that something must have happened that no one knew about, because they felt what they felt and wouldn't deny it. It was meant to make a point about how we trick ourselves into feeling things, but really, it made a point about how we trick *other* people into feeling things.

Ava is pissed. It's fucking *rude* that they were brought here under false pretenses. Lied to. Misled. Maybe the early contestants were in on it. Setting up things for the others to find, like the lost jewelry. Hell, with her conveniently horrifying backstory, maybe Mack is a plant. She could be an actress.

Ava stumbles, Jaden's arm around her catching her. If Mack's a plant, and Jaden's the one who told the story about her, then he's in on it, too. That would be super unethical, right? To get into a physical relationship with her—what little they had managed on a cot in the middle of other people, but still—when he was an actor and she wasn't in on it? Surely that wasn't legal. Had she signed something in the NDA that made it okay?

No. No way. Besides, how good would an actress have to be to be Mack? Ava has a sense for bullshit—she's worked enough service jobs to be able to bullshit with a smile in the most aggravating situations—and nothing about Mack seems fake or like a performance.

It doesn't make sense.

But none of this makes sense, and the idea of the whole game being a mean-spirited deviation from what they were told is more comforting than the idea that there really was something violent that went down at the camp.

Maybe Jaden's right. Maybe Ava and creepy LeGrand set it up to freak them out. She could see Ava being that ruthless, that clever. Almost admires her for it.

Or maybe Mack really did do it, either to win, or because she's so completely twisted from what happened to her that she wants to break everyone around her. Again, doesn't seem like Mack. But Ava doesn't really know Mack, does she? She doesn't really know any of them. Except Jaden, and she doesn't know him, just his type.

Still, he's being nice this morning, and she can sense an impending ending, but she'll take this calm before the storm. Maybe tonight they'll part ways. She'll break it off with him. But in a friendly way, so he doesn't retaliate. *I don't want to hold you back.* Or, *I don't want you to feel like you have to worry about me. You should focus on winning for yourself.* Those are both good options. Implying that it's obvious he'll win, and she's happy about it. Bullshitting with a smile.

She wonders what the other Ava and Brandon and Mack and

LeGrand are doing right now. If they're freaking themselves out even more, or if they're having fun at her expense. She hopes not. She'd rather they be scared than laughing at her. She doesn't know that's the biggest thing she has in common with Jaden.

A slight but telltale gush between Ava's legs rips her back into the present. She swears softly.

"What?" Jaden snaps.

"Nothing." Her period, right now, of all times. Another reason to wish she had gone with the others. At least Mack and the other Ava might have something on them. She really doubts Jaden thought to grab pads from the bathroom before they left.

Praying that it's not her period, or that it'll be a trickle of a first day before her usual apocalyptic bleeding, Ava scurries to catch up to Jaden. "It's almost light," she says, noticing how soft the night is getting, the sky shifting from indigo to something weaker, watered down.

"It's fine," Jaden says. "We're almost there."

The tracks would have been a good spot, and they seemed stable enough, but it was nice of him to worry about her. Maybe she's wrong about him. Maybe underneath the muscles and the posturing he's not like every other version of him she's dated before. She should give him the benefit of the doubt. She's the one who's being unfair.

They keep walking and she wants to ask again when they'll get there. It's definitely dawn. They should have been settled in a spot thirty minutes ago. But if she asks, she'll sound like a nag, and nothing turns guys off faster than a nag. A nag who is definitely starting her period right now. And she's not even wearing jeans, she's wearing a cute, sporty skirt. God. This is the worst, it's all the worst.

If she doesn't win, what will she do? She's lost a week of posting, a week of content. And yeah, she has no momentum, no sponsors, hardly anyone liking her photos and videos, but it's important to be consistent. It's going to be expensive to redo her now-ruined nails, though. And she'll have to get her hair done, too. She knows there's been damage from the cheap shampoo and conditioner here, and from having to pull it back into ponytails.

Maybe she should quit trying. Get a real job. But any "real" job she could get wouldn't pay enough to live on. Her chance—her only chance—is to somehow hit it big. To find a windfall, to claw money from the world around her, however she can.

Maybe things will actually work out with Jaden, and she can be in charge of the social media for his gym. It's a nice thought.

Who is she kidding, it's an awful thought. But what else is she going to do? Work for twelve dollars an hour for the rest of her life? Go back to school and get into debt she'll have to work off for the rest of her life? Or attach herself to Jaden and hope one of them manages to get lucky?

She's obviously already chosen the final option.

At last, the sky almost fully bright, Jaden stops at their destination. On this long, curving section of the path, there's nothing but the horrible overgrown bushes around them, no other structures she can see, nowhere else to hide. But she can't understand how he thinks they can hide here. It must have been one of those big swing rides, back in the day, where a central pole holds up bars that extend out, swings hanging on the ends, spinning in circles so the people go in wider and wider arcs. She always loved these types of rides, loved the thrill in her stomach without the jarring drops and turns of roller coasters.

But it's not a swing ride anymore. The chains for the swings hang down like strands of unwashed hair, clumped together in some parts, broken short in others. A few of the chains still have swings at the bottom, or what's left of the swings, anyway. The thick central pole seems stable enough, rising straight up to where the system of swing arms extend out. The whole thing is stark and depressing, like a giant denuded umbrella.

"Where are we supposed to hide here?" Ava asks, genuinely baffled. The platform is open, the central pole solid. She can't see anywhere obvious—or even unobvious—to hide.

Jaden looks over his shoulder at her, flashes her a grin. "*We* aren't supposed to hide anywhere. Good luck, Ava." He jumps, catching one of the swing chains, and climbs hand over hand straight up, disappearing onto the top of the central pole. Whether it's hollow inside or has enough space that he can settle in the center without being seen from the ground, it doesn't matter.

What matters is Jaden's hidden, and Ava's not, and it's fully daylight.

She thinks about screaming at him. But that would give away her location. Her shock and anger deflate, leaving her flush with shame. The others had known when they looked at Jaden. They had seen it. And she had seen it, too, and she had picked him anyway because the optics were better. And then she had doubled down rather than admit her mistake.

She's not surprised, not really. But she's disappointed. Ever since the other Ava introduced herself, Ava was worried about being the afterthought. And now she will be, because she's getting out today.

It should be a relief, in a way. An ending to all this shit, a return to all the shit she knows and is comfortable with.

But as she looks around, morning breaking without a cloud or a breeze, the air heavy and expectant, she can't stop thinking about that dark pool in the middle of the camp, the smears trailing away from it.

Without Jaden by her side sneeringly insistent that it's all a game, it's much easier to wonder if maybe, just maybe, it's not.

Ava turns and runs. She can find a spot. She has to.

As though summoned by her fears of blood, she feels a hot gush between her legs, soaking through her cute underwear and running down her skin. At least Jaden betrayed her early. At least she doesn't have to sit next to him, soaked in her humiliation. And at least she knows that period aversion is so strong in America that they'll never air this footage, even if it is a mean competition, even if it is a manipulative horror reality show.

There were pads in the bathroom. They might have abandoned camp, but that doesn't mean camp's not still there.

She doesn't know where *she* is, though. Jaden well and truly fucked her in so many more ways than he knows. Her sense of direction has never been great, and even though she can tell east because of the rising sun, knowing east does her no good when she has no idea where the camp is relative to her current position.

She stops, catches her breath, tries to figure out where she is. She doesn't deserve this. Not the betrayal, not the humiliation, and not the ever-increasing sense of wrongness, of dread, of fear pricking at the back of her neck.

A branch snaps somewhere behind her, and Ava takes off like a frightened rabbit, certain that, whatever's there, she doesn't want to see.

It's day now, so Mack's awake, but it feels like she's sleeping. She has that floaty sensation she craves, that she sleeps just to find: hovering between conscious and not, weightless and warm and free.

Maybe it's Ava curled against her on one side and Brandon's cheerful presence on the other. Maybe it's the fact that this is a genuinely good hiding spot, and for this day, at least, she thinks they'll be safe. This day is all she's thinking about. This hour, this minute, this second, this moment. She can float here, exist here. She's safe.

A ticking noise filters through the flimsy, dry wood separating them from daylight. It drags her back into reality, back into the passage of time. Tick, tock, time's almost up.

No. Not a ticking noise. A *clicking* noise. LeGrand. Ava hears it, too. She tenses, then shifts to crawl to the exterior wall. Mack and Brandon do the same. The nice thing about being in a building that could fall apart at a strong breeze is that there are plenty of cracks and holes they can press their eyes to, seeing outside without being seen themselves.

"What—" Brandon whispers, but Mack jabs him hard in the side, and he cuts off his question.

Mack holds her breath and keeps her eye on the path beneath

them. She doesn't know what she's waiting for, but it's going to be bad. She knows it will, because she was happy, and what right did she have to feel that way?

She half-expects screams like with Rebecca, so it puzzles her when it's only beautiful Ava, stumbling silently past. Then beautiful Ava glances behind her shoulder, revealing a face contorted into a mask of silent horror. Of absolute, devastating fear so complete no sound can hold it, no breath can expand to fill the void of terror ripped into the soul of a person.

Her face is bleeding, dark trails already soaking down to her shirt, and there's a streak of blood down the inside of one leg, too. She continues past their hiding spot, oblivious to their observation.

"Shit," Ava breathes.

"Could be a trap," Brandon whispers, but he doesn't sound certain. He *shouldn't* sound certain.

Ava grabs Mack's arm, so hard it hurts. Mack puts her own fingers over Ava's. Not to peel them away, but to increase the pressure. To keep Ava here, to be the one to make *her* stay this time.

"If it's a game, win," Ava says, her voice fierce. "And if it's not, survive." Ava turns in their tiny space, her shoulder slamming Mack into Brandon.

"No," Mack hisses.

"Keep her safe," Ava commands Brandon, and then she slides out of their spot. Mack is frozen. She wants to follow. Not to help beautiful Ava, but to stay with her own Ava. Whatever happens, to be with Ava, to not be left behind again, hidden and safe and alone.

She's already survived alone once, and it's not all it's cracked up to be.

Mack turns around so she can scoot toward the exit to their wooden womb. It's harder to maneuver in here with Brandon sprawled out, inadvertently blocking her. He still has his eye pressed against the crack in the wall.

Ava, already outside, shouts, "Stay where you are!" either to

LeGrand or to Mack and Brandon, or maybe to all three. Mack reaches for the edge of the platform, but Brandon's hand grabs her ankle, his grip a vise.

"Let go," Mack whispers, but his grip is so tight it's shaking. No. *Brandon* is shaking, trembling all over, his face still pressed to the wall, his whole body seized up with whatever it is he's witnessing.

"Don't move," he whispers. "Oh god, please, please don't move, oh god, oh god, oh god."

The tone of his voice is exactly how she felt when she heard what was happening in the family room, tucked away safely in Maddie's hiding spot. It sounds like someone who knows death is right there, praying that somehow, some way, it will miss them.

Mack doesn't move.

Ava has a thick pipe in hand. The contours of it fit her palm exactly right, the heft and weight of it comforting. She'd prefer a gun, but this works, too.

"Stay where you are!" she shouts, waving the pipe in the general direction of where she thinks LeGrand is hiding, an overgrown stand of trees. If she's getting out now, fine, but one of her friends is going to win.

Mack.

She wants Mack to win. Or survive. And she knows Mack will do it, too.

"Ava!" she shouts, running after the other woman. Ava Two is ahead of her on the path, a stumbling shamble of a run, like someone who's been bitten by a zombie and still thinks they can outrun the infection. Blood trails down her leg, though it's a smaller path than the blood from her head, soaking into her shirt so thoroughly Ava can see it from behind, now, too.

Ava Two twitches when she hears her name, a puppet with the wrong string pulled, but she doesn't stop moving. "No," she moans. "Run! Hide!"

Ava looks over her own shoulder. There's nothing back there.

Nothing. But *there*—the crunch of a dead leaf. And there, a shuffle of dirt over the cracked and pitted pavement.

The tiny hairs left on the back of her neck rise, and, for the first time in years, she wishes she had hair there, irrationally longs for the false sense of protection a curtain of hair would provide for the base of her skull, the skin at the back of the neck, a cover for the sudden overwhelming sense of her own absolute softness and vulnerability.

Her hand tightens on the pipe. Fuck that. Ava is not vulnerable. Ava is a fucking warrior, and anyone who tries to hurt her or Ava Two or anyone on her watch is going to find that out the hard way. A pipe-to-the-face hard way.

Ava puts on as much speed as she can, her leg screaming in protest. Her knee doesn't bend much anymore, and her ankle is basically soldered in place, so running isn't really an option. Fortunately, Ava Two isn't moving very fast, and Ava catches her, puts a hand on her shoulder.

Ava Two stops so suddenly Ava loses her balance and falls flat on her ass. She holds her hand up to the other woman for help standing, but Ava Two doesn't even seem to see her.

Ava Two is staring back at where they came from. A low groan, an animal sound of terror escapes from her mouth, and Ava wants to vomit. She knows that sound. She made it when she looked down and saw her leg crushed, and looked to the side and saw Maria *gone,* body still there but vacant eyes where Ava would never again see herself reflected back in love.

Ava doesn't want to look at what the other Ava sees, but she does anyway.

There's *nothing.*

Nothing is there.

The winding walkway behind them, curved so they can't see the Lovers' Hideaway anymore, is empty.

But.

Ava scoots backward on her ass, fingers around the pipe scraping and bruising on the ground, eyes locked on the path. The ivy trail-

ing down from an overhanging tree drapes across something, hanging as though suspended by the wind, or pulled aside like a curtain.

But there's nothing there.

"Oh god, oh god, oh god," Ava Two breathes.

"What is it?" Ava demands, her voice high and tight with panic.
"I don't see anything. I don't see it. Can you see it?"

The other woman's gore-painted face turns, and she looks down
at Ava as though only now realizing she's not alone. "I'm sorry,"
she whispers. "I didn't want you to get found."

And then Ava's world breaks neatly in half, tipping her sideways
out of reality and into something new, something worse.

Nothing picks the other Ava up.

Nothing pierces her torso so it blooms with blood as the other
Ava screams, a sound like being torn apart.

And then the woman's head disappears.

Ava's mind rebels against it, telling her she's not seeing what
she's seeing. But the other Ava's head is *gone,* her scream cut off,
her neck gushing blood, her whole body still somehow suspended
in the air, and there's no head, there's no head, there's nothing.

Ava scrambles to her feet, watching as the rest of the woman
disappears. And still, there's nothing. Nothing there, and now no
body, either. Only the other Ava's blood on the ground, fresh and
hot, so much Ava can smell it.

That's not all she can smell, though. There's a musk, something
far older than fresh blood. Left to rot day in and day out, a layer of
putrescence beneath the smell of the world around her.

Ava grips the pipe. She knows what death smells like, and it's
here for her again, at last.

She opens her mouth and screams defiance, then swings at *nothing*.

They hear both screams.

There's no question which Ava is which.

And there are no more questions, really. At least not about the
nature of the competition.

Mack struggles free of Brandon, slides out of their hiding spot, and bursts into the sunshine. It feels wrong, already, moving around in the open during the day. How quickly she's been trained.

Brandon shuffles out after her. There's something off about his face, something missing that was there before, but now that it's gone Mack can't say what it was.

"Which way?" Mack demands.

Brandon shakes his head. "It's too late," he whispers.

"No, we can—"

LeGrand walks toward them, his expression resolute and settled, some truth confirmed. He is no longer haunted. Whatever Brandon saw broke him, and whatever LeGrand saw either gave him strength or broke him so completely he came out a new shape.

"What was it?" Mack asks. Because LeGrand ran to help before, and if he isn't running now, it means he doesn't think there's any possibility of help. Mack clutches her stomach, wanting to cry or scream, to run after Ava. Join her, however that's possible, whatever that means. She can't help but wonder, if she wasn't here, would Ava still be? Did Mack make this happen? She cracked the shell, her protective shell, she let hope in, she let Ava in, and now this.

Now this.

"What was it?" she repeats.

LeGrand shrugs, twitching to the side with the movement as though he has something on his shoulders he's trying to get off. "I don't know."

"It was the devil." Brandon's voice cracks on the verge of tears. He keeps jerking his head, looking at the other building near them, checking to make certain the old rusted frame of a demon is still where it should be. His eyes are wide, too wide, like he can't close them. Whatever he saw has opened them to something they never considered before, and he can never shut it out again, never blink away the truth.

"What does that mean?" Mack demands. Brandon needs her to be gentle, but she has to have answers.

"That's two." LeGrand's tentative features have shifted, a subtle change that rewrites him. He still has a baby face, but gone is the expression of a lost child. "So we have until tomorrow morning. We need to get out."

"What do you mean, the devil?" Mack presses.

Brandon rubs his eyes as though trying to physically remove an image. "It's a monster. The devil. I don't know what else to tell you."

Mack looks to LeGrand. He nods in silent agreement.

They're not making any sense, but Mack can't dwell on it. It doesn't matter. *Ava* matters. "We have to look for Ava."

LeGrand doesn't argue. Brandon shakes his head. "It won't help," he says, but he drifts in the direction he saw Ava run anyway.

It's not hard to follow the trail, even for three people inexperienced with such things. Beautiful Ava's drops of blood are fresh enough they catch the light, a thread of violence unspooling to lead them to what they need to see. To the final destination, the end of Mack's infant hope. A new thing, so fragile, drowned in the pool of death they stop at.

"Can someone survive after losing that much blood?" LeGrand's deep voice is soft but practical. He's not asking it hypothetically, or hopefully. He's asking whether they should keep looking. He's letting Mack make the decision.

Mack stares at the only evidence remaining that a few minutes ago, she was happy. There's nothing around the blood. No drag marks. No sense that someone ran, that they made it out, that anything happened here other than two violent, final ends. It's an exclamation mark of blood, not an ellipsis. And certainly not a question mark. The story is ended.

There isn't any more.

Beautiful Ava is gone. And so is Mack's Ava. The first person who became a person to her since her family died, the first person who made Mack wonder if there could be more in her life. If there could be *life* in her life.

It's over now. For Mack, at least.

She looks at LeGrand. Sad, haunted LeGrand, who Ava wanted to protect and help. "Why are you here?"

He doesn't seem to consider her line of questioning odd given the circumstance. Perhaps none of them will ever find anything odd again, as long as they live.

The smell of blood and something older, more decayed, *wronger,* is overwhelming. *As long as they live* is feeling like not a very long time at all.

"I was banished from my family for trying to get a doctor for my sister. It's against the rules to go outside the compound."

"Compound?" Brandon asks.

"My father's the prophet," LeGrand says.

It doesn't answer Brandon's questions—raises far more of them—but Mack understands as much as she needs to. LeGrand was a prisoner. He broke the rules to help. That makes sense for the type of person who runs toward the sound when someone is screaming. He's here because he was trying to save his sister. Mack is here because she didn't try to save her sister. Because she hid and did nothing while her world was cut apart.

"If you get out," LeGrand says, looking toward the trees where the fence looms somewhere in the impenetrable, winding green, beyond the ever-present stone pathway walls, "will you help her? I'm from Zion Mountain in southeastern Colorado. Her name is Almera. She can't talk or walk, but she likes bubbles and the color yellow. They won't give her the care she needs. You'll have to kidnap her." LeGrand nods, as though he's made up his mind about something. "It's the only way. I should have done it that way."

Mack looks at Brandon. Brandon's eyes are filled with tears, and she can't imagine him kidnapping anyone. "Give us the details of how to break in and find Almera, just in case. But LeGrand gets to win," Mack says to Brandon. "If there's such a thing as winning. And if there's not, he's the one who gets out." She's afraid Brandon will disagree, that he'll insist it's not fair for them to decide on LeGrand without discussing it.

Brandon swallows hard and nods. "Anyone but Jaden." His voice cracks and Mack can't help it. She laughs. Anyone but Jaden.

Her laughter breaks the spell of the blood, releasing them. They walk on, like Ava would have wanted, like Mack wants. She has one goal now, one goal only: Get LeGrand out. Let him go save his sister, because he still has one, and he can.

Get LeGrand out, and whatever happens after, she will accept with open arms this time.

It's almost over. Two more days, and Linda can close her family's journal and not have to open it again for seven years. Well, six. They do have to plan these things well in advance to make certain everything is in place. And *she* shouldn't have to open it again at all, but she will. She knows she will.

She taps her manicured fingers—an abrasive coral that she thinks looks youthful but that makes her skin look dead—against the leather cover of her family's book. How long has she kept it? How long have the Nicely women kept everything running? And does she really trust Chuck Callas of all people to take over when she's done?

She prefers to think *done* rather than dead, teasing herself and others with plans to retire to Florida and leave all this behind. But she knows she won't. Even if Chuck does take over, nominally, she won't trust it to him alone. It's too important, and she likes that. Likes that she's important, likes the feel of the weight of generations who depend on her, likes that she took up the mantle from her parents and their parents. She likes to think of how proud her grandparents would be, that they might not have been the venerated *Callases* who started it all, but that it was *their* daughter, and then *their* granddaughter who safeguarded their gift.

The thick, heavy journal, far larger than that *other* book, stolen and lost now, sits on her coffee table next to a stack of *Good Housekeeping* magazines. No one reads it. After all, Linda knows the stories by heart, the other family representatives know them by reputation, and the rest of the town and everyone it feeds doesn't know them and doesn't want to. Linda's own daughter doesn't want anything to do with it. That's what hurts the most—the lack of gratitude, the lack of respect. That her daughter is as selfish as the rest of them. Angry at the very thought, Linda takes her family's sacred history and puts it in the special hidden shelf of her china hutch.

Her walkie-talkie radio crackles to life. She thinks how her daughter would mock her for using it instead of a smartphone, but sometimes old-school is better. Especially when you still have all the cellphone signals jammed. Which reminds her, she needs to follow up with Leon Frye, make certain he does his job—or rather, his *team* does his job—with the various competitors' social media accounts for the next few weeks, keeping them active just in case. She can't trust that anything will get done, that any *just in case* is covered, unless she does it herself.

To be fair, though, she has no idea how installing his app on their phones lets him impersonate them through all their accounts. She actually doesn't even know what an app is, but at least the Fryes have managed to contribute *something* to keeping the last couple of seasons running smoothly.

Linda lifts the walkie-talkie to her mouth. "What?"

"Three of them approaching the fence," Chuck growls from his end of the radio signal. He's up in the Mary tower, named for his great-grandmother.

"Which three?" Linda asks, though it doesn't really matter. It feels macabre to be curious, but that doesn't stop the natural impulse to want to know. Who is still alive?

"I don't remember their names." He sounds angry. How is he supposed to take over if he doesn't even want to know their names or their faces? What a privilege, not to carry them with himself. What a privilege, to have the Callas name but let the Nicely line continue to do all the actual work.

Linda is strong, though. She cares enough to learn every name, to acknowledge every sacrifice. She tilts her chin up proudly, knowing she's a credit to the Nicely name. "Well, shoot them when they get too close. But only arms or legs."

"Right." Chuck knows the rules. They all do. But when they ask her what to do, it makes them feel like it's her choice, not theirs. They're just following orders. *Weak.*

Linda taps the glass hutch door, and then goes into the kitchen to make tea. Her soap is almost on. She's resolved at last not to worry about the lost book anymore. It's not her fault Susan had it on her when Linda took care of her. And besides, it's a historical document at this point. They don't need it. The season comes and the season passes, like clockwork, no matter what. All they have to do is be ready, and thanks to Linda, they always are.

Unlike Christian, Brandon immediately recognizes the hum of the electrified fence and holds up a hand. They stumble to a stop as the first shot hits the tree next to Mack, flinging shards of bark in refreshingly forest-scented shrapnel. Mack ducks, then rolls behind the nearest tree. Brandon stands there, staring, shocked.

He knows there's violence here—he can't deny it—but it's one thing to see a monster and another to be shot at by a human. Thirteen years of active shooter drills in school, and all he can think is there's no door to shut. No desk to hide behind. No teacher to put herself between him and a bullet.

LeGrand shoves him, and they join Mack behind the tree.

"Are they just going to kill us now?" Brandon asks, choking back tears.

"They're trying to keep us in." LeGrand grew up behind a fence he was told held the world at bay, but really it was meant to keep them in. And then to keep him out.

Mack agrees. Whoever is in charge put them in here, and they won't let them out until it's over. She stands, brushing splinters of wood embedded in her cheek, leaving tiny smears of blood in their wake.

The three friends cautiously work their way away from the

fence, keeping to the cover of trees. Eventually they hit a pathway going deeper into the park. Mack steps out into the open, waiting for a bullet. Nothing happens. They're not trying to get out anymore, so no one needs to do anything to keep them in.

"The fence was electric for sure." Brandon's hands twitch as though he, too, has a current running through him, amping him up. "Lots of farms where I live."

"So we need to figure out another way to get LeGrand out," Mack says.

"What if he wins?" Brandon asks.

"I don't think there's going to be a winner." LeGrand doesn't sound overly concerned, but he also doesn't say it harshly. He's being gentle with Brandon, the way Ava was with him.

Ava. Ava, Ava, Ava. Mack wanders down the path, deeper into the park.

Brandon is desperate, his voice rising. "No, they said. There's one winner. The winner gets out. So we make sure LeGrand is the winner. That's how we do it. Right, Mack? Right?"

Mack nods. Maybe there really will be a winner. And Linda neglected to tell them the permanent cost of getting out.

Ava.

She wants to see Ava again.

Mack rubs her eyes, gritty with either exhaustion or tree shrapnel, she can't be sure and she doesn't really care. "So we make sure LeGrand wins, and in the meantime, we try to find a way out."

"No, first things first," Brandon says, distracted as he looks around them, as though seeing everything for the first time. Wide-eyed with wonder or horror as he takes in the towering trees, the creeping vines, the rusted remains of a kiddie roller-coaster car sitting alone and abandoned in the middle of the path ahead of them. "We find Jaden."

"I know where he is." LeGrand turns and heads down a new path.

"Tell us about your sister," Brandon says. He's distant and unfocused, but keeping pace.

"She's—she—" LeGrand struggles for the words. Almera didn't get enough oxygen at birth, and because his mother couldn't go to a hospital and was helped only by the other wives, Almera nearly died. He once heard an aunt whispering that Almera should be totally healthy, and it makes him sad to think about. Sad because of who Almera could have been if his father allowed real medical treatment. And then sad to wonder about it, as though he's betraying who Almera is, what a wonderful sunshine piece of happiness she is, by wishing she could have been someone else.

Everyone always told his mother, told him, that Almera was lucky. Incapable of sin. Heading straight for the highest degree of glory. They dismissed who she was on earth, focusing on who she'd be after.

But who she is on earth is a girl who is suffering and can't help herself. Who she is on earth is a girl who is suffering and can't help herself and is locked in a compound where no one will help her, either, because she's already saved, so what's a little suffering in the meantime?

If Almera's saved either way, why does she need to suffer to follow the rules of their father, the prophet?

"She likes the color yellow, and bubbles," LeGrand repeats. "She's thirteen. She can't walk or talk." How else can he sum up the only person he was ever sure loved him? "She's not too heavy. You'll be able to carry her. Break in at night. My mother's house is in a corner of the compound, southeast. Go over the wall there. You'll know it's the right house because there's a wheelbarrow in the vegetable garden with pads in it for moving Almera around. The gun shed is close by, so you can get some of those before going to the house."

Brandon misses a step, but Mack nods. Then she adds, "You're going to get her, though." She wants LeGrand to know she's listening, but she has no intention of doing any of this. LeGrand will. She'll make sure.

"I'm going to get her," LeGrand repeats softly. He takes another branching path, seemingly at random.

"How do you know where Jaden is?" Mack asks.

"Direction the other Ava came from."

Mack experiences a pang of guilt and sorrow. She hasn't mourned beautiful Ava at all, because LeGrand is right: She was the *other* Ava. Not the one who mattered.

All these people, locked in here together, and none of them mattered to Mack. She had tried not to learn their names. She treated some of them like enemies, when really, they were all just trying to win. Now they're dead. Soon she will be, too, and no one will remember her name. And that's okay. It's what she deserves, and more or less what she's expected and wanted out of life. To disappear. She hoped to disappear while alive, but something about all of this feels inevitable. The end of a game that started so many years ago when she took Maddie's hiding spot.

She was always going to be found by something terrible.

LeGrand puts a hand on her elbow to guide her to a tiny sliver of path shooting off from the one they were following. He'll remember her. He'll remember Ava, too. He'll remember them all, she's sure of it. Brandon would, too.

"The direction she ran from?" Brandon asks, staring up at where the sun stretches toward them between branches. An enormous clown head, once brightly painted but now chipped and muddied and missing its nose, leers at them with a mouth gaping open, an unnerving invitation.

"A ride," LeGrand answers. "I saw Jaden hide there on the first day. It's a good spot."

"What kind of ride?" Mack asks.

LeGrand shrugs. "Dunno. I've never been to a place like this."

"No one's ever been to a place like this." Brandon laughs. It's a broken sound, gaping open, an invitation, like the clown behind them, to explore the darkness inside. "I always wanted to go to Disneyland. Or Lagoon, in Utah. Have you guys ever been? But my dad would never take me on his visits. It was only ever fishing, once a year. Sometimes not even that. I wonder if he's related to Ray?"

"Who?" Mack asks. She isn't following Brandon's train of thought. Maybe there's nothing to follow; it's jumped the rails, like her own mind.

"Ray, in the diner. His last name is Callas. Same as my dad's. I thought that was a funny coincidence, but he didn't want to talk about it." Brandon's steps slow as he pauses in front of the tracks of a miniature roller coaster. Several cars shaped like bugs are lined up, waiting to go. Each car is filled with decades of seasons, layers of leaves from green to brown to a fine leaf powder at the bottom, black water sludging where tiny feet would dangle.

Brandon sticks his hands in his pockets and keeps walking, catching up to LeGrand. The train of his thoughts continues, crashing down a hill, engine on fire. "Jaden got her killed. Ava. Both of them, really. Sydney, too."

"He didn't know." Mack wishes she could blame Jaden, but he thought it was a game. He was playing.

Then again, she knew. Just like she knew the game of hide-and-seek with their father had higher stakes than simply winning or losing when she stole Maddie's spot. It was in his voice. She might have forgotten her mother's laugh, but she hasn't forgotten his voice that night.

People pretend things aren't wrong, even when they can feel the truth, because they're too afraid of what it means to look right at the horror, right at the wrongness, to face the truth in all its terrible glory. Like little kids, playing hide-and-seek. If they can't see the monster, it can't get them. But it can. It always can. And while you aren't looking, it's eating everyone around you.

So. Mack knew then, just like she knows now. And if Mack's guilty in her sister's death, then Jaden's guilty in at least three women's deaths here.

And Mack *is* guilty, isn't she?

"Here," LeGrand says. They've walked long enough. They're far from the fence, far from the gun waiting there. Is the whole fence guarded? It has to be. The odds that there would be a guard on watch exactly where they appeared were too small. LeGrand wonders how they'll sneak over, why they're wasting time with Jaden, but Mack wants to check for Ava and Brandon wants to find Jaden, so who is he to argue?

They all stare up at the skeletal structure LeGrand brought them to. The swing chains hang heavily down, nothing drifting, nothing moving. That's perhaps the most unnerving thing about it. A structure built for movement, for joy, rusted and stripped to stillness.

"He's up there?" Brandon squints upward. "How?"

"Climbed the chains." LeGrand stares upward, too. He's good at climbing trees, but this is a very different skill. Mack certainly can't do it. It's nothing like scrambling up the water heater and climbing into rafters. Brandon grabs one of the chains, the whole structure shaking and groaning metallically as he climbs a couple of feet before stalling out and dropping back to the ground.

"So do we wait for night? For him to come down?" LeGrand asks. "Do we *need* to wait for him?" They're wasting time, and LeGrand doesn't want to be rude, doesn't want to push them, but they only have this day and this night before the morning comes and resets everything.

"No," Brandon says, and there's a strange new quality to his voice, a sort of dreamy vacancy. Maybe the train has finally ground to a halt. "No, we can't wait."

Brandon's father had another family.

Grammy believed in telling the truth, so she never lied to Brandon. His mother was a teenage dropout, and his father visited every time he was in the area on business. When she fell pregnant, Brandon's father insisted she keep the baby. She had, of course, thought it meant he loved her and wanted a family together. Grammy didn't agree. She knew that men like him didn't have families with girls like her daughter.

But Brandon's mother saw it as a fresh start. The beginning of a new life. So she kept the baby, and got a job at the local gas station, a way of passing the time until her true love left his other family and joined them.

He never did. But he did check up on them, keep tabs on them, stop by enough that she could never settle into another relationship, never give up the hope of him.

Brandon was six when she died. He took up his mother's torch and spirit of infinite waiting. His father came once a year, spent a day with him, disappeared again. Brandon lived for those visits.

But between visits, he had Grammy. A kind, practical woman, raised on a farm, as blunt as the tools she used to help her family break the hard earth and coax potatoes free.

When Brandon was twelve, recently dumped back on his grandma's doorstep after a day of fishing with his dad, bereft, knowing it would be at least a year until the next bright shining few hours with him, Grammy patted him on the shoulder.

"He doesn't love you," she said matter-of-factly. "He didn't love your mother, either, and I don't want you to spend your whole life waiting for something he can't give. Men like that, people are things to them. That's why he can pick you up and drop you as easily. But you're not a thing, Brandon. You're wonderful, and if he can't see that, *he's* broken. Not you. Don't ever forget it."

Her words had stung. Brandon ran and cried in his room, but after he cried, he felt . . . relieved. Like someone had taken a burden off him. He didn't have to try to make his dad stay, didn't have to try to earn his love, because it wasn't possible.

So Brandon kept going to school, getting bad grades because his brain didn't work well for school things. He took his mom's old job at the gas station, and he watched television with Grammy at night, and it was okay, really, because he didn't have to do anything to earn her love. He just had it. Even after she died, at least he had the memory of it. But it wasn't quite enough, so when he got a call from his father, he couldn't help that old lure of happiness, that old twist of hope.

That hook cast into the water, snagging him.

And because of that call, Brandon knows something LeGrand and Mack and Jaden don't.

He knows *exactly* where his invitation to the competition came from.

Brandon understands that Jaden isn't his father. Obviously, on some level, that's clear. But Jaden set people up to die. Sydney, maybe Rebecca, and definitely the pretty Ava and his friend Ava.

His friend Ava who loved him. And Jaden will let Mack and LeGrand die, too, and he won't care, because to him, they're all just things.

Brandon feels like a *thing* for the first time in his life, like Grammy was wrong all those years ago. Brandon is a thing to be used and discarded, and this is it. The final place where unwanted things are dumped. He's trapped with the devil, his friends are dying, and he can't—he can't— He can't.

He can't.

So he jumps and grabs one of the chains, and he climbs.

He climbs for Ava. For Mack and LeGrand. For his dreams of roommates and pizza parties, a shared life. And, inexplicably, the kindest gas station attendant in Pocatello, Idaho, who has never set foot in a gym, manages to climb the chain all the way to the top. He scrambles for a grip, and when a normal person would be terrified of the fall, he stays calm until he finds a lip on the circular platform above himself. Just enough to fling his leg up and roll onto the top of the swing ride.

"What the fuck?" Jaden demands, curled fetal style in the center of the platform, sweating and sunburned and perfectly safe. He gets on his hands and knees, face red and furiously contorted.

"You killed them." Brandon turns his head to the side to stare at Jaden. He doesn't quite see him, though. He sees a white smile and a swig of beer, a lure sent flying into the water.

"What are you talking about? Why are you up here? This is my hiding spot!" Jaden's having a difficult time puffing himself up to be threatening without standing. He's adopted an awkward crouch, balancing on the balls of his feet.

Brandon looks upward. Up here, they've broken through the surrounding trees, and there's nothing above him but sky. Clear blue, so blue it makes his eyes tear up and everything blurs. It's a nice blue. A good blue. An honest blue.

He closes his eyes against the brilliance. There are monsters, real monsters in the world. His friends are dying. They're all going to die. And his father knew, he's sure of it, and once Mack and LeGrand are dead, there's no one left in the world who cares about him. But if one of them wins, then in a way, Brandon wins, too, doesn't he?

Making sure that happens is the least he can do. The only thing he can do. The only thing that makes sense in an absolutely broken reality.

"You killed them," Brandon repeats, not opening his eyes. "There's a monster out there. And you got both Avas killed."

"Don't be a jackass," Jaden scoffs. "Did that bitch put you up to this? Listen, it's only a game, and if they got out, then——"

Brandon grabs Jaden's ankle. The other man is yanked off balance in his crouch, and as he teeters, Brandon rolls, using Jaden's momentum to launch him off the side of the platform.

"One," Brandon calls down to his friends.

Two people get out a day. So two people have to get out tomorrow, and it won't be Mack and LeGrand. He can give them that. Because he's not just a thing. None of them are. He's a person, like his grandma taught him to be. A kind person, and a good friend. He doesn't want to live in a world where he's a thing, or where he's a bad friend, or where monsters are real.

Brandon stands up, taking a deep breath. He steps to the edge and looks down. Mack and LeGrand are waving and shouting. He waves back down, then takes one last long look at the perfect blue of the sky.

"*Two,*" he says, loud enough for them to hear. He steps off the platform.

Mack stares down at the mess. It feels callous to think of two people—one she liked, one she didn't—as a mess, but that's the only way to describe it. Maybe something is broken in her, too, but she doesn't look away. It feels important to witness.

Brandon is clearly dead. He tipped as he fell, neck snapped on impact. She can't understand why he did it.

"Two a day," LeGrand says, solving the mystery. He's not looking at the mess, but staring into the trees, watchful.

"He's making sure they're easy to find." Mack closes her eyes at last, cutting off the view of Brandon's empty stare. "Giving us an extra day." She knows she's talking about him in the present tense, like he's not already past tense, forever. But it's better to think of him like that, like he's still playing the game, still playing it for his friends, still the same sweet guy who offered to let three strangers come live with him just because he had a house, because he *could* help.

He'd figured out a way to help now, too. She wouldn't have asked this of him. And she wouldn't have done it herself. She knows death is coming for her, sure. Long overdue. But she's going to let it find her, not rush to meet it.

Besides, she still has to figure out a way to let LeGrand win. Thanks to Brandon, now she has an extra day to do it.

A terrible gurgling sound rips her eyes open, and she turns to the jumble of bones and burst skin and pooling blood that once was Jaden. Still *is* Jaden. He's not dead. His fingers twitch as he claws at the ground, his goal unclear. Bloody bubbles ooze out of his mouth, and Mack is sure that means something medically, but she has no idea what.

"Dammit," she whispers. Because Jaden got her Ava killed, but he didn't know. Not all the way. And even if he did, this seems crueler than the universe should allow. In this state, odds are he won't even survive until tomorrow. There's no hope of help coming, no potential for rescue. For medical intervention. Even if there were, she doesn't think it would matter.

Mack looks at LeGrand, who is equally horrified. Jaden has started groaning in a low chorus of agony.

Mack knows if she says it out loud, she's asking for permission.

And she shouldn't make LeGrand complicit. He's got to get out, after all, and save his sister. He'll need to be whole for that. Mack doesn't need to be whole, and besides, has she ever really been?

She searches the ground for a big rock. The area they're in is littered with small rocks and unidentifiable trash, but nothing as heavy as she needs. She'll probably have to find one of the sections of collapsed wall. Get a chunk from that. "Go into the trees," she says to LeGrand. "I'll be right there."

"Mack," LeGrand says.

She doesn't want to argue with him. It's the only kindness she can offer Jaden, the only—

"Mack!" This time there's a quiet warning in LeGrand's tone, a quality of fear that makes her go still.

That's when she hears it. The soft padding of something drawing near, the long, slow sounds of something inhaling deeply. Of something following a scent. LeGrand backs away, melting into the trees, and Mack looks at Jaden, suffering. Then she takes a step backward, and another, and another, her eyes on the path they had come from.

The walled walkway curves sharply, hiding the full length from her. But the sounds are getting closer, and she wonders how she could have ever attributed them to a person, or even to an animal. She takes another step backward.

Another.

Another.

She should be running, but she can't make herself do more than creep backward, timed to the steps she can hear shuffling ever nearer. One step forward, one step back, a careful choreography.

And then her dance partner is revealed.

"Oh," Mack breathes out, because as soon as she sees what's coming, she realizes what she expected to be revealed. She expected a person. Not just any person, either. Some part of her expected to see her father come around that bend, knife in hand, thin lips a grim line, eyes blank and emotionless, here at last to claim her.

So she can't quite understand what it is she's actually faced with.

She stands still, watching, as it shuffles forward, turning its head side to side as the wet snuffling noise continues, the flat broad snout of it searching, two tear-shaped nostrils flared. Above that, where eyes perhaps once were, are a patchwork hatching of poorly healed scars, pink and gray, a story of violence.

Violence, too, in its hands, almost human but too large, each finger a blunt, thick instrument, tapering to claws that are jagged, broken, crusted in blood.

It's the blood Mack can't look away from. Is that the last of Ava, *her* Ava, crusted and drying into flakes on the ends of the monster's hands?

It stops, swings its head to the side. Its nostrils flare bigger, and it takes a deep, lingering breath. Her eyes drift up to massive horns erupting from its head, five of them, almost elegant in comparison with the rest of it. Gray at the base where they sweep out from the head, then curving back toward each other, tapering to white tips that nearly meet in a single point eighteen inches above its skull.

Ivory, she thinks, remembering a nature program she and Maddie watched about poachers. It made them both cry with such desperate snotty gasps that their mother ran in and turned the TV off, scolding them. Mack could never understand why she was in trouble for being sad about the cruelty of the world.

Maybe even then their mother knew what her fate held, what both her daughters' fates held, and was only trying to spare them for as long as she could. To lie to them about what the world lets happen. But their mother's protection, even her own body, wasn't a strong enough dam to hold back the coming violence.

One hoofed leg slides forward, a long strand of spittle falling in slow motion from the monster's mouth to the matted, filthy hair of its chest.

A hand clamps down on Mack's shoulder and drags her backward. The monster, suddenly spurred into action, lunges forward with surprising speed. But it stops at the gasping remains of Jaden, left there for it by Brandon.

Its movements are oddly tender, smooth and unfrenzied, as it reaches down and gathers Jaden's broken body up in its arms, then lifts him toward its mouth.

Mack can almost see—in that mouth, in that gaping maw, there aren't teeth, there are—

LeGrand tugs her hard and she nearly falls. It's enough to jolt her out of her reverie, and she catches herself, then tears through the undergrowth and leaps over fallen trees, guided by LeGrand, leaving behind the sounds of death.

She understands, now, why Brandon decided to jump. Knows she owes her life to the fact that Jaden fell between her and the monster.

But—

"Three." She grabs LeGrand's arm. She recognizes where they are and points in the direction of the bumper car trellis. Up there, they can see and hear what's coming for them.

LeGrand nods, expression grim.

Three. That means their security, their idea that it was only two a day, was wrong. It could and probably would come for them next. Maybe it was only getting two a day because that's all it could find.

"Four," LeGrand quietly corrects. Because surely the monster wasn't going to stop at Jaden.

Mack is fiercely glad that Brandon's already dead. He knew what was coming for them, and he chose how he would leave the world. She's choosing, too. She's going to get LeGrand out, and then she's going to walk to her first hiding spot—where Ava slept against her, where Ava trusted her, where she remembered Maddie and her absurd yarn duck—sit on the ground, and wait.

"There." Mack points again. The trellis is up ahead. LeGrand goes first, then helps her up. They lie flat, faces pressed against the ivy, hearts racing.

So now she's seen it. She knows what's out there. It doesn't make any more sense than it did before, but at least she can move from horror, the fear of the unknown, and into terror, the fear of the known. Terror is almost a comfort at this point, a familiar friend.

"We wait until dark," she whispers. "Then we go for the fence."

"But the electricity, and the guards."

"Maybe you can find a tree overhanging, climb that. I'll distract the guards."

It's a hazy plan, and she can feel somewhere deep inside that it's hopeless, but she has to have a goal, has to have a focus, has to have something to think about other than that those sightless features were the last thing Ava saw. Those claws the last thing she felt.

"You're getting out," she whispers.

LeGrand nods, the ivy trembling beneath him. "We can both get out."

But Mack knows she's not. She was never going to. It settles over her and she feels her heart calm, slowing, something like peace wrapping itself around her.

They will wait until night, LeGrand will escape, and Mack will finally meet the same fate as the only people she has ever loved. Death would come for her, and at last she wouldn't be left behind, hiding alone in the dark.

LeGrand next to Mack is such a different presence than Ava. Ava's body was somehow both familiar and thrilling, a comfort and excitement at the same time. LeGrand just . . . takes up space.

It's late afternoon, and Mack feels the slow trudge of the sun in her soul. The waiting is terrible, and the fact that the waiting is *boring* feels somehow crueler. Terror shouldn't be boring, shouldn't be a slog through infinite empty hours. It should be sharp and quick and final.

Maybe Maddie really was the lucky one. Her terror was over quickly. Mack has been living in it for so many years, but she's almost at the end. She's nearly done now.

LeGrand grabs her arm, his tight fingers a warning. He needn't have. She hears it, too.

They both press their faces against the trellis, finding an empty space to look through, but they're not close enough to the edge. They can really only see straight down at the cracked and pitted cement beneath them. Whatever is coming is getting closer. Not satisfied with four in one day, then. Maybe the monster, too, wants to get it over with. Mack doesn't blame it.

"We jump down," Mack whispers. "I'll distract it, and you run."

LeGrand's watery blue eyes, not piercing or beautiful, dull eyes in a dull face that she hopes see his sister again, narrow as though he is considering disagreeing.

"Almera," Mack reminds him. He relents, nodding once.

A crunch of leaves signals the monster's proximity. "On three," Mack whispers, surprised at how calm she feels, how steady her heartbeat. A smile creeps across her face, and she knows it's absurd, but she can't help it. Olly olly oxen free, and it's not the winning she'd expected or the freedom she hoped for, but isn't it a sort of freedom nonetheless?

"One . . . two . . . three." She rolls and tips herself off the edge of the trellis, grabbing hold of it to stop her fall and then dropping to the ground. Her ankles absorb the shock with protest, but she doesn't need them for much longer. LeGrand lands heavily next to her and runs without pausing. Mack turns to greet her fate.

Her step freezes before she can take it. Her eyes snag on the rifle. She can't quite make herself look at the face, can't quite accept it.

"You're dead," Mack whispers.

Staring at Mack, Ava wants to tell her about the past few hours. Wants to explain. But she can only remember, because even remembering has so many questions she doesn't know how to put it into words.

Death had come for Ava, unknowable, unseeable, a mystery and a stench.

As the other Ava was consumed into nothingness, Ava screamed defiance and rage that it had to happen now, just when she had reason to hope again, to have something in this damn world she cares about.

She swung her pipe and connected with nothing.

Spinning in a wild circle, balance thrown by her desperation, she swung and swung and hit only air.

Fight or flight had long since been trained into fight or fight, but even Ava had enough training to know that this time, fleeing was the only option. She turned in the opposite direction of whatever the thing that ate Ava Two was, and she ran. Her leg screamed, not fit for running, but she knew the limits of her body better than anything, and she could push them.

Though her own uneven gait was painfully loud, she trained her ears, listening for pursuit, for that terrible wet breathing noise, waited to be assaulted by the death-rot smell of it. But she broke free of her path near the fence and heard nothing. Smelled nothing. She crouched, hidden in the undergrowth, and caught her breath.

"Motherfuckers," she gasped. She had noticed the weird material of the fence the first night, but she didn't put together why it was made of metal wiring. She could hear the electric hum, the slight crackling in the air. That also explained the periodic towers she saw. Not a remnant of the old park. A new addition. Guard towers.

She needed to get back to Mack, Brandon, and LeGrand. To warn them. She stretched her leg in front of herself, wishing she could take the damn thing off. Wishing she could run like she used to. Wishing a lot of things. Three minutes. She'd give herself three minutes to catch her breath, and then—

A shot rang out nearby. Not shooting at her, but shooting at someone not too far away. A voice of strangled confusion drifted on the air. Brandon. Safe to say he wouldn't leave the hiding place without the others. Which meant they were on the move. Ava could join them.

But.

There was a gun somewhere along the fence.

She took stock of her supplies, what she could access, what she could use. She gently silenced the panic blaring in her mind and packed it away, because it wasn't going to accomplish anything. She had work to do.

Mack doesn't throw her arms around Ava. She can't believe what—who—she's seeing. She stands there, staring, her eyes roving over Ava's face like fingers, trying to memorize the contours, the freckles and scars and lines of a face she had thought was gone forever. She knows how fast she forgets, and she wonders what she had forgotten already in these few hours.

LeGrand is less emotionally overwhelmed. "You're alive," he says, walking up from his aborted escape route.

"Yeah. Let's move." Ava slings the rifle over her shoulder, hands him a bag of rubber duckies.

"No, we have to hide." Mack feels slow and muddled, her brain still not caught up to this new development, this new tectonic shift in her reality. Why does Ava have rubber duckies? "Until dark."

"It's taking more than two a day," LeGrand adds. Then he frowns. "Oh, except. It didn't get you. That must be why it took Jaden."

"How did you get away?" Mack looks like she's staring at a ghost. She had never imagined this reunion, had never considered that something taken could be returned, and she doesn't know how to process it. Maybe another person would have cried, hugged her beloved, felt happiness or relief.

Mack feels numb. She was finally at the end, and now . . . she doesn't know what to expect. She had been sure she was going to win, then she had been sure she was going to die, and maybe in her head the two things had become one.

Ava shrugs. She sorts through her memories, reports what happened as though typing it up after the fact, removing herself and her emotions. Nouns, verbs, stripped of feelings. "Something ate

Ava Two. I swung at it, but I didn't hit anything, and since I couldn't see it, I—"

"You couldn't see it?" LeGrand asks.

Ava tilts her head, puzzled. "You could?"

Mack nods.

"What? Why can't I see it? What did it look like?"

Mack understands now why Brandon couldn't describe it. She ends up shrugging, too, echoing LeGrand's movement. The monster is a weight on her shoulders, a psychic wound she worries will never scar over.

Ava's frustrated, annoyed by their lack of helpfulness, and weirdly feeling left out. But she doesn't have time. There is no time. "Fine. Whatever. You can tell me where to aim if we run into it. Where's Brandon?" Ava looks around, expectant. They aren't safe yet, not by a long shot, and she won't stop until they are. She won't *feel* until they are.

LeGrand shakes his head.

This one hurts, in spite of her determination. "The monster?" Ava's worried now, too. Maybe it really is eating more than two a day, in which case waiting until nightfall makes more sense.

"No," Mack says, and she doesn't elaborate.

Anger flares in Ava's heart. Whatever happened didn't need to. Maybe if she had joined back with them immediately. But then they wouldn't have a gun, wouldn't have a plan. She made the right tactical choice. Stupid, sweet Brandon. All he had to do was wait. All they had to do was wait and trust that she—well, what? Trust that she would come back?

None of them have ever had that trust rewarded. Oh, Brandon. Ava takes the anger and the sorrow and tucks them away with the panic and the pain. Not now.

"Where did you find a gun?" LeGrand asks.

Ava's itching to run, needs them all to move faster, to go *faster,* but she can't push herself or her leg any more than she already has. She starts walking and they fall in with her. "Guard tower. I remembered the duckies from hiding with Mack." She turns and winks at Mack, trying to draw her out. She needs everyone here, present. "Saved me twice over."

Mack looks bad. She's back to the Mack who wandered away, the Mack who left them. Empty. What had they seen that Ava somehow hadn't? But this Mack, at least, walks close, offers her arm to Ava so Ava can lean on her and relieve some of the pressure on her ankle and knee. Mack is right here, but she isn't, and Ava can't have this, can't have her people distracted, drifting. They have to focus. She has to get them out.

"Anyway," she says, talking as though she's not afraid, to show them that it doesn't matter whether they whisper because they're safe, she's in control, she's back and they're going to be fine, "I found a stretch of fence without any guard tower sight lines. They probably assumed the electricity was enough. Made myself duckie gloves. Boots are already rubber-soled, thanks to my general practitioner, Doc Marten. Climbed over the fence, worked my way back to a tower. They switched shifts a couple hours back. The new guard stayed at the base smoking for a few minutes. Mean right hook." Ava squints where she can feel a bruise forming on her cheek. She doesn't mention it was someone they knew, the man from the diner. Not the really awful one. The other one. Didn't matter who it was. "I won the fight, took his gun and his radio. No one has tried to check in yet, but it's only a matter of time before they realize he's gone."

"Gone?" Mack asks.

"Him or us. I chose us."

And Mack realizes Ava *did*. She was out. She faced death, she beat it, and she escaped. Outside the park, outside the fence, free and clear. And then she climbed back over and found them.

Mack feels number than ever. Ava should have kept running.

"Not that way," LeGrand says in response to Ava's direction. "That's where we left Brandon and Jaden." He doesn't want to go there again. Not because he's worried the monster is still lurking, but because he doesn't want to see where it happened, doesn't want to think about it.

Ava frowns. In this damn loopy park, it's the most direct route to the section of fence they need. "Doesn't matter," she says. "They'll be gone, right?" She doesn't want to upset LeGrand or Mack any more than they already are, but they can't risk wandering off course, like the paths want them to.

"Yeah," Mack says. Gone. Brandon's gone. Could she have saved him? Maybe if he had known Ava was coming back. Or maybe if Mack had been the one to go after beautiful Ava, been the brave one. She's sure Ava would have seen what was going on with Brandon, would have been able to save him, or talk him out of it.

Shaking her head to try to shift the memory of the sound—all the hard and soft bits of bodies hitting the ground—Mack focuses on walking, supporting Ava, trying not to think about where they're going or what they'll do when they get there. She feels dizzy, disoriented, oddly disappointed. Like she was robbed of the first good decision she's made in her life.

"Oh shit," Ava says, stopping. They've reached the swings.

Jaden is gone, yes. But Brandon is there, lying broken and still, exactly as they left him.

"It didn't eat him." LeGrand states the obvious, but the obvious is all his brain is able to latch on to. There is a monster. It did not eat Ava. Ava is going to save them. The monster ate Jaden, but left Brandon. Suicides don't get to live with their families in the highest degree of glory, or be with Jesus, his brain tells him, but he dismisses that. It's not fact. It's what he was taught, but he knows now that no one who taught him anything knows how the world really works. He thinks Jesus would like Brandon, would understand that Brandon made his choice to save others. They have a lot in common, really.

LeGrand is relieved in more ways than one that Ava is back. Because with Ava on his side, he has a real chance at escaping, yes, but also at kidnapping his sister. Saving her from the monsters of men keeping her prisoner, letting her suffer when they could all help her if they wanted to. If they chose to.

Ava means he lives. Ava means Almera lives. Ava is everything the elders would warn him about, and he understands at last why they are afraid of people like her.

"I'm sorry," Ava whispers, not closing Brandon's eyes. He has a nice view of the trees overhead, after all. Why take that away from him? They walk on.

The day is muggy, the late afternoon sullen with impending pressure. Clouds have overtaken Brandon's blue sky, building fast with a breeze, piling on top of one another. The park forces them through several winding misdirections, but between Ava's sense of direction and LeGrand's ability to climb trees to reorient them, they make it to her section of the fence.

Ava holds a fist in the air, and while only Mack has seen enough shows to know what that means, LeGrand understands the way Ava stands, taut and ready. She pulls out the radio, a walkie-talkie of sorts, and listens, but no one is sending out a warning, no one is using the devices. No one is calling Ray. Inside the park, Brandon Callas is lying, eyes open to the clouding sky, and outside the park, Ray Callas is lying, eyes against the dirt beneath the bush where Ava dragged him.

"Here." Ava limps along the fence border, taking them to Ray's empty guard tower. "If you climb on the tower only, you won't get electrocuted. Don't touch the fence, though." She's relieved she doesn't have to climb the fence again. It had enough give to move around, making it a nightmare to scale. It took forever, carefully placing each hand, maneuvering her leg. The tower hurts, too, but at least it's steady. She has Mack go first, spurred by the irrational fear that if she let Mack go last, Mack would disappear back into the park.

At the top, Mack turns and surveys what they left behind as Ava and LeGrand climb. From the tower she can't actually see much. They have the section all around the fence cleared, a naked buffer circling the entire park, but beyond that it's only trees, with the occasional landmark rising in the distance. The Ferris wheel. The peak of a roller coaster's spine. The swing ride. The other guard towers are hidden by the trees and the landscape, none of them tall enough to be viewed from this one. If the guards wanted to actually see what was happening in the park, or to see the maze and what it leads to, they'd need much higher towers.

They don't want to see. They want it all to happen without having to look.

Ava arrives at the top, grimacing as she adjusts her pants as though that will somehow give her leg some relief. She can imagine her doctor's concerned expression, his warnings not to push it. Bone on bone in her knee, no cartilage there or in her ankle, more metal than bone in her foot. *You don't want to lose the whole thing,* he'd caution, reminding her how fucking *lucky* she was. Lucky, lucky her.

"Okay," she says, trying to distract herself from the agony pulsing through her ankle, spreading up her leg. "Now we have a decision. He came in on a four-wheeler like Linda's. If we take that, it'll be loud but faster. But we'll also have to stay on the road. We'll be vulnerable."

"Going on foot would give us more time until they figure out we're gone," LeGrand says.

"Unless the guard changes again soon, in which case they'll figure it out regardless." Ava knows sneaking out is the best idea, but the pain is so bad she can't keep it boxed up for much longer, and she knows she won't be in fighting shape then.

Mack points to a sheet of paper tacked to the post of the guard tower. It's a schedule, carefully written in blue ballpoint pen. Cursive, even. "No new guard until midnight."

"Dammit," Ava says, flinching. Daydreams of riding out, a roaring motor beneath her, her leg relieved of any weight, fade into nothing. They still have a shot at secrecy, so they have to take it. "Okay. We walk. Sneak into town. No way of knowing who's in on it, so we treat everyone like they are. Steal a car and go. Car will draw less attention than a four-wheeler, anyway." Even with the length of the bus ride in here, and her leg paining her, Ava knows they can make it to town and get a car well before midnight. It's the safer bet.

The fucking agonizing safer bet. She grits her teeth. "Let's get moving, then."

When they climb down and head into the trees to walk parallel to the road, Ava doesn't spare so much as a glance for the man she left dead. Her only regret is that she didn't kill him fast enough to save Brandon. It seems unfair that they should both be dead, that she couldn't trade one life for the other.

LeGrand feels lighter. He knows they escaped something terrible, but that's not the main reason he feels like he could sprint, like he could fly. He's going home, finally, at last. And he's doing it with Ava, and Mack, and a gun.

Mack walks with Ava on her arm, and she knows they're outside of the park, that they're moving toward freedom, but she can't shake the feeling that she's going the wrong direction.

Late afternoon stretches infinite before them, the day loath to leave, lingering on their skin in the muggy heaviness and droning of insects, lingering on Mack's soul and mind with the sheer enormity and impossibility of everything this day had contained.

All they can do is walk. LeGrand leads as Mack supports Ava to ease the burden on her leg. He keeps them parallel to the road, the asphalt in sight through the obscuring trees and undergrowth. It's harder going than the road—which is not good for Ava—but it means they can see anyone coming and going. And no one has come or gone, which means their escape has still gone unnoticed.

"Smug bastards," Ava mutters, slapping at the back of her neck in response to a biting insect. The aggressive movement shifts her balance, and Mack grunts under the increase of weight until Ava adjusts. "One electric fence and a few old men with guns. That's it. That's all they thought they needed."

Mack doesn't share the sentiment. It was more than enough to keep the rest of them inside. Just not Ava. The lure of the money and the fear of being embarrassed for being afraid kept them in to begin with. Then, after seeing the monster, what could they do but run and hide? The terror was too loud, too immediate, to leave room for anything resembling a plan.

Maybe that's why Ava was able to function, to take charge. Why hadn't she seen it? Mack feels almost lonely, knowing that Ava didn't share that dread knowledge with her. Hadn't been changed by it the way she had, LeGrand had, Brandon had.

Mack's surprised to find that thinking of sweet Brandon, neck snapped, eyes opened to the heavens, doesn't make her mind recoil. She wishes he had waited, that things had gone differently, but really, he *chose*. And he made his choice to save other people. Brandon was better than Mack, too. Everyone here is. Brandon, dying to give them a shot at living. LeGrand, banished for trying to save his sister. And Ava, with the chance to be free and clear, willingly climbing back into hell to get them out.

Mack imagines another scenario, where she's more like them. A past in which she gives Maddie the good hiding spot. Or, better, pulls Maddie up with her, somehow finding room for both their bodies above the door. Or, best of all, realizes what her father is going to do and warns everyone, saves them all. Because hadn't she known, really? Hadn't the tone of his voice convinced her to hide, sent her scurrying into the dark?

But the others in the park had known something was wrong—of course they had, how could they not?—and they had denied it, had kept moving forward as though the world were not laced with violence, as though they were not all walking corpses already. They were told everything was fine, and so they clung to that promise until they died.

Ava stumbles, and Mack catches her automatically.

"Almost there," LeGrand says, although he knows no such thing. It feels like they'll walk through these woods forever and, after an eternity, find themselves once again at the gate of the park. The maze, at their backs, somehow growing to ensnare them once more, following them for the rest of their lives. The idea that they're being punished is one he can't shake, though it occasionally retreats in the face of his anger.

He keeps almost praying, then stopping himself. He had been taught what the Holy Ghost felt like. That if he prayed, God would tell him that his father was right about everything. That's what prayer was for. So that those wicked parts of your heart, those doubts, those questions, could be burned out by God and replaced with faith. With knowledge.

LeGrand had prayed so much in his life, but he still always felt scared, and that didn't seem like something God would give him, something the Holy Spirit would do. It was terrifying, having a prophet for your own father. Knowing who and what you came from, who and what you could never live up to, who and what would judge you for failure.

LeGrand's father hadn't even shown up to excommunicate him, though. He'd let a lesser elder do it. LeGrand's failure, the end of his life as he knew it, was not important enough for the Prophet Rulon Pulsipher.

Maybe LeGrand is already dead, and this is outer darkness. Another reason to find Almera. If he's reunited with Almera, he'll know he isn't dead, because if he were dead, he wouldn't be with her. She gets the highest heaven, and he gets—well, he doesn't care. He wants *this* life. He wants it for himself, and for Almera. He's damned or he isn't, he's dead or he isn't, none of it matters as long as he can help her.

Besides, if the elders *are* right, Almera is saved no matter what. So if LeGrand spends his life easing her pain and is cast into outer darkness for it, well, Almera will still be exalted. And he'll be happy for those lonely eternities, because he'll have saved her a lifetime of pain and suffering she didn't need to endure on behalf of other people's fervor to prove their commitment to God.

The presence of an actual monster behind them doesn't factor into his internal wrestling. He was raised in a world of angels and devils, of gods and prophets and miracles. Why shouldn't there also be monsters?

Ava's leg rises to a crescendo of agony, bone on bone and metal on bone providing the instruments, her own swearing the percussion. The box in her head has disintegrated, burst at the seams with everything she tried to shove in it today.

The town, a car, escape. She repeats it in her mind, going over and over the elements like they're beads on her mother's rosary.

The town.

A car.

Escape.

They almost don't notice when the forest begins to thin. LeGrand barely stops them before it abruptly ends, spitting them out into a carefully manicured lawn leading to a white Greek Revival house, ostentatiously blocking their view of the surrounding neighborhood. They're on the side of the house, but they can make out the pillars serving no apparent function at the front.

After their time in the wild chaos of the park, the rock-lined flower beds with orderly rosebushes, punctuated by miniature versions of ancient statues, seem as unreal as anything they left behind. LeGrand doesn't understand ornamental gardening. In Zion Mountain, all the gardens were actual gardens, tended by the women and providing food. What's the point of this?

Ava picks up a smooth rock from a pile of them filling a garish birdbath with a round cherub pouring water out. Theoretically, anyway. It's dry.

"Live, love, laugh," Ava reads. The words have been carved into the manufactured rock. The impulse to throw it through one of the house's windows is almost impossible to resist.

"No lights on," Mack says. Houses like this always feel vaguely accusatory. Every perfect line, every well-chosen accessory says *You don't belong here,* like the spa. The windows watch her, making sure she knows they see her.

But it's twilight now, and no lights are on. The window eyes are blank.

"Let's go." Ava limps straight through the grass, deliberately stomping every flower bed on her way. The back door is unlocked. She checks for an alarm system, but there doesn't seem to be any.

"It's a good town." Mack drifts into the house, remembering the bus driver who wouldn't meet her eyes. "A safe town."

"Look for car keys." Ava tracks dirt across the spotless tile. If Mack is afraid of leaving a trace, Ava is determined to muddy the whole fucking place. But it's hard to tell, since the kitchen is all browns and oranges, a relic of another decade, meticulously kept up but woefully dated. The fridge has several children's drawings displayed with magnets. Mack trails her fingers along them; they're brittle with age. One falls, dislodged, drifting to the floor like a leaf. Where the magnet held it is a single pristine circle, untouched by the sun, protected from time. Mack leaves it where it lies.

Ava opens the door from the kitchen to the garage. Inside, there's only a four-wheeler and the empty space where a car doubtless goes. "Dammit." She retreats inside and careens through a fussy dining room, the large, polished table dominating the space, unsoftened by yellowing lace doily place mats. Unlike Mack and LeGrand, Ava has references for what a nice house is, and this definitely was one, but hasn't been updated in decades. It's a time capsule of expensive poor taste.

Mack and LeGrand trail after her, unsure what to do. Ava finds the family room—though it lacks any of the warmth or chaos of an actual family—and collapses onto a floral couch, the fabric shiny in a way meant to look elegant but that makes it slick and uncomfortable. She eases her leg in front of her with a hiss. She doesn't want to admit it, but she can't do much more. She's at the limits of her pain tolerance, genuinely afraid she's doing further permanent damage.

"Two choices," she says. "We keep going, look for another house, another car. Increases our odds of being found. Or we wait.

Doesn't seem like someone young lives here, and old people don't stay out late, right? Plus the four-wheeler makes me think the owner is in on everything. So we wait, and when they come back, we take their car."

LeGrand wants to keep going, is almost as uncomfortable as Mack in this house, but he can see how much pain Ava's in. He doesn't want to ask her to walk any more. He looks to Mack to make the call, but Mack isn't listening. She's examining a china hutch filled with porcelain figurines.

Imagine having enough money for the things you need, and deciding what you want next is a collection of little boys and girls with garishly cherubic faces in a variety of poses and outfits. The exaggerated innocence of the little girls in pink, frilly dresses, gazing over their shoulders with o-shaped lips, feels almost obscene.

Mack looks over her own shoulder. Ava and LeGrand are watching her, waiting for her decision. No one should make her decide anything. She still feels sure she's forgotten something, left something crucial behind. The park tugs on her, like she's a compass and it's true north. The idea of driving away from it all, just . . . leaving? Seems more surreal and impossible than the monster waiting for them in the maze.

But Ava is in pain. She gave more details for the option that involved staying here, which makes Mack suspect it's the plan Ava prefers. "We wait," Mack says, then walks into the kitchen to look in the fridge. She lost her bag with all her carefully hoarded protein bars. Left it behind in the park. Maybe that's what's drawing her back. She laughs quietly to herself at the thought of going back in to retrieve it and literally entering the belly of the beast for her troubles.

Ava doesn't know if they're making the right decision, but she wants to cry with relief that she doesn't have to stand up again yet. She has to do something about the pain. The pain is distracting her. It's going to make her a bad leader, and it's going to get someone hurt or killed.

"Do you know how to use a gun?" she asks LeGrand, who nods

in response. He sets down the bag of rubber duckies. She didn't notice he kept them. Useless now, but of course LeGrand would carry them until instructed otherwise, in case she needed them. In case he could help.

Ava passes him the rifle and leans back, wishing she could go to sleep, knowing she won't sleep again until they're the hell away from this nightmare. She's seen a lot of weird shit in her life, but invisible monsters eating women will probably take the top spot forever.

God, she hopes it does. What else is there out in the world that she doesn't know about, hasn't seen? Though technically she also hasn't *seen* this. Why could LeGrand and Mack when she couldn't?

Mack licks the spoon clean, quickly finishing a pudding cup. She grabs a second one and wanders into the dining room. Another massive hutch, filled this time not with figurines but delicate dishes that look like they're never used, only displayed. Baffling. But a hand-embroidered napkin—handkerchief?—folded on the bottom of the display case catches her eye. *Nicely* is delicately stitched onto the edge of the cloth. Nicely was her father's middle name, given to him to carry on his mother's maiden name. What is it doing here?

Mack sets her half-eaten pudding on the table and opens the hutch. She picks up the handkerchief, and that's when she notices there's a little compartment beneath it. Tucking the handkerchief into her pocket, she eases the board off the compartment and pulls out a large leather-bound tome.

The name NICELY is engraved on the front. For once, she has found something in a house that makes her feel like she belongs.

She doesn't like it.

She takes the book into the family room, sits next to Ava, and opens it.

I, Lillian Nicely, begin this record of my time in charge of
the season.

I have studied the records—both Tommy Callas's and that
old dirty drunk Hobart Keck's. (We do not know if he is
dead or merely wandered away. Either is fine by me. Why
we ever let him have a hand in overseeing the season is
beyond me. Hobart's bleak and negative views of our
parents and their sacrifice for us—their divine endowment
of both prosperity and the responsibility thereof—are not
shared by the rest of us. We view our inheritance not as a
burden or a curse, but a great gift and a solemn duty. Good
riddance to him.)

Of course, I am left with almost nothing in the way of
preparation, which does not surprise me at all. This is what
happens when you put the important work in the hands of
those who cannot be trusted to be worthy of it, someone
outside the seven families. Though, to be fair, Tommy Jr.
has been no help, either. When I called a meeting to discuss
Keck's disappearance and unveil my plans for the next
season, he barely spoke. He didn't even want to read his
father's journal, insisting we put it in a safe in the meeting
house. And to keep things "fair," only the Stratton family
has the combination. Their role will be to read the book
once a generation. Certainly an easier task than any others,
and hardly enough to pay for their keep in this town.

But it doesn't matter. I've read it all. And I'll keep my
own records.

I have laid out a new plan that will not require any of our
people to break the barrier of the gate during the seven days

of the season. As we have learned from Hobart's egregious errors, even if you are not the intended sacrifice, you can still be mistakenly consumed.

Our first step was the most perilous, but the deed is done. To say we were frightened is a grave understatement, but we have accomplished our task, and without any fuss! As ever, the beast remains so fast asleep as to be almost dead—at least, until the season is upon us. We crept into his temple and put out his great burning eyes.

I say we. I mean, of course, the youngest Callas and Pulsipher sons, who must learn to bear their share of responsibility. But they both returned unharmed and boisterous, thrilled with their success.

We will see if now, deprived of its sight, the beast is quite so picky about who he will consume.

We have secured fourteen distant relations and one unrelated woman, plagued with madness and taken from a sanitarium three states over. It is unfortunate that we must send in people who do not know what they are embarking upon, but we cannot deny the power and goodness the sacrifice continues to give all of us—and the world, by extension!—and we are certain they would agree if they could truly understand the sacrifice our parents made, and the incredible chain of selfless blessing they are part of.

Down to details now:

The night of the fourteenth, they will be drugged with a concoction formulated by Joel Young Jr., at which point we will take them into the temple clearing. Chains have been well-fastened into the concrete poured around the temple last year, and they will each be secured along with enough food and water for seven days (though, clearly, not all of them will need that much. Still, better to have waste than let them suffer needlessly since we cannot predict what order they will be taken in). We will chain the madwoman closest to the temple, to tempt the beast first.

With this method, we need not venture in and out of the grounds. The gate will stay closed, and once the seven days are over, we can safely enter to tidy and make whatever adjustments we deem necessary for the next season, as well as determine whether without its sight the beast can pick us out.

It would be wrong to say I am excited—of course I am not excited, that would be ghastly—but I am eager to do my part in ensuring the unbroken chain of prosperity so dearly bought.

I have even decided that, as gratitude for their unknowing contribution and as an homage to our parents, we will spend the day before we take the fourteen sacrifices into the grounds pampering and preparing them. I think our parents would like that.

JULY 22, 1946

Disaster. Who could have guessed that, once they figured out their fate, they would choose to end their own lives rather than wait? Their deaths served no purposes, had no meaning, did no good. Selfish. Foolish. And we only knew because the beast came to the gate, moaning and slathering, searching sightless for us. I thought nothing could be worse than those twin points of flame, but I think this is.

Fortunately, I had planned for contingencies. Two spares were already in town, working in my house. They were offered, which bought us time to range out and find more. We sent the replacements in two by two to "work" on the building in the woods and by the time they got close enough to know something was wrong, it was too late for them.

Wasteful, and embarrassing, and the beast did not even consume the madwoman or the dead bodies. At the end of the seven days, she was sitting in the midst of the remaining corpses, filthy and crying. It was horrible to have to see, and I wish someone else had taken care of it all so I did not have to.

I am ashamed at my arrogance in assuming I had designed a perfect system, but who could have foreseen this? There were rumblings that it should be Tommy Callas Junior in charge, but he did not step up. And why should he? He has no more right to lead than I do. The seven families are equal, no matter whose idea the sacrifice was.

Still. I will be humble going forward, and far cleverer. No more waste.

But I also wonder if Hobart really tried hard enough to find other options to feed the beast. We now know it will not consume dead things, and it does not depend on sight, both of which are a pity.

I will think on it, and come up with a perfect system. I know there is one to be had. One that keeps the beast far from the gate, one that keeps him fed, one that keeps us safe.

JULY 15, 1947

I feel the weight of July most keenly. Though I have six years left to plan, each July feels like a claw descending onto my shoulder, pressing down. It does not help that I have children of my own, demanding my attentions, and a husband who does not understand why I must meet with the other families, what "secrets" we are up to.

Sometimes, as he sleeps next to me, snoring gently, I want to smother him in his ignorance.

Sammy Frye whines that he is being run ragged, tracking down distant relatives and sleuthing far-flung cousins, as though his is the difficult task. Our men are virile. We have not discouraged them from sowing wild seeds with low

women. It is a sacrifice easy for them to make on behalf of
our community. Between them and the siblings of our
parents, there are plenty of sacrifices to choose from, plenty
who do not know what we keep in the forest outside
Asterion. Plenty who do not know by what means their
sons have been kept safe in the war, what miracle protected
their money when the banks fell, what secret wind lifts
them all to ever-greater heights. But the more diluted the
blood, the more diluted the people, and there are enough
who are disposable.

That is all distasteful to dwell on. I will have a better plan
by next season.

MAY 23, 1948

My husband has returned from New York and a trip to
Coney Island with the girls. I do not leave Asterion—I am
its guardian, and I do not take that responsibility lightly—
but hearing their breathless reports of roller coasters and
games and rides, how easily they lost an entire day there,
sparked a brilliant new plan. One that means we can send in
the sacrifices happy, and let them be consumed with no one
the wiser! A minimum of suffering. A garish, cheerful
solution.

An amusement park! Low entertainment for the low
classes, and perfect for our needs.

The plans are elaborate, yes. Tommy Jr. complained
extensively, surprising no one. But the Pulsiphers, Youngs,
Harrells, and Fryes are all on my side. Besides, I am not
doing this on a whim. The labyrinthine structure of the
park serves a purpose, turning the beast in circles and
keeping him near the center, away from the gate. And with
our sacrifices lured in ever deeper by the promise of delight

and fun and excitement, they will escort themselves to the slaughter.

The downside, of course, is that all the sacrifices must pass through Tommy's gate, so during the season we will have to leave it open. In normal times, we can let guests in and out through a meaningless side gate. But not when it matters. It makes us all nervous, but the ingenious design of the park and the flood of potential sacrifices means that the beast will never get far from the center. We will, of course, still guard the gate, but I am confident we need fear neither discovery nor escape. It is a perfect system. Everyone is fed, and we will also bring extra jobs and prosperity to the region, which will doubtless alleviate some of the resentment the surrounding towns always feel toward us.

Much to do to prepare. I am including my youngest daughter, Linda, in the plans, though she is barely old enough to read. It is never too early to prepare the next generation for their responsibilities. I fear I've already waited too long with her older sister.

JULY 22, 1953

The Amazement Park is a success! Not only did this year's season pass without a single hiccup, the park itself is lovely and very popular all summer long. It's nice that we can use the space more than once every seven years.

Of course, none of *us* go in. Just in case. But I've read such glowing reports in all the local newspapers.

We have already made a list of the people we will invite to the park during the next season. What we initially thought of as a curse—that only we could see the beast—has become an unexpected boon. It walks among them and none see it save those who need to be consumed.

And if anyone witnesses a sacrifice disappear—like magic!—well, it is an amusement park, and filled with wonders. One distant Harrell cousin saw his brother eaten and ran out, screaming, but of course he ran to the Harrell house. He was escorted back into the park under cover of night and left, unconscious, outside the temple. These dregs of our family lines are so often disappearing or running away, it is a small task to sweep up any bits of evidence in their wake.

I suspect we will be able to use this system for a very long time. I am so proud of how Linda has embraced our heritage, and I know my parents would be, as well.

JULY 22, 1974

I resent that my first entry in my mother's book must be about disaster. I should have wrested control from her senile hands years ago. Perhaps then it would not have come to this. I am humiliated, though none of it is my fault. And still I am left with the mess!

If we had wanted Mister Jones's family to come to the park, we would have invited them! Obviously his family was not the type of sacrifice we make. And of course the Strattons are beside themselves, because the little girl was from their line. Susan Stratton actually wept that a child was dead because of them.

No! She was consumed because we let so many be ignorant about what they owe their prosperity to. I have argued with my mother and the other families that we should bring everyone in on the truth, but they say it is too much, that others might not be comfortable. That they might want to stop it.

Would they, though? If they knew that, without what dwells in the center of the park, they would lose everything?

I do not think they would! I think they would see the sense of it, the necessity, the honor of the responsibility. I think it is the secrecy that drives people away, like my father and older sister. Indeed, only those of us in the direct lines of the original seven families seem to stay in Asterion. Everyone else embarks for the world, leaving us behind, carried on the strength and support of what <u>we</u> do.

My park is closed. At least that fool lost his daughter on the last day of the season and we did not have to try and find another sacrifice. It is the only good thing that can be taken from that little girl's death.

I will have to go back to the drawing board. All those years of faultless seasons, and now we must start anew. My mother is too old for this task, and no one else is up to it. It is mine now.

JULY 1, 1981

Before, when we could send in dozens of our undesirables to the Amazement Park and let the beast take its pick, we felt safe leaving the gate open, knowing on any given day of the season, more than two of our blood stood between us and the beast.

But now we are limited once more, and faced with the dilemma of sending fourteen in at once, or sending them in two by two.

I do not like having the gate open any longer than absolutely necessary. We have something special, something precious, both inside and outside the gate. We must guard it with everything we can.

I have hired fourteen people—none are aware of their connection to our families—to "clean up the park for potential reopening." They are under strict instructions to work in pairs, but never in a group larger than two. They

will sleep in the park. My hope is that, with our labyrinth of
walls and trees and paths, they will not realize what is going
on until it is too late. We have also reinforced the fence
along the borders of the park, and set up fourteen watch
towers. One for each of the original sacrifices. Their spirit,
still watching over us, keeping us safe. Sometimes I climb
into the tower named for my grandmother and gaze over
the park, feeling connected to her as I will the trees and
bushes to grow faster, higher, thicker, so I cannot see the
temple and can simply enjoy the view.

JULY 22, 1981

It went as well as can be expected. At least Ray is good at
shooting to wound, not to kill, so there were no escapes and
no wastes.

I am getting married this fall. I do not know what, if
anything, I will tell Dick about my family or why we must
always live in Asterion. How much does he really need to
know? After all, I'm giving him and our future children the
blessings of my grandparents. We are moving into my
mother's house. He asked where I am getting the money to
redecorate it, and I laughed. It's <u>mine</u>.

I've earned it.

JULY 22, 1988

This year the biggest challenge was finding fourteen people
who accepted the job. We know they are all worthless,
scrounging, contributing nothing. Drains on the society we
help build and bolster. They are too good for a week of
honest labor?

It makes me so angry, the entitlement, the laziness.

Perhaps we will have to think of a different tactic moving forward, if these young generations are so opposed to good hard work.

I often wonder how far the net extends. Our generation is so successful, and our children, and our cousins and nieces and nephews, but we can always find someone desperate on the edges. Perhaps the blessings of the sacrifice are more powerful the closer the bloodline. Thank goodness the beast doesn't seem to mind diluted blood.

Today I was going over how much we have done, how much we have built, how much we have given our own community, yes, but the world as a whole! If only people knew, if only our parents and grandparents could see. We have worked so hard and done so much with what they gave us. Truly, we are their dreams realized. It makes me laugh, thinking of how my mother wrote about Joel Young Jr. concocting a mix to make the sacrifices sleep. Now Young Pharmaceuticals leads the entire world of medicine. From seemingly small beginnings, our parents' blessing creates truly astonishing results.

You wouldn't know it to speak to some of the others, though. Susan Stratton showed up on my doorstep yesterday, a drunken mess. She acts as though it is such a burden, having read Tommy Callas's book, having shown it to her own daughter. It is a privilege. I would do anything to read the book, to understand more fully what our grandparents did for us.

But no, there she was, crying about whether the cost is worth it, about whether we have the right, about that little girl she never even met or knew.

If we didn't have the right, we wouldn't have the responsibility. I reminded her of her children's degrees, their places at tables in major businesses, courts, Congress. We deserve those roles, and we get them, and we do good with them.

Is the equivalent of a life every six months really such a sacrifice in the grand scheme of things? I do not think it is too much to ask, and I told her so. Besides which, when has she ever done more than attend our meetings, a sullen, cow-eyed presence?

Still. It reminds me that I was wrong to want to tell everyone. Best to keep the information close. Contained. Who knows what other people would do if they knew, what they would decide. I have seen Dick try to get his hands on this journal. Casually ask me what I'm up to when I meet with the families. As if it is any of his damn business what I do with my time, in my house, in my town. He's lucky I let him stay.

I will keep an eye on Susan.

JULY 22, 1995

Tragedy this year, as Susan somehow got inside the gate during the season. No one saw her go in. We only knew when her daughter Karen reported her absence and we realized the beast was behind on its eating schedule—which meant it had consumed someone else. Susan is the only candidate.

It's a mystery, and a tragedy. I already said it was a tragedy, look at me, so upset I'm repeating myself.

Well. Nothing to do but move forward. Everything else went smoothly.

FEBRUARY I, 2000

That bitch. That absolute <u>bitch</u>. I finally cracked the combination to the safe—a task that took me years!—so that I could read the rest of my heritage, my inheritance, and it's gone. The book is gone. That night, Susan must have had it with her. Had it on her. I should have known when I saw her slinking out of the spa. Why else would she be there? But I cannot tell anyone without admitting that I threw her into the park. I did it for us, for Asterion, to protect us all, but will they see it that way? Of course not.

No one can know that it's missing. If they do, they'll ask questions about Susan. Or they'll go into the park to search for the book. And who knows what else she left behind, what evidence they might find.

Fortunately Karen has already had her lookie-loo at the book. And Karen's own daughter is still a child. I have a few years yet to figure out a replacement before the safe is opened again.

JANUARY I, 2002

I have discovered reality TV. What a nightmare. What a glittering example of everything that is wrong with the younger generations. But . . . what an opportunity for us. I think I have finally solved the issue of how to get people to come gladly, to stay in the park willingly, and to stick it out the whole time in spite of what they may or may not suspect is happening.

More pressing is the issue of inheritance. I've had to run the last two seasons with only Ray and Gary to help me manage, though their sons are always good for guard duty. I don't see true leadership or innovation in any of them. Tommy Callas would be ashamed, I think. At least he was a visionary. None of his descendants have been the same. Certainly I can't depend on any of Rulon Pulsipher's children. He's seen to that.

My own children, of course, have such happy, successful, busy lives elsewhere. Dick wounded me the only way he could, poisoning them against me. I sacrificed everything for my family and they left me behind. Sometimes I think my grandparents were lucky that they never had to see it happen. Their sacrifice was instant and complete.

Doubtless Chuck Callas will be groomed to take over. I know the families have been wanting to push me out for decades. I'd like to see how he does. A woman's touch will be sorely lacking.

JULY 22, 2002

I will try not to exult in my cleverness, but I was right. The "contest" lured them far more easily and permanently than the promise of honest work did. They all want something for nothing.

JULY 22, 2009

Another perfect season. I think I have finally done what no one else could: created the ideal sacrifice scenario. You're welcome, Asterion.

JULY 12, 2016

Another successfully planned year, but does anyone give me credit?

I used to think perhaps we should aim for older people, sparing the youth in the hopes that they could still make something of their lives, but I look at this group, at their young faces, their smooth skin, their utter disrespect for experience and labor, all their years spreading ahead of them already wasted. They contribute nothing to society, and they complain at being asked to work like we did, to build themselves like we did. And honestly, I think I'm doing them a favor. I'm giving them purpose. I'm making sure their lives <u>mean</u> something.

JULY 10, 2023

A new season is nearly upon us. This may be my last one. Is it odd that I'm sentimental? I have the names and photos of my final fourteen in front of me. So young. No idea what a great, noble thing they're about to do.

I wish I were passing this torch to my own daughter. I wish she could have worked side by side with me, like I did with my mother. I wish she could be grateful for what we have given her, instead of taking it and me for granted. The poison of her father. I should have married a damn Harrell or Young, kept it within the families.

Regrets. But I do not regret what I have done to protect this legacy, and what I will do this last time. My legacy would be perfect, were it not for stupid Susan and her theft. But maybe I'll die before they ever discover the missing book. It would serve them right. A tremendous mess, and no Linda to the rescue! Let them clean up for once.

No need to think on that right now. Another season. Another sacred week to remember those who came before us, to be grateful for all we have, to acknowledge the sacrifice it takes. My life's work, ready to pass along, to give this trust to those who will linger after me, who will protect the temple and our blessings.

Oh, who am I kidding. They're all idiots. Let Chuck Callas try to do better than I have. I pity whoever is in his first season. My contestants will never know how lucky they were that I saw them through their sacrifices. They have no idea. No one appreciates the things I do for others.

T WILIGHT RELEASES ITS GRASP ON THE TOWN, letting night draw a blanket of darkness. The families let out a breath of relief, a sigh of tension released. It's almost over. Two more days. No one goes out much during the season's seven days, fear lingering even though the gate is there, even though the beast is fed. At the end of the week, without agreeing to, they'll have a big cookout, laughing loudly and drinking too much, the end of another season, the promise that things will continue for them as they always have, without struggle, without interruption, the sacrifice finished on their behalf, where they don't have to hear it or see it or make it.

And Linda's Jell-O salad is divine.

Meanwhile, in Linda's house, three stunned people sit on the couch and stare at the end of the journal entries.

"Rulon Pulsipher is my father," LeGrand says.

"My father was a Nicely." Mack closes the book, running her fingers along the name stamped there. "And Brandon's a Callas."

"How many people have they sacrificed?" Ava asks, aghast, then closes her eyes and shakes her aching head. "And who the *fuck* is Hobart Keck?"

The garage door groans, announcing an arrival.

Mack picks up her discarded pudding cup on her way to the kitchen, licking her spoon clean before setting it in the sink. She opens the junk drawer she discovered while searching for a spoon and pulls out a heavy roll of duct tape.

Ava limps in, followed by LeGrand, rifle at the ready. The pain in Ava's leg is colonizing the rest of her body, invading and settling in places it has no right to be—her head, her neck, her left shoulder. Her last physical therapist, before a paperwork error stopped Ava's insurance and she couldn't afford visits anymore, advised her to avoid stress and actively work to release tension from her body. That's why Ava gave the gun to LeGrand. The trigger feels like a release, and she trusts him to make a less tense decision.

The door from the garage opens. Linda's looking down as she roots around in her enormous alligator-skin-patterned pleather purse. Linda, who welcomed them with smiles. Linda, who stroked Isabella's hair with maternal tenderness the night before Isabella was fed to a monster. Linda, who has planned and run this entire thing with *pride*.

Ava regrets surrendering the gun. A stream of words so foul they hang, almost palpable, in the air leave her mouth as she lunges across the linoleum and punches Linda in the jaw.

Lucky for Linda, pain has thrown Ava's balance off, and her blow glances rather than pulverizes. Still, Linda is so shocked by the bright overwhelming reality of pain that she stumbles and bangs her hip against the counter, adding another burst of disorientation.

Mack takes her wrist and gently leads her to one of the ornate dining room chairs, sitting her there and getting to work taping her arms to the scrolling woodwork. It's the most use this chair has gotten in more than a decade, a far cry from the dinner parties newlywed Linda imagined for it when she claimed and refurnished her mother's house forty years ago.

Mack has a brief worry that Linda's paper-thin skin will tear when the tape is removed. She tugs Linda's jacket sleeves—another blazer, this time in a blindingly bold blue—down, but the material is stiff and won't stretch. At least Linda is old enough that she still wears pantyhose, so that can tear instead of her legs.

This close, taping her ankles to the legs of the chairs, Mack can see the discoloration, the fine purple and blue webs of veins that have strayed from their original purpose, floating at the surface and feeding nothing.

What would it be like to grow old? Mack's never imagined such a thing, never saw it in her own mother, can't remember her grandparents well enough to picture them. Were they this fragile when her father took a knife to them? Mack's so distracted, she doesn't realize that Linda has been speaking to her, or that Ava and LeGrand are still in the kitchen, having a quiet argument.

"Did you hear a word I just said?" Linda whispers, lipstick bolder than ever against her pale cheeks, the blue of the bags beneath her eyes peeking through her thick foundation a prettier shade than Linda's actual murky irises.

"No." Mack steps back to check her work. She couldn't get out of it, and she doubts Linda will be able to.

Ava lurches into the dining room, dumping Linda's purse on the table. Gold lipstick tubes roll free, along with a massive pink leather pocketbook, an address book, a walkie-talkie radio that matches the one Ava has tucked into one of her many pockets, throat lozenges, a small handgun with a pale pink pearlescent handle, baby wipes, tissue, and, at last, car keys.

"How did you get out?" Linda demands as Ava opens the wallet and removes all the bills there, shoving them into yet another pocket.

"That's enough gas money to get us a few states away from wherever the hell we are," Ava mutters. "We'll need food, too."

"How many of you got out?" Linda's not asking to be freed, not bargaining. There are more important things to her. "Please, Mackenzie."

Mack looks up, startled. The only people who call her that are people reading her name off a list. That's all she is to Linda—a name on a list.

"I need to know," Linda continues. "How many of you got out of the park? Was it fed today? *Was it fed today?*" Her voice goes up an octave with panic.

Ava can't reach the old woman across the table, and that's probably good. She sits in one of the chairs instead, leaning back and lacing her fingers behind her head. "That's what you care about right now? With us here, armed, knowing you knew *exactly* what you were sending us in there for?"

"Kill me, if you want," Linda snaps. "But it *was* fed today. You wouldn't leave friends behind if they could join you. And the guards would have radioed if it was at the gate." She closes her eyes and sighs in relief. "Okay. That's good. That gives us some time. Don't touch that!"

Mack freezes with her hand on the china hutch. She was going to replace the handkerchief.

Ava smiles. "No worries, Linda, we already found your journal."

Linda's eyes bug out in outrage, her drawn-on eyebrows not quite matching the sheer levels of pissed off the rest of her face is giving. "Who did you leave in the park? There are only three of you."

"Why the fuck do you care?" Ava asks.

Linda flinches, scowl deepening. "Don't use that dirty language in my house. I care because I need to know—" She pauses, then sighs. "No, I suppose I don't need to know exactly how many replacements we need. It's not my problem anymore. Ray can deal with it for once." She lets out a hiccup of a laugh. This is the end, then. All her work, all her sacrifice, undone by these ungrateful little shits.

"Ray, the one from the diner? The cook?" Ava spins the handgun on the table, scratching tiny patterns in the polished surface.

LeGrand is standing in the entry to the kitchen, rifle held at the ready as though Linda might break free of her bonds at any moment, transforming into a monster to devour them all. It's not an unwarranted fear, really, not after what he's seen, what Mack read to them. He can't shake the feeling that Linda can still hurt him, *will* still hurt him, will hurt them all.

Linda nods. "Yes, that Ray."

Ava stops the gun mid-spin. It's pointing right at Linda. Then she casually spins it again. "Oh, he's dead."

Linda lets out an aggravated huff of air. Her breath is stale, competing with the punch of her spiky floral perfume for olfactory dominance. "Wasteful," she mutters.

"Wasteful?" Ava laughs. "I knew you were a cold bitch, but wow, this is a whole nother level."

"If you were going to get rid of Ray, the least you could have done was force him into the park." Linda twitches to rub her forehead, but of course her hands can do no such thing. Perhaps most impressive is that her hair has not migrated a single centimeter from where it is curled and shellacked into a blond sculpture. "Who did you leave behind, though? Jaden?"

"Already gone," Mack says, staring at her reflection superimposed over the delicate china. Her eyes look like blank hollows, her face white, her hair black. Like an artist's impression of a person, but one they didn't think was worth finishing. Tear it out of the sketchbook, start over.

"You didn't leave sweet Brandon, did you?" Linda has the audacity to sound aghast.

Mack shudders, remembering the sound of Brandon hitting the ground. "We would never," she whispers.

She would have, in another life. But not this one.

"He's dead, too." Ava spins the gun so hard it slides off the table and falls on the floor.

Linda sucks her teeth, a habit meant to clean lipstick off them, now done automatically. "Consumed, or dead?"

"Dead." Mack finds herself once again happy for him. Sweet Brandon. "The monster got Jaden and the other Ava."

"Another waste. He died for nothing."

"As opposed to the rest of them?" Ava's voice sharpens with a hysterical edge, her face contorted in a smile of disbelief.

"Yes, as opposed to the rest of them! You read my journal. Do you think we do this for *fun*?"

"I don't know. White people. You really never can tell."

"Don't be racist," Linda snaps.

Mack never knew her father's reason, whatever Jaden and that fucking podcast might have projected onto him. It suddenly feels urgent to understand the exact reason so many people were ended in the park. Why she should have ended in the park. "Why?" she asks. "Why do so many people have to die?"

The journal they had was unclear, but Ava knows enough. "Because they're a bunch of demon-worshipping predators."

"I am a Christian!" Linda huffs. She rushes to correct Ava's assumption. "We don't worship it. You don't understand that all great things require sacrifice," Linda says, and her voice takes on a slightly different quality. A sheen as polished as the table. This is something she has recited before, the shape of it familiar and smooth as it leaves her mouth. "And the seven families who founded our town have shaped the world in great ways. Pharmaceutical advancements, surgical innovation, technological titans, not to mention the myriad of judges, senators, local leaders, and business giants that guide our country and provide jobs for countless people."

"And this requires feeding people to an invisible monster *why*?" Ava asks.

"You couldn't see it?" Linda's voice snaps back to the present, derailed from its well-worn track.

"Nope."

"Could you two?" She looks at LeGrand and Mack, then laughs. "Of course you could. I can tell. Besides, we never have any question about your father's lineage, LeGrand. The most prolific Pulsipher."

LeGrand frowns, but says nothing.

Ava kicks the table. "You were explaining why you need to feed people to an invisible monster?"

"Do you know how many of the founding families of this town lost everything in the Great Depression? How many of their sons were killed in World War Two, Korea, Vietnam?"

"How the fuck would I know that?" Ava mutters, increasingly

annoyed. This isn't getting them anywhere. They should leave. But Mack is hanging on the words, a hungry look on her face. Ava will let Linda finish explaining, and then she'll tell LeGrand and Mack to get in the car, and then she'll shoot the old lady. For Brandon. Because he's dead, and because this woman declared it a waste because it didn't do her, personally, any good.

"*None.*" Linda smiles, triumphant. "No one lost everything, no beloved sons were killed on foreign soil. We were protected. We have been protected, since my grandparents' time. They performed the first sacrifice, made the covenant, traded their blood to protect their blood. Which *you* are obviously not, Ava. I should have known. Your slut mother must have tricked your idiot father."

Ava leans down and retrieves the handgun from the floor, setting it on the table with her fingers caressing it. "Say something else about my mother." A wild grin splits Ava's face. Her father always knew her mother got pregnant just before they met, put his name on the birth certificate anyway. He never cared, and he never once looked at Ava with anything but love and pride.

Of *course* he didn't belong with these people.

"Oh, shoot me then, you filthy little animal. It doesn't matter. They'll figure out you've escaped, and they'll get more. Probably from Rulon. He's always good for it. There's doubtless a dud daughter or two he won't mind shipping to us." She glances at LeGrand, her smile coy.

LeGrand raises the rifle in one smooth movement. "I'll kill you."

"Once I'm dead, who knows who they'll pick to replace you? You're signing death warrants."

"We're not doing anything," Ava spits. "Don't turn this on us!"

"Aren't you? You're choosing to leave, knowing that someone else will have to take your place. Your whole generation is so selfish, it disgusts me. This was the most noble thing you could possibly have done with your lives, and instead you're going to turn your backs and run, leaving someone else to die in your place."

Ava lets go of the handgun and lifts her hands in the air, incredulous. "Do you even hear yourself? You're batshit. Completely fucking batshit."

"Watch your tongue," Linda snaps. "I will not tolerate such language in my home."

"Oh my god. If you love your legacy so much, sacrifice yourself."

Linda scoffs. "You'd like that, wouldn't you! All of us, gone. Then no one would be in charge. *My* grandparents sacrificed so *we* wouldn't have to! We earned our success. We earned our lives. We earned this world, and I'll be damned if I let you take it from us."

"Come on." Ava stands and gestures to Mack and LeGrand. This is pointless. She half feels like she's back on Facebook, arguing with her pervy grandpa. Maybe she *is* losing her mind, after all. Pain delirium has set in. "Let's go. We're done here."

"My father will send someone?" LeGrand asks, his voice soft.

"Oh, yes," Linda replies. "He's good for at least one replacement. He mentioned her when we spoke about you. Alma? Almera? Something like that."

LeGrand swings the rifle, the butt catching the side of Linda's temple. Her head snaps to the side, skin broken and blood finally ruining her hair.

Linda gasps in pain, blinking, still alive. Still conscious. It's the first and only time LeGrand has struck anyone. It feels like someone else did it. He can see evidence of it, feel his heart racing, but he didn't choose to hit her. It was automatic.

"How do you know it works?" Ava demands.

"What do you mean?" Linda groans, closing her eyes and shaking her head.

"I mean, how do you know it's this deal with a devil that keeps you all successful and shit? You're white. You're well-off. Pretty sure people like you have been gliding through life for generations. No mystical protections needed."

"Don't pretend like I've had an easy life! You have no idea what I've had to do, to face, to decide in order to take care of my family, my people, my heritage."

Ava laughs. "We read your journal. We know exactly what you've done. God. I can't. I can't talk with her anymore. Come on." Ava stands and holds a hand out to Mack.

"What happens if the monster isn't fed?" Mack asks. "Will it get out?"

"It will be fed, no matter what. I already told you. Besides, the gate keeps it bound."

"Will you promise that LeGrand's sister isn't touched?"

"*Mack,*" Ava warns.

Linda looks up at this, eyes narrowing shrewdly. "In exchange for?"

"We go back in," Mack says. "That buys you a day, and then you only need one more person." Mack has finally figured out why it felt wrong to leave the park. They weren't running away. They were *hiding,* just in a different place. Mack would hide, and someone would die in her place, just like before. Just like Maddie. And this time she knows it.

Never again.

"*Mack!*" Ava grabs Mack's shoulder, but Mack doesn't stand, doesn't move, doesn't look away from Linda.

"Two more," Linda corrects. "It won't eat her." She jerks her chin toward Ava, her tone indicating she thinks that's an insulting thing to say. Lowly Ava, not good enough to be devoured by a monster.

"Okay," Mack says. "Two more. But not Almera. She's safe forever."

"Stop." Ava tugs on Mack's arm, trying to get her up, trying to move her. "Stop."

Linda is fixed on Mack, a shark on the scent of blood. She can turn this around. She's still going to win. Of course she is. It's her divine right to win. "I can guarantee that. But only if I'm alive."

"You swear?" LeGrand asks. "I go in, and Almera stays safe. Really safe. You take her away from my father and put her in a good house. A place where they'll take care of her."

"I swear on the lives of my grandparents. On their sacrifice. I will see to it that your sister is safe and cared for, for the rest of her life."

"You can't be serious!" Ava lets go of Mack's arm and paces, but the pain is too much. It's all too much. She can't catch her breath as her vision tunnels, and she leans heavily against the wall. "No. *No*."

"I never had a choice." Mack stares at the wood grain of the table, the tiny scratches Ava made. Wonders if they can be buffed right out, erasing the fact that they were ever here. "No. That's not right. I had a choice, and I made it, and I let my sister die in my place. I took her spot, and for what? What have I ever done with my stolen life?"

At last, Mack looks up, but not at Ava. At her ghost of a reflection in the glass of the hutch. The glass over the Nicely family china, china that Mack could never touch, could never use, could never have. "This time I know what the stakes are, and I get to choose the sacrifice. And I'm not going to make the same mistake." Mack glances over at LeGrand. She's making this deal for him, too.

He nods. Whatever it takes for Almera.

"Okay," she says. "We'll go back in."

"Fuck!" Ava screams, slamming her fist into the wall. "No! I won't let you."

LeGrand calmly points the rifle at her. "Ava. Get in the car and leave. Go. This isn't your problem, not anymore."

"You can't—this isn't—god, *no*. No." Ava's voice breaks, tears pooling in her dark eyes.

"You can go back in with them," Linda offers. "Stay with them. Be their witness." Linda smiles, and the red of her blood dripping down her cheek clashes with the pink of her lipstick, a garish mess of colors. "You'll be perfectly safe, and you can make sure I keep my word. That'll make LeGrand and Mack feel better, right? Ava will keep me accountable."

LeGrand nods, quick, small movements. "Please," he says, still pointing the rifle at Ava.

"You really think they'll let me live, after?" Ava's voice is strangled with the strain of holding back tears, with the terrible weight of despair.

Linda's tone is back to the chipper one of the woman who greeted them on the bus a lifetime ago. She absolutely will not let Ava live, but there's no reason not to play along. "We've done it before. Doreen, a maid. The second sacrifice season. Back when we still thought we could offer the beast lesser prey. It rejected her, of course, and we let her go. Because who would believe a—" Linda stumbles, making it clear she was about to use a different, more familiar-to-her-tongue word before she course-corrects. "A poor Black uneducated maid over us?"

"And who would believe me over you?" Ava laughs, shaking her head. "God, you're right. You're absolutely right. I can't tell anyone about this."

Linda settles on what she believes is a warm, motherly smile. Ava would try to tell. It wouldn't get her anywhere, but it would bring more attention than is worth dealing with. She'll be easy enough to kill once Mack and LeGrand are gone. "You're welcome to leave. I won't stop you. Or you can keep vigil with your friends and then leave after. It's your choice."

"Give her the money, too," Mack says.

"What?" Ava and Linda both say at once.

"The prize money."

Linda's eyes go wide and she looks at Ava as though to confirm that at least someone here is smart enough to realize there was never any prize money. No one was ever getting out alive. "Yes, of course," Linda says, her tone placating. "We'll give her the fifty thousand dollars."

"Okay." Mack feels peaceful. Truly peaceful. She's not hiding anymore. She's in control for the first time in her life. "Right now, though. Give her the money right now."

"I don't have fifty thousand dollars on me!"

"Whatever you have in the house." Mack shrugs. She can wait. The night is long, the dawn and its approaching death far enough away still.

"Oh god." Linda closes her eyes, but her tone is less worried and more annoyed. "In my bedroom, in the closet, there's a safe. The code is seven-fourteen-seven. You'll find cash in there. Don't touch the jewelry. It was my mother's."

"Mack," Ava pleads.

"Go get it," Mack says. "I'm gonna untape her, and then we'll drive back to the park. No one else needs to know what's happened, right, Linda? You tell them the monster rejected Ava and Brandon died in an accident, so you need two more."

"That's acceptable. How did you kill Ray? I'll need to do damage control."

"Bashed his head in." Ava walks away to find Linda's bedroom. She doesn't know why she's doing it. Why any of this. She's lost control. She's not in the lead. It's all impossibly fucked. She can't drag Mack away, can't force LeGrand into the car. What is *happening*? What did they see that she didn't? She thought she was too late to save Brandon. It turns out she was too late to save them all.

Linda nods, organizing her thoughts. "Bashed in the head. That's easy enough. He fell off his tower. Too old to be doing that, anyway." She puts on her best let's-get-to-work smile as Mack carefully peels back the tape one limb at a time. She rubs her wrists and stands. "Let me get cleaned up and then we'll get you kids back where you belong."

Mack nods, sweeping Linda's things back into her purse, bending down to retrieve several of the lipstick tubes where Linda can't see. Mack keeps the car keys out. She's ready. She knows Ava is hurt—wishes she could make it better—but she's so glad Ava decided to come with them rather than leaving right now.

She could do this alone, if she had to, but it's a relief that she *doesn't* have to. Ava cracked her open, started this whole business. She wants Ava with her to finish it, too. Mack follows Linda into the kitchen, hovering nearby.

LeGrand keeps the rifle. He's cradling it, gaze indistinct, the resolve that had reshaped his face softened once again. He saved Almera. Not the way he wanted to, or the way he hoped to, but it makes sense. God is letting him save her, but only at the cost of himself. When he tried to help her before, he thought it cost him everything. Now it actually will.

Ava reappears, face grim, pockets bulging. She shakes a prescription bottle at Linda. "This label accurate?"

Linda frowns, offended, gently dabbing the side of her head with a washcloth. "Why wouldn't it be?"

Ava takes two pills, swallows them dry. "I can't afford this shit, and I actually need it."

"It's not my fault you're poor," Linda snarls.

Ava takes the car keys from the table. "Agree to disagree." She's not looking at Mack, deliberately avoiding her gaze as they get into Linda's massive sedan, Ava driving. Mack can see the pain around Ava's eyes, the strange bravado that has settled in now that Ava has accepted her fate.

Maybe Mack wishes Ava *had* decided to leave them, had opted to get into the car and drive away from all of this madness that has no claim on her. Ava didn't see the monster. She can't understand, not really, why Mack has to go back in.

Ava backs up recklessly, knocking over Linda's floral-painted mailbox and taking out several of her flower beds. Linda hisses in displeasure, but apparently thinks better of calling her on it.

Once on the road, though, Ava drives with a steady hand in spite of her pain and her painkillers. She knows Linda and her cronies will try to kill her. She's looking forward to it, actually. At least that'll be an enemy she can face, can make bleed.

How can she fight back against Mack's decision to self-destruct though? Ava gets it. When she was in the hospital, alone, being pinned back together, she had wished more than once that her life had ended on that road next to Maria. She nearly drifts off the road, remembering Maria. She's going to watch Mack die, too.

She course-corrects roughly. No. She'll come up with a plan. Something. Something. But she can help only if she stays with them. She grits her teeth against the fading pain, steels her head against the impending disconnection of the really good drugs.

Either way, Mack's been alone. So long. And so has Ava. They'll have a last few hours of not being alone, and then Ava will figure something else out. She will because she has to.

LeGrand stares straight ahead into the night and sighs, so tired. At least this way he's being consumed, and not consuming others. In another life, he would have grown. Become an elder. Become the same as his father, a devourer, a small, petty god of a small, pathetic world. It's in the blood of this town, after all. Rulon Pulsipher just went a different route than Linda.

None of it matters. Almera will be safe, and that's all he ever wanted. Though now that he's flying through the night back toward the park, he has to admit: He would also like to live.

"Where did you climb out?" Linda asks as the road turns to dirt and gets bumpy.

"Ray's guard tower."

"And I suppose that's where you left his body, as well." Linda sounds cross.

"Sure is!" Ava chirps.

"Pull over here, then, before the gate guard sees us. You can go back over the fence that way."

Ava pulls to an abrupt stop, then climbs out of the car. She leads them through the woods, her sense of direction unerring. At the base of the empty guard tower, she points to where Ray's body is.

"Drag him out," Linda says.

"Drag him out yourself. You're not my boss."

"Leave the rifle," Linda snaps. "Otherwise they'll know something happened."

LeGrand holds it out, but Ava grabs it before Linda can. Rifle in hand, she briefly considers holding Mack and LeGrand hostage. Forcing them back to the car. But she knows they won't go, and she won't shoot them. She should dump Linda into the park, let the monster eat her. But LeGrand is depending on Linda to protect Almera. He wouldn't allow it.

Okay, so, make it so that they don't need to bring in new sacrifices. Get Linda into the park. Then somehow find three more guards, and, not getting shot, lure or throw them into the park, too, all while going undiscovered by the rest of the guards and the town. And without full use of her leg, and this crescendo of pain, and maybe having to fight LeGrand and Mack, who seem bent on self-sacrifice, and—

It's all hopeless. Ava pulls out the firing pin of the rifle, instead. "Just in case you decided to shoot me in the back as soon as we're over the fence."

"Such a nasty girl," Linda mutters, taking the rifle. "What will they think if they examine the gun?"

"That Ray didn't know how to handle one. Don't know, don't care. Good luck with the body, he's a big dude." Ava grits her teeth. She's in hyper-focus mode, one task at a time, not letting herself think about tomorrow, what will happen, what she'll do. She's so mad, she wants to strangle them all. All she knows is she has to stay with Mack and LeGrand. She's their only hope. So she climbs, up into the tower and then back over and down into the fucking murder monster park.

"Your grandparents understood covenants," LeGrand says, his deep voice firm. "You'll keep yours." It's not a question, it's a statement, as forceful as he's ever been in his life. Except when he hit Linda in the head. That still feels like someone else did it, like the hands weren't his.

"Of course." Linda's head hurts, and she neither forgets nor forgives as she watches him climb. Since they already passed through Tommy's gate once, this shouldn't be a problem. All it takes is one cross of that threshold.

Mack is last. Linda goes stiff with shock as Mack embraces her in a hug. "Thank you," Mack says.

Linda hesitantly pats Mack's back, then something inside her loosens and she really returns the embrace. Linda's so relieved that Mack understands. At last, finally, *someone* understands the weight of this responsibility, this duty. Linda's surprised to find herself suffused with pride for this unnerving, strange girl. A girl who understands that sometimes, sacrifices have to made. Of course she's a Nicely. They always have been the best family.

This is all going to be fine. Linda's got it back under control, somehow, against all odds. She'll even keep her word to LeGrand and move his sister to a care house, since that means knowing where a spare is at all times. She most certainly will not keep her word about Ava, though. Ava will die.

"Goodbye." Mack pulls away and climbs up the tower.

By the time she gets to the other side, Ava and LeGrand are both on the ground, waiting. Ava's shoulders, so strong, are slumped. Being here, again, has broken her. She doesn't know what to do now. She has no idea what to fight, or how to fight it, or even if she has the strength left for any fight at all.

LeGrand sits on the ground. He might as well wait right here. Doesn't seem much point to doing anything else.

"Why?" Ava whispers, not reaching out for Mack, not wanting to touch her skin while it's still warm, while it's still here. She had felt safe with Mack, had felt a future in her touch. "Why did you do this?"

Mack took Maddie's hiding spot. But she hadn't known what the result would be. She hadn't killed Maddie. She can see that now, thanks to Linda. Mack crouches and pulls out the handgun she tucked into her sock instead of putting it back in Linda's purse with the fallen lipstick tubes.

"I said we'd choose what was sacrificed. I never said it was gonna be us."

DAY SIX

THE SUN BREAKS THE HORIZON, cracking the darkness and flooding an abandoned amusement park—a labyrinth—a cemetery—a place haunted by the living and the dead alike—with light. Three people are inside.

The sun hits the top of the Ferris wheel first, so brilliantly backlit it could almost look whole, like at any moment it will spin to life, rotating riders up and around, an orbit of wonder as they look down at the quickly receding and then breathlessly approaching ground, the stomach-dropping giddiness leading to a stolen kiss. A peal of gleeful laughter. A few minutes of freedom from gravity.

But no more. This particular orbit has been forever arrested, rusted into place. The view will never change.

A set of roller-coaster tracks, ancient and rotting, carpeted with so much ivy that it might be the body of some great sleeping beast long since forgotten, is illuminated next. But it's just wood and metal. The only beast within this park is neither forgotten nor sleeping for much longer.

Daylight pierces the trees, the ivy, the feral topiary. It can't break through to the center of the carousel, where both Rosiee and Rebecca ended, surrounded by the grimaces of flaking animal faces. It shines sideways into the base camp, where Ian's and Christian's blood has become a sticky black stain, an accusation with no one willing to answer for it. It winks along the chains of the swing, where Jaden thought he was safe and Brandon chose not to be. It lingers on Brandon's gaze, filmed over, no clean devouring disposal for his body. Who will be the kindest gas station attendant in Pocatello, Idaho, now?

The sun races along the ground, over countless winding maze walls, devouring shadow and piercing mist, throwing everything into sharpest relief. The bushes where Sydney crouched and closed her eyes so she wouldn't see what was chasing her. The leering clown mouth where Logan—out so quickly, forgotten now by even our three hiders, who will not be able to remember his name—fell asleep and never left. The clotted pool, a twin to the one in the base camp, a testament that beautiful Ava existed, that she was real, that she tried. She tried so hard.

And here, following arrow to arrow, the path Atrius left behind. His mark on the competition. Mack pauses at the discarded sensible pumps, tries to remember the woman they belonged to, can conjure only an image of a pantsuit and an aura of stress.

Isabella, lost first, lost forever.

Mack doesn't fail to notice the child's shoe, cracked and peeling leather, hooked onto a branch now grown to the level of her face. Mack nods, as though making a secret agreement with the shoe, and takes it off, tucking it into her pocket.

She pushes on, knowing this is far enough, but needing to see for herself the center of it all. What a generation long before her summoned and paid for, and what subsequent generations decided to make others pay for. Trickle-down economics. They got the economy, and the blood trickled down the decades.

Mack comes around a bend, almost trips on an old iron loop fixed into the cement decades ago. She stops, awed in the oldest sense of the word, where awe is soul-quaking fear and mind-bending wonder wrapped into one.

Here is the temple.

And here is the beast.

Elsewhere, ringing the park, surly but with shockingly little mourning for one of their own lost, men sit in their towers with their guns leaning against the walls, drinking coffee, glad that at least Linda is the one who has to clean up the mess. The least charitable among them resent Ray for dying and leaving one less guard in rotation so they all have to do more. The most charitable among them no longer live in the town or have anything to do with these families, so they have no presence in the towers.

Even Ray's son Chuck cannot muster stronger feelings than general displeasure over his father's death and the "whoopsie" inside the park, as Linda so annoyingly summed it up. They're really going to dump this all on him next time. He's a forty-five-year-old man, for fuck's sake, and he's still working for his father. Or he was, until a few hours ago. But where are his blessings from the great sacrifice? Why should *he* be tasked with making it run smoothly so other people can benefit? It's a good town, but sometimes it feels like a prison sentence.

His radio statics with life at the same time several *pops* echo through the air from somewhere in the park. He lurches upright, scanning his limited view. He's manning the guard tower nearest the gate, named Tommy for his great-grandfather, but he doesn't see anything.

The static eats several of the words, but one of the guys—Ted, maybe? Sounds like Ted—is saying something about being shot at.

Linda has settled in bed at last, a compress on her aching head, when her nightstand phone rings.

"What?" she snaps. It's got to be one of the men, probably wondering about the arrangements for Ray's replacement, as if she couldn't manage this all by herself, as if she hasn't been managing it all by herself for decades! Maybe if she had some damn competent help, last night's fiasco never would have happened.

"You aren't on your walkie. Is there any way they could have a gun in the park?" Gary demands.

"No, we checked their bags on the bus, how could—" Linda drops the phone on her bed and rushes down the hallway, banging her elbow against the wall. Her purse is exactly where Mack left it on the table after thoughtfully replacing the spilled contents. Linda dumps it out, desperate. But of course she doesn't find what she's looking for.

She goes to the phone on the wall and picks it up, the line still connected. "Sorry, I dropped the phone. Chuck must not have checked well enough. It's probably the military one. Treat her as extremely dangerous."

Those filthy little cunts. Linda throws on her house robe, grabs her keys, and gets in the car.

"Which tower?" Chuck demands.

"Ferris wheel! They're all here! Hurry!" The man is cut off. Chuck has a moment of confusion—the towers are named—but he knows which one Ted meant. Rose. Which is also weird, because Ted is usually on Ethel, but he must have swapped with someone. Bad luck for him. And for them all. Ted's the worst shot of anyone, so they'll have to get to him fast. And the Ferris wheel is on the opposite end of the park, a good two miles away since he has to go all the way around.

"Everyone! Get to Rose!" Chuck broadcasts, then climbs down and gets on his four-wheeler, gunning it away from his tower and its view of the gate.

LeGrand puts the walkie-talkie on transmit and holds it that way, jamming the line so no one can communicate. Then he fires one more shot for good measure at absolutely nothing and starts running.

"Goddammit, where is it?" Ava tears apart Ian's bag, left on the floor of the abandoned pavilion. She's the only one who isn't in immediate danger, but she feels Mack and LeGrand's peril acutely, a pressure in her chest, phantom claws piercing her own stomach. They're ending this today. She pulls out an old leather book and shoves it into one of her many cargo pant pockets. Could work as a wick. But not if she doesn't find the lighter.

"Ah!" she screams, triumphant, emerging once more from the

depths of Ian's bag with his sleek silver lighter. Thinking better of the book plan, she grabs one of Christian's *Athens Solar* T-shirts, takes hold of the monstrous generator, and begins to drag it.

Her still-intact stomach sinks. Maybe they should have chosen someone with two functioning legs for this task.

"Fuck fuck fuckity fuck." She grits her teeth against the pain. This should never have been her fight. But isn't every fight her fight, whether she benefits from it or not? She's so tired of having to fight.

"Mack," she whispers to herself, closing her eyes, taking a breath. Then she crouches as best she can with a right knee and ankle that won't bend anymore, shoves her arms through the metal roll cage around the generator—cheap fucks couldn't spring for wheel attachments?—and stands with a roar.

One foot in front of the other is good enough, she thinks, then she laughs because she only *has* one good foot. But she's enough. She has to be.

She is the goddamn strongest woman in the world.

In Mack's mind, scarred over with wounds from that night, her father had lost his face. He had transformed into something towering, bent at impossible angles, with black holes for eyes. He didn't hold a knife; he *was* a knife.

But Mack, staring at death, lets herself finally try to remember her father. And when she does, she laughs.

He had a beer belly. His arms and legs were thin, the hair there so sparse in some areas it wore right off. He couldn't grow a beard. His eyes were like hers, too big, wide set, so that he gave the impression of always being distracted or slightly puzzled. The fastest way to set off his explosive temper—which was never a difficult task—was to ask if he was paying attention. That lost him most jobs.

He'd always tried to fix plumbing issues, would swear and rage and declare he was taking a break, at which point he would go out to a bar. Mack's mother would quietly step in and finish the job so that when he got back, he could smugly explain he must have done it right, it just needed a few minutes to settle.

He yelled at his favorite television programs as though his feelings had any bearing on what might be happening on the screen.

He made pancakes with chocolate chip smiley faces, and whistled with the clearest, purest notes.

He hit their mother, and he hit them, not because he was strong, but because he wasn't. No one who is strong hits a child. No one who is strong does *anything* he did.

And Mack has no questions about that: He chose to do what he did. He looked at the world and felt it owed him more than he had, and when that didn't materialize, he took himself out along with everyone who had tried to love him, who might have been happier without him.

Finally, at last, Mack can form him in her mind as small, impotent, poisonously angry. Not a monster at all, but the most pathetically human of men.

The monster in front of her is not human at all, but there are traces in its hands. It doesn't have claws so much as thick, grooved nails that have never been trimmed, broken and growing and broken again into jagged edges. It shuffles toward her on legs that bend backward at the knee, like a cow's. At the end of those legs, covered in dense, matted fur tinged green with moss, heavy hooves fall on the ground not with cheerful clopping, but with careful padding.

Its shoulders are broad, too broad, rippling with power on either side of a massive chest, but its waist narrows to an almost delicate taper before turning into hips not designed for upright walking. It has no genitalia at all, just more of that matted, green-tinged fur. It hunches, head parallel to the ground. Atop a short, broad neck, its face is a flat expanse with two nostrils, flaring as the monster breathes in deeply, searching. The terrible scarring where they put out its eyes balances between incongruously delicate ears, velvet soft, sloping on either side of the head beneath the long, sensuously curving crown of horns.

They look heavy. She wonders if they make its neck ache after a day of hunting.

Unlike her father, there is nothing pathetically human about this monster, but it strikes her as pathetic nonetheless as it shuffles closer, bringing with it the scent of death and decay and rot to assault her senses, warning her that this is the end.

And even though this thing, this abomination, destroyed so many people and would consume her, too, she can't hate it. Whatever those families did to summon it, to make their deal, she can't imagine it *agreed*. It doesn't seem to have the capacity for consent.

It exists to consume. Who can blame it for following its terrible course, for being in a place it does not belong, for being forced into wretched existence and sustained and fed merely to keep existing?

Mack takes the sharp edge of Rosiee's silver heart pendant, rescued from the carousel, and drags it along her wrist. Blood beads along the line, the scrape enough to break the skin but not make her gush freely.

The monster stops mid-step, head snapping in Mack's direction, nostrils flaring wide.

Her task is to make sure the monster is where they want it to be, when they want it to be there. But instead of turning and running, Mack watches. She can't look away. She missed death the first time it came for her, and she was ready—maybe even eager—for it here. For that last, final, ultimate hiding place, the darkness in which no one could ever find her. Not her father, not her guilt or her shame, not hunger or fear or want.

The monster unseals the thin line of its lips and a spittle of drool drops down. But there are no teeth there. In its mouth, oblivion. A velvet black so deep and complete she has never seen its like, never will. And beyond the black, a hint of something burning. Not warm, hungry, orange fire, but the cold white pulse of a distant star.

Mack takes a step toward the gravity-drag of that promise.

Several shots fire somewhere in the distance, and Mack remembers herself. She remembers her own self, super-compacted, pushed down so deep all she had was the pull of her own misery, the terrible weight of her lonely shame.

But her shell cracked, and it didn't end her. She didn't burn up, or burst. She's not alone anymore, and she won't leave her friends, just as she knows—has seen, has felt, and would believe even without that evidence—that her friends, her Ava, won't leave her.

Mack turns and runs, and death follows quickly, drawn by the scent of her blood and the need for more.

Ava's going too slowly. She knows she is. But even her tremendous will can't make her body move faster. The generator, named PREDATOR with absolutely no irony on the part of the company, weighs nearly two hundred pounds. She's glad it weighs that much, because that means it still has gas in the tank. But it also means she can barely manage a shuffle, much less the brisk pace she had planned on.

They need her to be at the right place at the right time, or they have no chance. Mack will die, LeGrand will die, and then what point does Ava have? She finally found the borders of herself again, finally believes she can fill in the vast hollow that took claim of so much of her. Finally found a purpose and a family, two things that had been taken away from her right alongside a functioning leg.

She would give almost anything for that old leg now. Her knee trembles and almost gives out, her boot-encased metal ankle sliding dangerously far ahead of her. She stumbles to catch up.

Head down. Do the work. She's done harder things than this, hasn't she?

Has she?

Probably not. Fine then, this is the hardest thing she's ever done, and she'll be damned if she doesn't do it.

"You are the strongest woman alive," Maria whispers in her memory, both of them squeezed onto her cot, pressed so close Ava knew exactly where she ended and Maria began because she felt every inch of it.

"But what if I wasn't?" Ava had whispered, suddenly afraid that if she couldn't be strong, she couldn't have Maria.

"Impossible." Maria had squeezed Ava's bicep, laughing when Ava flexed as a matter of pride. "Even without these," she said, pinching, "even without any of this, you'd still be the strongest woman alive."

Ava is so *tired* of being strong. It hadn't saved Maria, and it hadn't saved her own soul, and why should she have to be so strong? The world demanded constant strength from women like her, displays of infinite grace and patience, proof of why they deserved to—

Ava stumbles again, and this time she doesn't catch it. She only manages to twist at the last second so the generator doesn't fall on top of her and pin her to the ground.

"Fuck!" she screams, face pressed against countless seasons of fallen leaves. An earthy scent, dirt and decay and life all in one, floods her nose and invades her mouth, trying to claim her.

Ava lies there for one second. Ten. Thirty. A minute.

Just because she shouldn't *have* to be so damn strong doesn't mean she *isn't*. Ava stands up. She grabs one of the cage bars of the generator, and she starts dragging it.

She moves without thinking, without checking her progress, mind on nothing but her goal. Not where she's going right now or what she'll have to do when she gets there, but the goal beyond that. Mack, and LeGrand, and freedom.

Her pocket with Ian's book bounces against her leg, while other pockets jingle, flush with cash and Linda's family jewelry—taken as vengeance for how many times her fucking *saint* of a mother was accused of stealing jewelry from the houses she cleaned for women like Linda—and her muscles tremble, and her spine aches, and her knee won't move right, and her ankle isn't functioning, and Ava keeps going.

She has no idea how close to the gate she is, and, with her back turned, she doesn't see the owner of that terribly gaudy jewelry standing beyond it, rifle pointed at Ava's back.

• • •

Mack follows Atrius's arrows, guided by his ghost. Her arm bleeds, cut by Rosiee's silver. Maybe because the monster is so close, padding turned to pounding as it matches her pace in terrible ravenous pursuit, but she can feel them with her. All these lost people, who had worked so hard to carve out a place where they could be successful, where they could be famous, where they could be stable, where they could be loved, where they could be safe.

They came here, desperate, lured by the promise of finally winning something, set up to be devoured so people who already had everything would continue having exactly what they already had, what they could have had anyway, what they felt was their due. What they were willing to let fourteen hopeful souls pay for.

Mack can't remember all their names, but it doesn't matter. They are no longer her rivals. They are her team. She will win this not in spite of them, but because of them. *For* them. For Isabella and Logan and Rosiee and Sydney and Atrius and Rebecca and Ian and Christian and beautiful Ava and even Jaden.

And Brandon.

And LeGrand.

And Ava. But she doesn't run *for* Ava. She runs *toward* Ava, trusting absolutely that Ava will be ready.

Another shot cracks through the air, this one much closer, and if Mack wasn't so focused on running, navigating this maze with a monster right behind her, she would wonder why there was another gunshot when LeGrand was done with his part and should be hurrying to meet them.

If it had been anyone other than Ava, they would have fallen to Linda's bullet.

But Linda hadn't counted on the time Ava spent in active combat. The fact that, even with her back turned and her body screaming and her whole mind focused on a singular, impossible task, Ava's instincts would remember the sound of a rifle being cocked and she would drop to the ground at the exact moment the trigger was pressed.

The shot passes precisely where Ava had been. Linda, in addition to being a bad mother, forgotten ex-wife, and the hopes and dreams of her grandparents utterly filled and wildly failed, is an excellent shot.

Ava rolls, crouching behind the generator.

"Oh, stand up, you worthless animal," Linda shouts. "Did you think everyone would be fooled into abandoning their posts? I will *never* abandon mine! This is my birthright, my legacy, and no one is going to take it away from me." Linda's naked lips curl back in an ugly sneer, her false teeth, white and straight, standing out against her gray gums. "Stand up and take it like the man you wish you were."

Ava examines her options. She has none. The road to the gate has been cleared well, and the nearest cover isn't close enough to make it against someone as good a shot as Linda is. Doesn't mean the plan is over, Ava tells herself. Just means her part in it is. She carefully takes the T-shirt and lighter out, setting them on the ground where LeGrand and Mack will be able to find them. One final offering of love.

Ava stands and turns, holding both hands in the air, middle fingers raised to the sky.

Linda jerks the rifle down toward the generator. "What were you going to do with that? Blow the beast up?" Her laugh is harsh and ugly, neglected and as thin and sour as the breath that carries it. For all Linda has done exactly what was expected of her, for all she has benefited from the horrible sacrifices of those who came before, her life has been absolutely devoid of happiness, of warmth, of joy. She has everything, and she has nothing, and some part of her knows. Some part of her knows, and needs to destroy Ava, needs to destroy whatever hope Ava still has before killing her.

She needs Ava to know that *she*—not Ava—will win. That she's better than Ava.

"You can't kill it," Linda says sweetly. "You could stand there and blow yourself to pieces with the beast right on top of you, and it would walk away. It's not an animal; it's not a person. It's a concept. It's a covenant. It's an agreement between my grandparents and the universe that, as long as we feed it, we will thrive. And we will *never* stop feeding it. It might not want you, but it will take Mack, and LeGrand, and all the other pathetic branches we prune to feed it. It will always be here, and there's absolutely nothing someone like you can do about it."

Ava's jaw clenches. She doesn't want her part to be over yet. She wishes it had ended differently. But the universe has never cared about her wishes.

"Shut up and do it, bitch," Ava says.

A shot cracks through the air.

Another shot, and this time it's close enough that Mack notices, and fears. She puts on a burst of speed she didn't know she had. For someone who often wondered if she would have been better off dying with her family, Mack is suddenly, desperately aware of how easy it is to die and how very much she doesn't want to.

Ava feels the crack of the gun, the power of the shot, reverberate through her whole body. And she watches Linda drop her rifle and stumble as her floral robe blooms with fresh scarlet before she falls back on the ground.

LeGrand steps free of the wall he was behind, tossing Linda's decorative handgun to the side. "Out of bullets," he says, matter-of-factly. "Come on. Mack should be here soon."

He grabs one side of the generator's cage, and Ava, still not quite sure how she's not shot, grabs the other. Together, they drag the generator to its place.

"Is this a good spot?" LeGrand asks.

Ava isn't sure, but they aren't exactly spoiled for time here. Mack will be here any moment. She has to be. Mack will make it.

Ava unscrews the gas cap and twists Christian's shirt so she can feed it in until it touches the gas. *Please,* she prays, careful to direct the prayer only to her mother's god and not to any others that might be listening in this cursed place, *please let there be enough gas.*

Atrius's arrows run out.

Mack is at a crossroads. Two paths diverge in a deadly maze, and she can't afford to take the one less traveled.

Maybe Atrius came from a different starting point. Maybe he didn't mark this one. This entire park was designed to keep a monster in, to confuse and twist and double back so that the beast never wandered too far out, and so that its prey was sucked in, too. The park does its job incredibly well.

Mack hears the pounding of hooves behind herself, all her gained ground covered in mere heartbeats counting down until her end.

"Ava," she whispers, closing her eyes.

Something nudges her to the right. Whether it's the pull of Ava's gravity, or hope, or folly, Mack doesn't know, but she'll find out soon.

Linda groans. Ava sweats. LeGrand stands on the waist-high stone wall lining the path into the park, looking. Waiting.

Mack stumbles to a halt, her heart seizing in terror.

She hasn't picked a path to the gate. She's run straight to her first hiding spot. To the sunken-roofed duck stand, the one that hid her, that bonded her with Ava, that gave Ava the tools to scale the fence.

But it's not safety anymore, it's not hope. It's exactly the opposite direction she was trying to go. She's deeper in the labyrinth now, heading the wrong direction. She knows how to get to the pavilion from here, but it requires doubling back. Going *toward* the relentless, patient hoofbeats heading her way.

Mack runs forward, trying to correct, trying to get back on the right path. She's heedless of direction now, turned and twisted.

Her heart races and her breath is ragged and she's going to die and then LeGrand is going to die and then Ava is going to die, and once again it will be her fault. It was her choice to come back into the park. Her selfishness.

Mack stumbles and careens off a lone roller-coaster cart waiting in the middle of the path.

She needs time. She has to buy herself time to figure out where the hell she is.

The roller-coaster cart eyes her wearily, the painted face of a long-suffering cow begging her to look at what it sees.

She turns her head. The tracks are right next to her, a wooden path leading off her traitorous trail and up, up, up into the trees. She can't see where it ends through the tunnel of branches and ivy. It's obviously not a path that will lead her to the gate. But maybe, just maybe, it will save her.

Mack jumps onto the track and runs straight up.

When it was built, the Cattle Run was a wonder of engineering. Most roller coasters were designed to be contained, portable, easy to dismantle and transport and reassemble, depending on where cash was flowing and where it wasn't.

As a demonstration of how flush with cash, how confidently permanent the Amazement Park was, Lillian Nicely Smith commissioned a wooden and metal marvel, the longest ever made. This was a roller coaster that would never be taken apart and moved elsewhere, a soaring, dipping, twisting testament to the fact that things built in Asterion are meant to last forever.

It was the most popular ride in the park, so fast and winding that there were dedicated vomit bins at the end for the unfortunate riders stumbling off to lose their overpriced lunches. Ian's favorite ennui-plagued Russian revolutionary would have written about it as a perfect example of both American ingenuity and excess.

Indeed, until the unfortunate incident with the little girl lost, the Cattle Run was the most notorious and famous aspect of the whole park.

But all things end. The park closed. Even if the roller coaster had been portable, no one would have taken it, because no one needed anything from the park except the thing that never left it, that slept in the center, that woke only every seven years to consume and bless and sleep once more.

And it turned out this roller coaster was not, in fact, built to last forever. Halfway up the first great climb, Mack's foot goes right through a rotted board.

"Shit," she gasps, falling hard on one knee as her calf is gouged by the wooden shards around the hole she's made. Without concern for doing more damage to her skin beneath her pants, she yanks her leg free. She runs up the steep incline with all the speed and lightness she has, with an empty focus honed by years of doing and being nothing. She is as light as the memory of her mother's laughter, as soft as the touch of Ava's buzzed hair, as weightless as a child's duck made of grubby yellow yarn.

Mack crests the top of the roller-coaster track, and her stomach drops as the park falls away around her, the trees at last defeated.

There, the gate! And there, a path through the labyrinth, a winding return to hope.

Mack can feel the hot, wet breath of death on the back of her neck. She doesn't turn. She throws herself down the track, her feet barely keeping up with her momentum, and leaps over a gaping hole where the track has completely fallen away. She lands hard, rolling and coming up decorated with splinters. There's a terrible crash behind her and she doesn't look back, but she waits for something—a low animal moan of pain or panic, some indication the monster has fallen, has slowed—but it doesn't come.

Still, she's bought herself a few precious seconds. She keeps running, eyes tracing the track, searching for where she needs to exit to meet up with her escape plan.

Everywhere paths in the park wind around and away, intended to corral the monster's prey, to make it easier. Easier on the monster, easier on the prey, easier than fighting and running and hoping.

Hope is exhausting, and Mack is nearly spent.

A dip, a turn, a stumble, and Mack's stomach drops with fear that she's lost where her path is. That she'll be running this track forever until she is caught. An infinite, futile loop, the same she has always been stuck in.

Ava's smile, she thinks and puts on a burst of speed, leaping another gap and barely noticing when she trips and her palms are speared by rusted nails. She tears them free and continues.

LeGrand's sister, she thinks, climbing one last rise, the rise she needs most, and looking down at the pool of water beneath her, a layer of green sludge on the top making it impossible to gauge the depth. Across it, access to her path out.

She doesn't have time to climb down, and she doesn't know how deep the water is. If she jumps and it's only inches, she'll break something and be devoured.

If she climbs, she'll take too long and be devoured.

She thinks of the bird, living forever hidden and alone in the dark of the rafters. Safe. But never free.

Myself, she thinks, *and Maddie.* Mack leaps into the air, floating impossibly long, suspended by hope and fear and desperation and something, at last, like peace.

"Come on, come on, come on," Ava whispers, crouched next to the generator. They can't do it too soon, or everything will be lost. She has to time it exactly right. LeGrand has moved to a tree, watching. Waiting.

Linda is on the other side of the fence, letting out small whimpers of suffering. Her breaths are panicked and shallow and sound wet. Ava knows from experience that's not a good sound. Feels good to hear today, though.

At last, LeGrand shouts. Ava lights the end of the T-shirt, now thoroughly soaked in gasoline where it's been twisted and worked through the open gas cap down to whatever is left in the tank.

"Go!" Ava shouts, waving at LeGrand. He jumps down and ducks behind the stone wall. Christian's shirt is well and truly on fire now, and if all goes to plan, there will be shrapnel.

So much shrapnel.

LeGrand pops back up to help drag Ava over the wall and they crouch together next to a spot where a little girl once sat, kicking her heels against it, patent leather shoes still new and shiny.

"Come on, come on, come on," Ava prays again.

The explosion is deafening, a tremendous boom punctuated with the terrible scream of metal. Ava and LeGrand are thrown back, stunned, as shards of iron and clods of dirt and a few pieces of stalwart concrete rain around them.

They stand hesitantly, checking for injuries as they brush themselves off. A gasping laugh greets them. Linda, still lying flat on her back, gurgles and laughs again. "You did it too soon. The beast wasn't even there yet."

Ava walks to the blasted remains of the generator, then looks through the gate at Linda. "Silly Linda. We weren't trying to blow up the *monster*."

Linda's laugh turns into a choke as she pushes up onto her elbows to see what they've done.

Mack bursts through the trees, covered in green slime and soaked through and the most beautiful thing Ava has ever seen.

Mack stops, chest heaving, and takes in the destruction. The gate, wrought with ancient symbols, kept closed against a monster for nearly a century, hangs by one hinge. It's destroyed beyond repair. Only the word MAZE—carefully soldered to the top of the gate when they made the theme park—remains.

But the maze, too, has been defeated, the beast led out of the labyrinth designed to keep it far from the gate, far from the people beyond it.

LeGrand, Mack, and Ava almost don't remember there's an unknowable horror pursuing them, they're so happy to be reunited, so in awe of the destruction. But a pounding of hooves *felt* more than heard spurs them on. They climb through the twisted remains of the gate, helping each other. Linda's car waits for them, keys still in the ignition.

"Stop," Linda gasps, waving red-soaked hands futilely in the air as though she could grab them, make them stay. "You can't let it out! You have to go back in! If you feed it before it makes it to the gate, it'll go back to the center! Please. You don't know what will happen."

Ava, Mack, and LeGrand share a look.

"Maybe it'll eat its normal amount from the town, and then go back to sleep for seven years," LeGrand says. "Or maybe it'll disappear."

"Or maybe, now that it's not bound, it'll eat them all," Ava says. "Which means eventually it could come for you again."

Mack looks back at the maze that housed a monster that fed on youth and hope and stalled dreams. That ground up vulnerable people so the ones in power could *keep* their power, could keep their safety, could keep everything.

The monster emerges from the trees, ravenous, unstoppable, unbound at last. It stretches its head, rising to its full, wondrous, height, the sun framed atop its crown of horns like a burning golden disc. It takes a step toward the gate, no longer snuffling, no longer searching. Its next meal is not hard to smell.

Mack tosses Linda's abandoned rifle to Ava, then gestures for LeGrand and Ava to get in the car. She crouches next to Linda, the fresh blood painting Linda's abdomen a siren song leading the monster the last few steps to the ruined gate.

To freedom.

To who knows what end of destruction.

"Please," Linda whispers, blood painting her pale lips. "You're a Nicely. You understand. Help me, or it will destroy us."

Mack pulls out the shoe and the delicately embroidered handkerchief from her pocket. She sets the shoe on Linda's chest, then drapes the handkerchief on Linda's stomach wound. The cotton soaks up the blood first, a crimson background with the word *Nicely* in stark white before that, too, is claimed.

With a shrug, Mack stands and turns to the car. "Who fucking cares."

ACKNOWLEDGMENTS

When my oldest child was in eighth grade, the yearbook did a feature on her special faux–stained glass classroom window art. The purpose? To prevent active shooters from being able to see inside. From age five, American children have to practice hiding from bullets, and to protect themselves we let them have *art*. In a game of Gun, Paper, Scissors, which wins?

So: All I have is art, too, and I wrote *Hide* as a scream of rage, but I had help.

This book benefited from two soundtracks: Joywave's album *Content* while I was letting the ideas simmer for a couple of years, and The Smashing Pumpkins' "Eye" on repeat while I was writing and needed to tell my brain where to be. Though not music, Maksim Gorky's "Coney Island" rivals any song for sheer lyricism and also has the only detailed description of the infamous Hell Gate ride that tragically burned down Coney Island's Dreamland. I was also inspired by the myth of the Minotaur and the ways we keep living the exact same cycles.

There really is an international hide-and-seek competition, the Nascondino World Championship, and it really did take place in an abandoned resort town one year, a fact that lit my brain on fire when I read about it. But it has too many rules and too few monsters, so I made my own.

The editor I most hoped would want to shepherd *Hide* into the world was Tricia Narwani, and I feel so lucky she felt the same way. I'm immensely grateful to her, Sam Bradbury with Del Rey

UK, Alex Larned, Bree Gary, David Stevenson, Michelle Daniel, Angela McNally, Simon Sullivan, Ella Laytham, Pam Alders, Craig Adams, and Del Rey as a whole. As a child obsessed with fantasy, I looked for Del Rey on the spines at the bookstore, and it's a tremendous honor to join those ranks. Most of my books live in the Penguin Random House now, and it's a very very very fine house.

My agent, Michelle Wolfson, has seen me through so many stories she never expected when we started working together thirteen years ago, and I'm forever grateful to have her as friend, advocate, and business partner. And not at all sorry I keep writing things she has to read with all the lights on.

Special thanks to my earliest readers for their invaluable encouragement and feedback: JS Kelley, Lindsay Eagar, and Stephanie Perkins. Stephanie and Natalie Whipple provide constant friendship and sounding boards, and I'm glad every day to have them. Thanks as well to Eliza Jane Brazier, for being an example of fearlessly forging ahead in new directions. And Ian Carlos Crawford, someday I'll put your name in a book and not kill that character. Maybe. Probably not.

My spouse and three children are the foundation of my entire world, and everything I write is possible because my days are filled with love and support. It's a tremendous honor and constant delight to navigate life alongside you all.

Finally, to everyone who still insists they pulled themselves up by their own bootstraps: For fuck's sake, look up the origin of the saying.

ABOUT THE AUTHOR

KIERSTEN WHITE is the *New York Times* bestselling, Bram Stoker Award–winning, and critically acclaimed author of many books, including *The Dark Descent of Elizabeth Frankenstein,* the And I Darken trilogy, the Slayer series, and the Camelot Rising trilogy. *Hide* is her adult debut. White lives with her family in San Diego, where they obsessively care for their deeply ambivalent tortoise, Kimberly.

kierstenwhite.com
Facebook.com/KierstenWhite
Twitter: @kierstenwhite
Instagram: @authorkierstenwhite

ABOUT THE TYPE

This book was set in Bembo, a typeface based on an old-style Roman face that was used for Cardinal Pietro Bembo's tract *De Aetna* in 1495. Bembo was cut by Francesco Griffo (1450–1518) in the early sixteenth century for Italian Renaissance printer and publisher Aldus Manutius (1449–1515). The Lanston Monotype Company of Philadelphia brought the well-proportioned letterforms of Bembo to the United States in the 1930s.